LAST MERCY

EMMA LAST SERIES: BOOK SEVEN

MARY STONE

Copyright © 2023 by Mary Stone Publishing

All rights reserved.

No part of this book may be reproduced in any form or by any electronic or mechanical means, including information storage and retrieval systems, without written permission from the author, except for the use of brief quotations in a book review.

❦ Created with Vellum

This book is dedicated to the children who have faced more shadows than sunlight in their young lives. May you find strength in your resilience, hope in your journey, and know that you are deeply loved and valued.

DESCRIPTION

At the mercy of a killer.

Overwhelmed with grief and anger, Special Agent Emma Last is now haunted by more than the ghosts who seek her out. Guilt becomes her constant companion as she attempts to unwind the clock, undo what's been done to yet another person she loves.

Will she ever escape the weight of her past?

When a fellow agent rescues a little girl hidden in the tunnels under the Washington National Opera House, Emma finds a focus for her energy. And she's determined to find the person responsible. Especially when two more children are found in the same tunnel network, their lives gruesomely claimed by blood-sucking leeches.

With no clear connection between the young victims other than their impoverished backgrounds, the investigation hits a dead end. But Emma isn't alone in her quest for justice. She receives cryptic clues from ghosts that only she can see.

The challenge for Emma isn't just finding the killer—it's convincing her team to believe her insights, especially with her reputation tarnished by recent transgressions. She's on thin ice, but her resolve is unshakable.

She can't—and won't—let another child's life end tragically on her watch. No matter the cost.

Last Mercy is the seventh book in the suspense-filled FBI series by bestselling author Mary Stone. You'll be at the mercy of your imagination as the curtain falls on one of the most horrific crimes yet.

1

Carla Alvarez tried to forget about the C-minus she got on her last times tables test, but it was impossible to ignore as she carried the weight of her mom's sacrifice—a neon-blue backpack that had cost much more than they could afford.

The Christmas gift represented Carla's failure. Her broken promises. With each step, it tapped against the rigid shell of her back brace, a staccato beat that echoed the sharp jabs of her classmates' taunts.

Why did life have to be so hard? She was only ten and already knew her battles were just beginning, far from over.

She paused by the old oak tree and dropped her backpack to the ground. Mom expected her to walk straight home to the apartment and get started on homework. Before her life got all twisted up with doctor visits and the stupid spinal cage, Carla hadn't minded the walk home. She hated the brace, temporary or not.

A lot of things in Carla's life were supposed to be temporary, like living in what she'd referred to as "the worst neighborhood in the whole wide world." Beyond the tree's canopy, the sounds of laughter and the thud of a soccer ball being kicked back and forth served as a bitter reminder of a carefree life that seemed just out of reach. The ball flew over a fence, and the boys climbed over to get it as if scaling the structure was as simple as walking.

The wind picked up, sending a whirl of empty soda cups and plastic bags dancing along the chain-link fence. She turned away from the litter. From the thing no one seemed to care about.

Carla swore when she and her mom had a house, they'd take better care of it than the awful places around there. They kept their apartment pretty clean "in case the landlord stopped by." Carla was super careful. No messes meant no bending over to clean things up.

Groaning, Carla straightened and stretched as best she could. The back brace made it impossible to move the way she used to. She inched one hand under the hem of her shirt to tug on the rigid plastic. It just wouldn't sit properly and dug into her skin whenever she turned or tried to bend.

The brace had been irritating from the jump, but today was extra rough.

Going to school used to be sort of enjoyable. Not exactly a party, but at least not torture.

Today, Brooke and Ava swatted her notebook out of her hands and kicked it under the lunch tables, apparently just to watch her crawl around like a cockroach.

And, of course, Matthew and Lucas had thought it would be funny to kick the notebook side to side while she grabbed for it. It took her three tries and a "Cut it out!" before Lucas pushed it her way with his foot.

She tugged harder at the plastic, knowing she shouldn't, but it didn't budge anyway.

Ava had said she was like a bug wearing an oversize turtle shell.

Way to go, Ava, coming up with an insult that doesn't even make sense.

But the words still hurt.

"If Ava and Brooke weren't such bitches, I'd still be on the honor roll."

The D.C. sidewalk didn't answer her. The afternoon air remained still, and almost a little too cold.

With great care, she leaned to the side and picked up her backpack, hating how hard it was to do such a simple task. Carla shrugged into one shoulder strap, grimacing when the backpack thumped hollowly against her brace.

Only last year, she would've been hurrying home to drop her bag, do her homework, and hang out with the girls down the street.

Now?

Now they pretended like she didn't exist. Street games were out because she could barely run. Hide-and-seek was hard because she couldn't crawl into tight spaces.

When she got back home to the apartment, she'd drop her bag, do her homework, and spend the evening watching television. That'd be the weekend plan too. Aside from stupid stretching exercises, there wasn't anything else to do. Mom wouldn't have time to take her anywhere.

And even when her mom did finally get home, Carla would have to tell her about that C-minus.

"I shouldn't complain." Speaking to the ground, she bit back tears. Other people had it worse. "Mom's doing the best she can."

The truth didn't change the fact that her mom had worked overtime, like, every day for the last month, leaving Carla mostly alone.

A shadow played in front of her, and she looked up. Far ahead, past the corner store and another empty lot, the turn that would take her home beckoned. But between her and the way to the apartment, a man in a tattered coat, stocking cap, and sunglasses stood directly in her path. He was maybe twenty feet down the sidewalk but focused on her.

No other movement on the street. No neighbors, no kids kicking a ball around anymore, no cars.

Carla stepped off the curb, thinking she would cross the street. But the Doberman that lived a few houses down let out a bark as soon as her foot touched the pavement. She jumped back onto the sidewalk and kept going, thinking she might just bull past the man.

"What's your name, little one? You look miserable."

Carla stopped, maybe five feet away from him. Were grown-ups going to bully her too?

She glared. "Who are you calling 'little one?' Get lost, mister, or I'll scream."

"No need to scream." His voice was soft, but that didn't make her feel any better.

Carla pushed forward, thinking he'd leave her be if she ignored him, but he walked backward ahead of her, his movement measuring hers and keeping the same too-close-for-comfort distance between them.

"Leave me alone, creep."

"You don't have to feel so miserable, you know."

He had the same sort of acne scars as her mom, the same tired circles showing under his eyes from beneath his sunglasses.

"I said I'll scream."

The repeated threat made him shake his head, but he stayed ahead of her, walking backward in a way that made her feel smaller, less significant, than she already did.

"Don't you need someone to talk to, honey? I can help you."

"I'm fine."

Tears burned behind Carla's eyes, but she kept moving.

This guy was bad news, and she knew it, but the street was empty.

Could she scream? It was so hard to imagine drawing that much attention to herself. Her mom would tell her to go on ahead, but the man hadn't done anything but be creepy.

Plus, what would Carla say if the cops came? If the guy disappeared before they arrived, the cops would think she was crazy or—worse—lying. They'd probably laugh at her like Brooke and Ava had.

On top of it all, they'd call her mom, pulling her out of work, like they did when Carla skipped school the first day she wore the brace. Ava had been up in her face the moment she'd walked through the door, making jokes and calling her names. The other kids joined in, and Carla ran off before she even got through the gate. The school security officer chased her down and called her mom when Carla refused to go back.

Her butt was still sore from the paddling Mom had given her that day.

"Life is a curse, isn't it?" The man huffed a plume of air between them. He was closer now. Walking backward ahead of her, but only maybe four feet away. "Wouldn't it be better to have never been born? To save yourself from this misery?"

The words echoed those of her bullies, which made it easier for Carla to speed up her steps. That was all this man was. A bully.

"Leave me alone, you creep. I'll scream, I swear."

The Doberman snarled behind its fence and let out sharp barks in their direction. Carla flinched at each one.

The man chuckled at her.

"Are you afraid of dogs? Is that what life is like for you, just fear all the time? I know what that's like."

"I said leave me alone. I'm going to scream."

The words sounded too small, even to her, and he kept talking as if he hadn't heard her.

"Life itself is a disease, little girl, but it does have a cure. I can help you with it."

They'd passed the house with the Doberman now, and its barks faded. The street remained empty except for some parked cars. No neighbors were out. If anything, the street looked more vacant than usual for a Friday afternoon.

The man stopped walking close enough to touch her. He bent toward her with gloved hands on his knees. "I'm the only one who can save you."

Carla froze.

His voice had gone darker, deeper. Terrifying. Plus, it was cold but not really glove weather, not for adults.

She whirled, almost tripping in her boots, and a scream finally broke from her throat. "Help! Help me!" The Doberman's house was a few houses back. She'd scream at that dog and—

A hand clamped onto her shoulder, yanking her backward. The hard, plastic brace made it impossible to lean away, and she fell. Her scream for help cut off as she hit the sidewalk and the air left her lungs.

His other hand had some fabric in it, and he covered her mouth, pressing hard. His fingers and palm smelled like hospital chemicals, burning her nostrils. She needed air, and she inhaled, pulling in the stink of whatever he had pressed over her face. Though she tried to scream, only gasps made it past his hand. He held her head steady with his other one.

She wanted to kick at him, but Carla's mind went fuzzy. She wondered how much trouble she'd be in when she got home. She wondered if the dog would save her. It was barking again, but the sound was so very far away. Carla was so sleepy, too sleepy.

Her eyes grew heavier. She knew she should fight, push him away.

Carla closed her eyes, thinking she'd try to scream and struggle again in a minute. She just needed sleep. A little sleep, and then she would scream.

2

Emma woke on her couch to darkness and the sound of a downpour hammering against her metal balcony. Her clock showed sometime after ten at night. The loosely capped bottle of pre-made margaritas judged her from the patio table on the balcony. Her good throw blanket was out there, getting soaked.

"Unbelievable." She shoved herself into a sitting position, instantly regretting the rapid movement. One hand went to her pounding head, the other over her mouth in case the inevitable decided to take that moment to announce itself. Her stomach churned.

The drinks had poured themselves when she began missing her boyfriend. Oren would have poured them real drinks, with fresh ingredients. He'd have made a plate of nachos topped with his own mango salsa.

Oren would've laughed with his deep voice, his eyes glinting in the lamplight, sending a warmth through her. Even hungover, Emma blushed at her thoughts of Oren as she imagined dabbing sweet, tangy salsa from his perfect lips, bringing out his rumbly laugh.

All that could have happened if Oren were still alive. If he hadn't been shot dead in his yoga studio by a deranged, schizophrenic murderer.

Almost a month had passed since he died, and Emma was trying to move past mourning. She was. But the future with Oren…well, she could visualize it like she could her hand right in front of her face. And then when she turned away for an instant and looked back, he was gone. Just like that.

She'd started her Sunday morning responsibly enough, until she decided that day drinking wasn't all that bad if it was just one. She even planned to make up a little vegetable tray for snacking. What better way to cheer herself up on a day off when the weather was too gloomy to go running?

Not that she'd gone running recently, or held herself to one drink, or made the vegetable tray. From the instant that first boozehound's margarita went into the mug, her fate was sealed.

Forcing herself to move, she got up and grabbed a fresh garbage bag from the kitchen, then ducked out into the cold rain to collect the throw blanket so it wouldn't drip all over her apartment. By the time she got to the bathroom and changed out of her damp, tequila-scented clothes—*did I spill the damn stuff on myself?*—she almost felt human.

Mostly, she felt an ache in her chest she knew was grief, but at least that meant she was still, technically, among the living.

In the kitchen, she pulled the water pitcher from the fridge and sat down to hydrate. Her gaze fell on the half-emptied liquor bottle outside.

"At least it kept the damn dreams away. Score one for drugging myself stupid."

She drank the water, pretending she was fine and that her insides weren't presently threatening to become outsides.

Pretending the blasted dreams didn't also haunt her when she was awake.

Oren's dead body. Emma couldn't decide if she preferred the memory of his staring, unseeing blue eyes or the white-eyed gaze of his ghost from the Other.

In the dreams, she crouched beside him to mourn, but he turned his head to her—still dead-eyed—and howled like a wolf. The howls always woke her, echoing in her ears, her body trembling.

"Coffee. I need coffee."

For once, her little pod brewer cooperated. She inhaled the rich, steaming aroma and almost took a sip before remembering how little sleep she'd managed the night before.

Should've brewed decaf, Emma girl. Just don't tell Denae about it, or you'll never live it down.

She set the mug on the counter and cradled her face in her hands, trying to think about dinner instead of the nightmares plaguing her sleep. Really, the endless parade of dreams and headaches was enough to make Emma hate life. Hate existence entirely.

The way her blood sometimes bubbled over with grief, heating her emotions from the inside until she felt like she might erupt in a fountain of pain and agonizing sorrow—she hadn't yet figured out how to manage that. And now here she was, hungover and feeling as damp and drippy as the throw blanket she'd left stuffed in a garbage bag in her tub.

If she couldn't even handle a simple task like hanging up a wet blanket, maybe she should just grab her margarita mug and finish off that bottle.

No. I can't think like that. That's a rabbit hole some people never come out of, and I will not let myself go there. Not today, not ever.

But the thoughts weren't new. She'd spent her week of

compassionate leave moping in her apartment, putting in more time on her couch than her yoga mat. Spending her nights wishing she could sleep. Dreading the moment her eyes slipped closed, because she knew the howling would begin shortly thereafter.

Jacinda had all but forced her to take advantage of the leave option, but Emma knew it was the right thing to do. Maybe she should've taken more time off. Even after she'd returned to work, Jacinda had only allowed her to do paperwork and desk duty.

What she wouldn't give for a serial killer right about now. Well, not now, and not really, but a case to sink her teeth into would have been welcome.

Or to return in time to the moment Adam Cleaver walked into Oren's studio. To be there and stop him, killing him if she had to.

Recognizing a bargainer's thoughts, Emma paused with her coffee cup halfway to her mouth. She'd picked it up without realizing. Taking a calming breath, just like Oren would have advised, Emma replaced the cup and stood straight, arms at her sides, shoulders relaxed.

Breathe, center, and refocus. Reframe. Everything is a lesson, and every breath is an opportunity to learn something new.

Letting her breath out slow and steady, Emma reminded herself that even desk duty and paperwork had their places in Bureau affairs, and they were just as important, if not more so, than getting into the field on the trail of a violent criminal. The tasks Jacinda gave her were just more opportunities to impress her supervisor with her ability to perform.

But your paperwork's been less than impressive, Emma girl. Jacinda's made that clear.

Painfully clear, in fact.

And just like that, all the centering and balance she'd

found from memories of Oren were swept aside, replaced with the unholy trinity of guilt, shame, and anger.

What did little errors and typos matter in the bigger scheme of things? Nobody could really complain if she wasn't up to her usual level of perfection. Not after what she'd been through. What she hadn't been able to stop.

Emma scoffed at her own attitude. She wasn't going to let grief be the end of her. A quick slug of coffee scalded her tongue and shook her from the downward spiral.

Quit it, Emma. No more coffee. Food, then sleep. That's all you need, and you'll be good as new.

She put a pan on the stove, thinking a fried egg might help the jackhammering in her head. Two eggs, maybe. While the pan heated up, Emma stalked to the couch. Her phone blinked with alerts for messages she had no intention of answering. As it had for days.

Mia and Keaton and Leo all checking in on her, seeing how things were going.

Leo had been especially insistent lately. Tonight, he left another message, promising he'd be there for her whenever she needed him.

The man seemed incapable of leaving her to her grief.

"Don't get too close to me, Leo, or you'll end up dead too." She wished she could say that to him rather than to her living room walls. She knew he meant well. Emma just wasn't in the mood for his support.

Yeah, he was a friend, but he was also a colleague, and one she'd twice now given reason to mistrust her. The last two cases had ended with her racing after the perpetrator on her own, first in a car, chasing Kenneth Grossman, and then pounding her feet into the ground on the trail of Adam Cleaver.

Sure, both cases had ended with the suspects in custody. But they also ended with Emma earning an earful from the

SSA about being a team player. Her colleagues depended on her to follow the game plan, but they couldn't if she was out in front.

"All because you decided to make the decisions for everyone."

Showing her weakness to Leo or anyone on the team wouldn't do anybody any good.

Emma turned back to her little kitchen and refocused, pulling two eggs from the fridge even though food held less interest for her than before. She got the eggs sizzling in the pan, lowered the heat, and leaned back against the counter. Her gaze caught the calendar hanging on the fridge.

How had nearly a month gone by since Oren died?

The loss still felt as raw as when she'd seen him lying in the Yoga Map, bled out and already going cold to the touch. That felt like yesterday.

"I'm going to be alone forever, aren't I? Doomed to never have a family again. Never love someone without them dying on me."

Emma stared at her eggs, shocked into a chuckle at the melodrama of the words that'd just come out of her mouth. A rush of anger straightened her back, and she flipped her meal as if to shut down the thoughts and fry them into oblivion. Being dramatic was something fourteen-year-old Emma would do.

She was twenty-eight and a federal agent, for crying out loud.

Boo-fucking-hoo that your boyfriend died.

People dealt with worse than that every day, and so would Emma. She'd just keep right on going without a family and be considered all the braver for it.

Biting her tongue as if to remind herself she was tough, Emma pulled out a plate and waited for her eggs to fry past the point when most chefs would have served them up.

She'd survive, just like she always did. Alone.

And hell, some alone time was good. She'd been enjoying it, really. Her ghostly neighbor across the street, Madeline Luse, had all but stopped trying to communicate with her. She only rarely turned to look her way and hadn't offered a wave in weeks.

Emma was at a stalemate with the whole of the Other, really. Even her most devoted ghostly visitor, Mrs. Kellerly, had cut back. The old woman's willowy ghost, once a daily "treat" for Emma's mornings, now appeared only every few days and never with more than a single word for her.

"Forget."

Emma took Mrs. Kellerly's advice at face value, doing her best to ignore the old ghost every time she oozed into the kitchen. In all honesty, she'd never felt less inclined to talk to the dead. Her psychic friend, Marigold, had sent a few texts since Oren had been killed. But they'd been easier to ignore than anyone's.

The Other has nothing to offer me right now. Maybe it'll even go quiet on me for good. Wouldn't that be something?

Emma flipped her eggs onto a plate and took the meager meal to the kitchen island.

The eggs had no taste—she'd forgotten to season them even with salt and pepper—but she forced bite after bite down into her tequila-addled stomach.

She kept her eyes down, though, away from the room at large. Because despite what she kept telling herself about not needing to see the Other, the truth was far simpler than ghosts changing their behavior and offering unsolicited advice.

Emma was terrified the next ghost she'd see would be Oren's, white-eyed and accusing, and ever so dead.

3

Carla's thinking was all fuzzy, like when she woke up late for school and her mom was calling to her from the kitchen. At least then she was wide awake, even if she didn't want to be. She remembered what happened, with the stranger on the sidewalk, and it was like a siren went off right next to her ear.

Carla blinked into the darkness, her throat burning from that smell on the stranger's cloth. She tried to swallow, struggling to get enough spit to make her throat work, wishing more than anything for a glass of water.

And at the same time, the brace bit into Carla's back worse than ever before. As if she'd been wearing it for days.

But the hard plastic wasn't the worst of her concerns. Staring into the dark, unable to move practically at all, she could hear a worrying rustling that reminded her of the hamster she had once. The way he'd rooted around in his bedding and buried snacks against the glass of his little home.

In the cold and the dark, with her hands and feet going numb from being tied together so tightly, Carla couldn't quite pretend it was hamsters scurrying around the edges of the room, much as she wanted to. She knew the sounds rats made when they would scratch inside the walls at home and when they would get into the cupboards underneath the kitchen sink or where her mom kept the cereal.

At least the humming man who came by occasionally hadn't taken her gloves or her boots, or she suspected she'd have had her proof that hamsters weren't sharing the space with her.

His footsteps clicked and slapped whenever he approached. Carla closed her eyes, ready for the sudden burst of light. He carried a big flashlight, or maybe a lantern, whenever he appeared. It was bright, but only in one spot, and it barely lit the shadows around her. She'd hear his humming soon too. Maddening and soft, so casual that she thought he intended it as an extra bit of torture.

Gritting her teeth around the cotton gag in her mouth, she blinked hard to keep more tears from coming. He'd ignored her crying before and only tightened her gag.

The light came closer, his humming and his footsteps growing louder at the same time. When the shadow came, she knew it was him. The man from the sidewalk. He'd kidnapped her after school…today? Yesterday?

Carla settled on yesterday. That felt right. She hadn't been here very long, but long enough to know her mom had to be home and missing her by now. Carla hoped she'd called the cops. Maybe the neighbor with the Doberman saw what happened and could tell them how to find her.

"How's the little girl?" The man stood in the arch of the doorway leading off to some hall, gazing down at her. His lips thinned out into a frown. "You wiggle a lot, you naughty thing. But don't worry. My friends won't mind unless you wiggle on top of them."

She swallowed behind the gag, trying to remember what

he was talking about, and flinched when he knelt beside her. He was wearing a mask, and Carla couldn't see his eyes well.

He held a box or something in one hand. From his other hand hung a lantern, like a soda can with a hat. It glowed with light all around. When he set it down, the light revealed a stone floor and brick walls covered in patches of green or black mold, like Carla saw in a friend's apartment bathroom.

The light also reflected off whatever the man held in his other hand.

Carla struggled, pulling away from him and bumping against a wall.

"Stay still, or you won't like what happens. You're almost at the final bleeding stage now. Don't you want the misery to end?"

That's right. Last time he was here, he said he would help me feel better soon. But what is he—

The thought cut off when she saw what he had been holding. It was a big glass jar, like for those giant pickles. But it was full of murky water, like the dirty sludge that sometimes came up from the toilet when the plumbing backed up in their building.

Something was moving in the jar, swimming in the filth.

He opened it and reached in to scoop out whatever was moving around in the water. Carla thought it might be some kind of fish. Was he going to feed her a fish from dirty sewage? She almost threw up thinking about it.

She squirmed away again, hating the brace that kept her from moving easily, even though she had nowhere to go and her hands and feet were still tied together.

He moved his hand out of the light, and she pulled her head back as far as she could, not wanting him to put whatever he'd taken from the jar anywhere near her face or mouth. But he just pressed it against her arm, right over the place where he'd cut a hole in her coat the last time she woke up.

It was slimy and wet, cold. But Carla felt something else, too, like pressing or pinching on her skin. And then nothing.

"What is it?" At least, that was what she tried to say. With the gag in her mouth and her throat so dry, Carla knew her words could only come out as muffled grunts or whining. And the last time she'd cried, he got very mad at her, saying he would "make the misery end faster" and that it would hurt more unless she behaved.

"Hush, little girl. We'll fix that consciousness of yours before you know it. This illness called life and that damnable brace. Isn't that the true torture?"

She shook her head, trying to pull away from the man again. He gripped her arm tighter and ripped her coat sleeve open more before returning to the jar and scooping something else from it.

That pressure and pinching feeling came again. Carla wished she could see what he was doing, but she also didn't want to see. It was better not to know, because she knew it couldn't be good. It wouldn't get her out of here or make her scoliosis go away.

The man reached into his jar two more times, pressing two more of his "friends" against Carla's arm. Whatever his friends were, at least they didn't hurt. And at least Carla didn't have to see them.

By the man's lantern, she watched a large spider making its way across the floor. She didn't have the energy to be afraid of it. Not anymore, when there were so many other, worse things to worry about.

The man shifted his position and kicked his lantern over, sending the light onto Carla's arm—the very one that had been trapped beneath the man's iron grip, pinched and prodded until it felt alien to her.

In that sudden illumination, her skin appeared alive, a writhing mass of thick, worm-like creatures squirming over her flesh in a grotesque dance she didn't understand. Terror eclipsed Carla's brain, and her breath caught in her throat as her mind struggled to make sense of the nightmare unfolding upon her. Her vision tunneled, the encroaching darkness a merciful curtain falling over the horror, until all was silent and void.

But the darkness was short-lived. A sharp sting spread across her cheek—once, twice, rousing her from the merciful abyss of unconsciousness.

"You got scared. But it's okay. Everything is going to be okay."

Carla knew it wouldn't. She knew with every brain cell she had that it was definitely not going to be okay.

And the man kneeling beside her looked like he knew it too. Like he was just waiting for the "not okay" part to happen.

"Why are you doing this? My mom—"

"Your mother? Is that what you're saying?" The man barked a laugh, like her math teacher. "Your mother is better off without you, just like you'll be better off after I'm done. Remember that." He picked up his lantern and his jar, humming to himself again.

Only then did fresh tears start drifting down Carla's cheeks.

"The suffering will be over soon. Remember that too. You should be grateful." He got as far as the door before he turned back to her, lips turned up in the first smile she'd seen from him. "Existence is a curse, and you'll soon understand that. And then you'll be ready for the end."

Carla wanted to explain that she was tired and needed to sleep, away from the cold and the things on her arm and the scurrying in the dark corners. And she wanted to explain that she'd done nothing wrong, nothing bad enough to deserve this, but he was already gone. Lantern light fading with his footsteps down into the dank tunnel he always came from. Leaving her in the pitch black once more.

She had to stay awake, though. Had to. What had her mom told her? If she ever got lost, stay put and scream for help. Well, the staying put was no problem. But once he left, she'd scream. And maybe he wouldn't hear her and someone else would.

Part of her wondered what would happen if the humming man *did* hear her, but she doubted things could get much worse for her.

She wiggled her tongue against the gag, biting and grinding at it with her teeth. When that failed, she leaned her head back against the cold stone behind her and rubbed the knot at the back of her skull up and down, up and down. It hurt her head and pulled her hair, but the gag began shifting, stretching and loosening with the friction.

Carla was just so tired. Maybe if she slept, she would feel rested, and then she could get herself free somehow.

The brace was hard against her back and hips, and she leaned sideways to make it dig into her skin, waking her up again. She couldn't allow herself to sleep. Not now.

She pushed with her tongue until she thought that might go numb along with her hands and feet, moaning when she accidentally bit down on it instead of the gag. But then, as if the blood from her tongue had been the magic sacrifice to get the job done like in old storybooks, the gag fell out from between her lips.

Carla didn't wait another breath. The humming man had to be far away by now. He just had to.

A faint melody echoed from somewhere, like a man's voice calling. Then a woman's voice joined it. Were they singing? Carla thought it could be singing, like the choir in church, all long words and moaning and really loud.

All at once, the singing stopped, and Carla heard a sound like quiet thunder and a few shouts.

She gathered what last bits of energy she had, blocking out the image of those things on her arm, the humming man's "friends." She didn't know what they were, but they couldn't be good. They weren't okay, and Carla wasn't okay.

But her mother told her what to do if she got in trouble. And it sounded like people might be nearby who could help. Carla took the deepest breath she'd ever taken.

And she screamed.

4

Mia clapped twice more as the lights came up in the Washington Grand Opera House, her elbow brushing Vance's beside her. The performers of *Tristan und Isolde* had just taken their last bow for the night, and the large audience nearly vibrated the whole space with their applause.

Vance's warm breath tickled her ear as they pressed up the aisle. "You ready to meet the performers?"

Part of her just wanted to call it a night, but she nodded. Vance was more excited for this portion of the evening than he'd been about going out on the date.

Neither of them really knew anything about opera, but when Jacinda had offered up free tickets, they both jumped at the chance for a fancy date. They only realized at the last minute that the seats came with special VIP privileges.

At the top of the aisle, the smiling usher glanced at their tickets before leading them through the door and along a hall toward the stage. A few people going in the opposite direction gave them curious smiles, and Mia glanced over her shoulder to Vance. "Having fun yet?"

"I feel like a celebrity." He straightened his suit jacket,

plucked at his shirt cuffs, and ran one hand over his perfectly coiffed hair. They approached a framed placard standing atop a stanchion that read, *Theater Personnel and Performers Only Beyond This Point.*

Backstage, the usher led them around hulking set pieces and a chaos of bodies in various states of costume removal. Jackets and wigs sat discarded on tables or draped over the backs of chairs.

Mia held Vance's hand as they wound through the crush until they reached a relatively calm space toward the back of the stage. The actress who'd played Isolde still wore the gorgeous red gown from the finale and sat on a chaise Mia recognized from early in the opera. The man standing beside her wore all black, as he had when lying dead on the stage. Unlike his costar, he also wore a tired frown.

"I'm Layla Simon," the woman stood and held out her hand, "and this is Jason Engelson."

Vance stumbled over introducing the two of them, and Mia couldn't blame him. Layla was gorgeous, and her low-cut gown left very little to the imagination beyond what was hidden beneath her superlong hair, so wavy that the woman might have stepped right out of a commercial.

"The performance was fabulous," Mia shifted sideways as a stage worker hurried by, "and that's coming from someone who didn't know they liked opera until tonight."

Layla laughed, her genuine smile growing larger. "What brings you to the show, if I may ask?"

Mia gave Vance a quick check-in look, and he nodded, gesturing for her to continue the conversation. "Our employer received the tickets and offered them to us at the last minute. She had something come up, but it's our good luck."

"Well, I'm glad for you and sorry for your employer. You

can't imagine how many people think they hate opera until they actually see it live."

Vance nodded. "It's certainly not the same as hearing snippets on the television."

Jason raised a sharp eyebrow. "You wouldn't think it would be, would you?"

"Oh, stop it." Layla gave Jason's arm a playful punch, and the man apologized with a wince. "Don't mind Jason. He's just a grump. So what was your favorite part?"

Mia allowed herself to relax a touch more, letting Vance answer Layla's questions and occasionally take another barb from her costar, Jason the Grouch. He seemed ready to do anything but talk to audience members, but Vance held his own, replying with all the grace Mia knew she could never muster herself.

He really is kind of adorable. We'll have to go to the opera more often, it looks like.

Layla bubbled out answers as fast as Vance asked questions, and Mia wondered if the woman ever got tired of talking about her role as Isolde. Beside her, Jason was reserved but polite, apparently willing to let his partner do most of the talking, just as Mia was.

A man cleared his throat, having come up just to the side of their foursome. Dressed all in black but for a gray tie, the man didn't appear half as animated as the performers. "If you'll excuse me, Layla—"

"Oh, Ted, of course." Layla grabbed his arm and pulled him into their little circle. "Vance, Mia, this is our talented stage manager, Ted—"

"And as I was saying," he pulled away gently, "I'm afraid it's about time to wrap things up here, if you could?" He pointed the last part of his comment at Layla, clearly understanding it was her and not Jason who could talk all night. "We need the two of you out of costume so we can all head home."

Layla patted his shoulder, even though the gesture only seemed to make Ted's expression grow grumpier. "Oh, we'll just be a few more minutes."

Mia tried to catch his arm to ask where she might find a restroom, but the man was already stalking away, muttering something about not waiting around.

Beside Layla and Vance, Jason seemed more politely bored than anything, so Mia leaned forward and whispered her question to him. "Restroom I can use?"

He gave a tired smile and pointed off the way they'd come. "Past the costume rack there, head left. Back corner of the room. There's a leads-only restroom that tends to be on the nicer side. Anyone asks, just tell them Jason said it was okay."

Mia excused herself and headed off the way Jason had directed her, weaving between stage crew dressed in black and hurrying back and forth with small props and paperwork. She glimpsed the grumpy stage manager they'd met slipping out a stage exit and wondered if she'd end up having to remind Vance the performers didn't have all night.

Chuckling at the thought, she found her destination tucked into the corner, labeled with its restroom sign and a slip of paper below that simply read, *Layla, Jason, Dressing Assistants Only*. Inside, she locked the door of the single-person bathroom and slipped her coat off, hanging it over yet another rack of clothes.

True to Jason's word, the little bathroom was neater than she might have expected of a backstage facility, but by the time she was pulling her dress back down, the glow she'd felt after the performance had bled into confusion.

Mia *heard* something…

For a second, she thought she was imagining it. While she

washed her hands, the sound disappeared. But then it returned. It was like a soft keening. Almost like a muffled cell phone video. Glancing around the space, she didn't see a potential source, and a quick glance at her phone was enough to remind her the device was still silenced.

She moved to the door and opened it a crack, but when she leaned her head out, the sound disappeared, so she ducked back inside and glanced around. The sound went higher for an instant, and goose bumps ran up her arms.

There was really no question. That had almost sounded like…a scream? She had to have imagined it…right?

Her training wouldn't allow her to dismiss it as a figment of her imagination—not when every fiber of her being was attuned to the nuances of human distress. As the keening resumed, another chill ran through her.

This wasn't her imagination.

Unbelievable as it felt, something was going on below the theater. There had to be other possibilities, but at the moment, they were hard to process, especially when she just couldn't shake the goose bumps on her arms.

Though the opera's final note had been sung, she wondered if the night's true performance was just beginning.

5

Maybe Mia's ears were still ringing with the orchestra music—they'd been so close to the musicians—but she'd been fine before she'd come into the restroom.

Without giving herself time to doubt what she was doing, she moved to the clothes rack and shoved it sideways, searching for the source of what she'd heard. Beneath it lay a grate, and even before Mia crouched down, the sound became louder.

She moved in close, nearly putting her lips to the grate. "Hello! Hello?"

No answer came, but the keening continued, and then it ratcheted up once more to what absolutely sounded like a muffled scream.

The cries were clearer now…high-pitched, shrieky, and interrupted by breathy sobs that made it sound as if the person were hyperventilating. A loud "Help!" bled up through the grate, shaky and full of terror, and Mia stood so fast she wobbled backward on her heels. Unless someone was playing a horrible trick on her, there was a person somewhere below the bathroom who needed help. A child, if she guessed right.

Stepping out of the bathroom, she considered whether or not to go find Vance, but maybe the best thing for everyone would be if he kept the performers distracted. Anyone left backstage would be waiting on Layla and Jason instead of trying to hurry her and Vance off into the night.

Outside the bathroom, though, Mia lost the child's calls for help. She paced back and forth along the back wall and searched for any additional grates. Without any other ideas, she headed toward an exit sign over to the right.

A glance out the door showed hallways leading in every direction. She used one of her heels to prop the door open and slipped out of the other one to leave it in the hallway. If all else failed and she got in trouble, Vance would recognize her troublesome shoes. He'd commented at dinner that they were the least practical things he'd ever seen her wear, and now she was proving him right.

Heading down the hall and hanging a left in the direction of the bathroom, Mia still couldn't hear the cries continuing, but she did find a stairwell. The light switch by the door responded when she flipped it, showing prison-quality cinder block walls, cement stairs, and pipe railing running up and down. Swallowing her nerves, she left her coat hanging on the doorknob and headed downward, thankful she'd worn a long-sleeved dress.

Her stockinged feet didn't make a sound on the cement as she moved down through pools of light that grew dimmer and dimmer, more and more bulbs having gone out over time. Apparently, nobody frequented this area—or almost nobody—so the lights went unfixed.

Two flights down, the stairwell ended, and a heavy, metal door stood as the only exit. It was unlocked, and it groaned in protest as she pulled it open. She peered into the dark hall behind it, finding only a deep, unforgiving blackness. But she heard the cries again, more clearly than before, even if she couldn't quite tell what direction they were coming from.

Slipping her phone out of her purse, she put the little bag between the door and the jamb, propping it open as another breadcrumb for Vance should he have cause to come looking for her. Realistically, though, she didn't think that would happen.

Before, she'd suspected she was imagining things. Now she knew she wasn't, but she was also close enough to feel sure the voice calling for help was alone in the dark, abandoned. She heard no sounds of fighting or threats, which meant whoever left the victim crying down here wasn't around.

Mia just had to find the child before the person responsible for the terror reappeared.

In front of her, dark passageways stretched off ahead and to her left, and the cries echoed off the dank surroundings. She turned on her phone's flashlight and shined it around the area, searching for any extra detail to lead her to the voice. The ground showed no signs of anyone having passed through, let alone a child.

Puddles of water dripped from a pipe running along the ceiling to the left. Mia followed the pipe first, thinking it could guide her toward the exit a level above.

But within forty feet of where she'd started, the cries faded, and she still hadn't seen any doorway. Swallowing down frustration, she headed back the way she'd come. Sure enough, the cries grew louder, proving that she'd simply gotten farther away from them.

Wrong way, Mia. Keep going.

She reassured herself that her purse still sat in the doorway to the staircase, a beacon to Vance if he were forced to come looking for her, then took the other passageway into the darkness. The cries got louder, but so did the echoes.

Disoriented, Mia forced herself to count the doors she passed, all of them leading to empty rooms or tunnels that seemed even narrower than the one she followed. For now, she kept going straight, praying the child in need of help wasn't too many turns from her current location. Already, she knew Jacinda would've told her she'd lost her mind, chancing getting lost in an environment like this.

How many lost field agents did it take to find one victim? She didn't know and didn't want to find out.

Mia focused on the cries, pushing aside the possibility of getting lost. The sounds still echoed eerily but weren't fading. So many doors and offshoots led away from the main hallway she'd found herself in, which was dank and damp beneath her feet, but sobs and an occasional "Somebody, help me!" pulled her forward.

When she passed yet another passageway and realized that the cries were, ever so slightly, getting fainter, she whirled around so quickly that she knocked her phone against the wall. The light disappeared.

"Shit! Shit, shit, shit." Fumbling, barely avoiding dropping the device, she found one button and then another, and pressed hard. The light came back.

What a time to be getting used to a new phone. Damn, that was close.

Leaning against the wall, Mia gave herself a count of three to catch her breath again. She then anchored herself back to the cries and gazed down the tunnel behind her. Taking a turn off the main passage was dangerous—she knew it was—but she didn't seem to have any choice.

Her throat clenched as she knelt, propped her phone carefully against the wall, and reached behind her neck for the clasp of the silver pendant necklace Vance had given her at dinner that night.

She gave it a quick kiss before setting it on the cold ground, placing it at the corner where the main passage wall met the tunnel she was about to venture down. Another tunnel went in the opposite direction, but with the necklace at this corner, she wouldn't bypass the hallway as long as she kept her eye out for this little signpost.

This was the one piece of jewelry she'd worn tonight, though. Heaven help her if she had to shimmy out of tights or underwear to continue marking her way.

Standing up, she clenched her phone tighter and moved down the slightly narrower tunnel.

Remember you turned left off the main passageway, so you're going to be looking for the necklace on the right when you come back. Just don't drop the damn phone.

Thankfully, she didn't have much farther to go.

Two doorways down, in a room as pitch black as the others, the cries drew her inside. Breathier now, they were closer and more desperate.

Mia held her flashlight up and froze in the doorway, her mouth going dry.

She'd thought she'd heard a child, a girl, but hadn't really believed it until now. Even worse was the slimy coating on the child's arm. It was moving, in waves, and as Mia got closer, her heart leapt into her throat.

What is that? Oh no, oh God, what is happening here?

A girl who couldn't be more than twelve was bound and slumped up against the wall in an otherwise empty room. Mia's light picked out rats scurrying off into corners. She brought the light back to the girl. Frozen tears coated her cheeks, and a gag was scrunched between her nose and upper lip so that her breath came out in wheezing gasps.

Even before Mia could fully process the sight before her,

she stumbled forward. "Oh, honey, you're okay. I'm here, and you're okay."

The girl's cries bled into whimpers as Mia skidded to a stop beside her. She was dimly aware of her dress tearing against the cold cement floor and the girl whispering what sounded like "Thank you."

She was delirious, exhausted, and probably dehydrated. Mia focused on the task before her, doing her best to calm the child and make sure she could be brought up from this awful prison someone had placed her in.

And to figure out what was all over the girl's arm.

As Mia's hand rubbed the girl's shoulders, she heard what sounded like "frightened" or maybe "friend."

"Yes, honey. Yes, I'm a friend. I'm a federal agent, and I'm here to help you. Let's get you out of here."

Mia balanced her phone against her knees and undid the girl's bonds around her wrists. She moved to untie the bonds on her ankles and stopped when her flashlight illuminated a tear in the girl's sleeve. She'd seen what looked like trails of blood. When she moved her light back over the girl's bared flesh, she had to hold in a shriek.

A cluster of thick, dark shapes clung to her arm. Mia had never seen a leech in real life, but she knew what they were and knew she had to get the creatures off the girl's arm. Plucking a few and dropping them to the floor, where they squirmed and wriggled in the dust, Mia realized the task would take more than she could do right now. The child's entire arm was covered in them.

Mia had to get her to a hospital immediately.

She held the girl's gaze while she tried to call Vance. Of course she had no signal so far underground.

Mia finally heard the girl's breaths coming more evenly and took that as her cue. "I'm gonna have you out of here soon, baby. What's your name? Can you tell me that?"

Last Mercy

"Carla." The girl shifted sideways, trying to come to a sitting position, but she was too weak, and Mia had to grab her to stop her from smacking her head against the wall as she slumped again.

"Your name is Carla, okay. We're going to get you out of here now, Carla."

"Please, you have to tell my mom. She's at home. She—"

Mia gave the girl a gentle hug, careful not to press hard because she was unsure of the extent of Carla's wounds. "We'll tell your mom, baby, we will. Let's get out of here first." She helped Carla to her feet, kneeling in front of her as she wobbled. "It's dark, but you just stay with me, okay? Can you walk?"

Carla nodded shakily and stumbled. Mia wrapped one arm around her waist for support, steadying her despite the awkwardness of some type of back brace. With her free hand, Mia held up her phone, using the flashlight to illuminate their path. She kept the girl beside her as best she could. Carla dragged her feet at first but leaned her weight on Mia's arm and managed to take full steps as they cautiously moved back through the tunnel.

The silver necklace glinted in the flashlight's beam, just as planned, and Mia's chest tightened with relief. She nabbed it. Once they took the turn, Mia sped up the steps, pausing to lift the girl into a firefighter's carry once they reached the main hallway. Soon enough, they arrived at the stairwell.

Mia set the girl down on the bottom step, forcing herself not to look at the leeches hanging from her arm. She tried Vance's phone again and saw a text from him.

Her thumbs trembled only a little when she texted him back.

Emergency. Stairwell, back of the theater. Ask Jason for bathroom.

That done, Mia helped Carla stand, and they slowly

climbed to safety. With every step up, Mia felt safer and surer of what she would do next.

First, Carla needed a hospital.

Next, Mia would begin hunting for the monster who had done this.

6

Leo had already heard Vance's rendition of events but listened along as Mia went over the unlikely ending to their date night yet again. Gathered with them and Denae in the little conference room tucked into an upper corner of the opera house, he didn't mind the repetition. Denae was enthralled, but he couldn't help being distracted.

Where was Emma?

Nearly two hours had passed since Jacinda had sent an *all hands on deck* alert to bring the rest of the team running to the opera house, yet Emma still hadn't shown up. Meanwhile, more and more cops were being pulled from other assignments and routed into the massive tunnel system below the theater. Soon, their own team—or some of it, at least—would need to head down there, and it wasn't as if they had a big team to start with. They needed everyone.

He glanced at Jacinda out in the hall. She still wore her formal getup for a dinner party at the mayor's house, something she'd hoped to avoid but couldn't legitimately blow off "just to see the opera." Hence the tickets having gone to Mia and Vance. Even so, Jacinda had ditched the mayor's event and made it here in minutes.

So where the hell was Emma Last? Her apartment couldn't be more than a half hour away. More like fifteen minutes, tops, the way she drove.

Denae hugged Mia, who'd started tearing up over how alone and little their victim had been, and how bravely she followed Mia back through the tunnel. She ushered the other woman over to chairs at the conference table.

Vance sighed, looking less sure of himself than usual. "So much for our fancy date night, huh?"

Leo clapped him on the back. "You grab some coffee. I think I'm gonna get the projector warmed up so it's ready for Jacinda."

At the front of the room, he took his time connecting Jacinda's laptop and getting the projector set up. He went through the motions casually, keeping one eye on the door, waiting for their last team member to show up.

Emma had been so distant since Oren Werling's death, Leo couldn't stop worrying about her. She remained cold and dismissive, regardless of how many times people reached out to her or who was doing it.

Leo was pretty sure the rest of the team had given up two weeks ago to let Emma make the first move toward heart-to-hearts. Lately, he'd been the only one trying to reach out at all, and still, she ghosted him.

Mia had told him to chill, that Emma would come up for air when she was ready. *"We just have to give her time to heal."*

He couldn't buy that.

Leo knew what it felt like to lose someone close and to feel guilt and shame over it. He still blamed himself, no matter how ridiculous it was to think he could have saved his papu that day. He knew the signs, knew the behaviors, of someone grappling with grief and losing the fight.

Some days, Leo got to see those signs again in vivid detail each time he looked in the mirror. He'd remind himself he couldn't have done anything in the moment and he couldn't change the past now. Sometimes it helped. Other times it just made him feel worse.

How many times had he reached out to talk with someone about those feelings? How many phone calls had he answered from friends or his brothers when they knew he was hurting?

Emma was cut from the same cloth. She was suffering in silence, just like he'd done. Knowing that, Leo recommitted to offering his support the instant Emma replied to his texts or answered his next call.

He was just sitting down by Vance when Jacinda and Emma appeared in the doorway together, Emma with a tall cup of coffee in tow. Raising a hand to her as she came to the table, he tried to catch her eye, but failed. Her scowl didn't falter.

With the door shut behind her, Jacinda hurried to the front of the room. "Thanks for getting us up and running, Leo." She opened her laptop and focused on the screen even as she began logging on. "As you all know by now, Mia and Vance's night at the opera turned up a kidnap victim, by sheer luck and Mia's canine-like hearing. Mia, you were last with her at the hospital, so tell us what you know while I get some files pulled up."

Mia sat a little straighter while Denae's arm remained loose around her shoulder. "The girl's name is Carla Alvarez, and she's ten years old. Unfortunately, she doesn't remember anything about being kidnapped except that it happened. The doctors are saying it's dissociative amnesia."

"That's generally temporary, right?" Vance asked.

"Generally. She remembers bits and pieces. Like she was walking home from school Friday. A man approached her and said something frightening. She remembers a 'hospital chemical smell' that burned her nose…chloroform, I'm guessing…which stuck with her after waking. The same man came to her down in the tunnels, below the opera house. He wore a ski mask, so she can't give us anything visual to identify him by. She said he hummed at her, and she recognized his voice when he said he would 'help her.'"

Vance grunted. "Humming and helping. Great. Don't let the press get ahold of that, or we'll be drowning in phone calls about everyone's great granny."

Mia frowned, nodding. "Yeah, well, that's about it. The doctors are hoping it's just trauma and that she'll remember something more soon. But for now, we have to assume that's all we have to go on. Her mother's with her at the hospital."

"Thank you, Mia." Jacinda glanced around the room, meeting everyone's gazes. "For now, I don't want any more questions directed at the girl. I know we sometimes circle back to witnesses and victims as needed, but any further questions, once approved by the mother, are going through me, then through Mia, since they've already connected, and that's it."

Leo managed not to look over at Emma, their resident rule breaker, but she must have felt Jacinda's gaze. Still scowling, she nodded.

"Okay, then." Jacinda laid her hands flat on the table, pausing for a deep breath. In that moment, Jacinda reminded Leo of himself, of his conviction to protect everyone who needed it. And his constant fear that when it really mattered, when the person at risk was someone close to him, he would be powerless to do anything but watch them die.

Jacinda straightened and addressed the group. "I know it's late, and we're all wired on adrenaline, but…I need you to focus. Two other elementary-school-age children were reported missing recently. Their bodies were recovered from another chamber in the tunnels below. The next two photos I'm going to show you are difficult ones."

Despite the warning, Leo jolted in his seat when the photos came up. Even without there being adults in the photos for reference, the bodies in the shots were clearly those of children. A Black boy with *Star Wars*-themed glasses lay curled on his side, in jeans and a long-sleeved t-shirt.

The t-shirt had a patch cut out from one arm, just like Mia had described when it came to the leeches set against Carla's arm. His hands were mostly gone—rodents, Leo assumed—and even in death, it was clear the boy had been too thin by half.

But he had fought, Leo guessed, if the gaping mouth was anything to go by. The boy had died either gasping or screaming.

In the other shot, a girl, further along in the decomposition process, was even harder to look at. He wouldn't have been able to even take a shot at ethnicity if not for the curly red hair sprouting out every which way from her head, which was canted at an odd angle.

Decay and whatever lived in the tunnels had destroyed what skin she had, leaving her looking more like a horror-movie prop than a child. The sweatshirt with a smiling llama in sunglasses, dressing the corpse, made him want to throw up the coffee he'd just swallowed.

So far, ethnicity didn't seem to be a common denominator, since little Carla had been Hispanic while these two were Black and white.

"Both bodies were found in the tunnel network below the opera house in just the last hour." Jacinda spoke in a quieter voice, as if in deference to the violent deaths before them. "We have positive IDs on both. Jessica Howard, age ten, and Daniel Jackson, age eleven. Both reported missing in the last few weeks, though nowhere near either the opera house or

Carla Alvarez's neighborhood. We have more cops on scene now, working to search the tunnels to make sure we don't have more victims. I'll receive alerts as any updates are available."

Leo struggled to form words, his gaze still focused on the bodies. Somewhere below them, maybe thirty feet down into the dark of the earth, an active crime scene surrounded these dead children. And maybe others. But these bodies were plenty bad enough.

Through the decay, he didn't see any blood, even though their clothes had both been cut to give the unsub a place to set leeches on their skin. "Cause…" His voice came out choked, and he cleared his throat and tried again. "Cause of death?"

"To be determined." Jacinda took her own glance at the large screen behind her, then turned quickly back to her computer. "Forensics say blood loss is a contributing factor, though there are also signs of strangulation. The states of decay, advanced as they may be, suggest the kids weren't killed shortly after being kidnapped but several days afterward. A short length of rope was found near Carla, as well, which may give indication to our killer's plans."

"If Mia hadn't found her…" Emma's voice was low but carried the weight of the room. But for the chance discovery by their teammate, there was no doubt about the fate Carla Alvarez would have suffered.

Denae gripped Mia tighter. "Do we have any security footage?"

"Nothing turned up yet." Jacinda finally moved off the shots of the bodies, pulling up a blueprint of the tunnels below the opera house. "But, as you can see, the tunnels are extensive. They're also unused, which means there's no effort made to surveil them on a regular basis. Not beyond keeping entrances and exits locked, particularly outside the opera house, and discouraging anyone from exploring."

Emma leaned forward. "What about outside?"

"We do suspect an external entrance, but these blueprints only cover the tunnels directly below the building, which means we need to find that outside entrance and get investigating. Mia went through the backstage area's access stairwell, and that's the one entrance currently being used by all law enforcement as we get the search and investigation underway."

Mia sat back in her seat, closing her eyes hard. Leo jutted his chin at Jacinda, drawing her eye to the other agent. She nodded.

"I think you've spent enough time down there, Mia," Jacinda said quietly.

Mia's chest heaved out a heavy breath, and she gave a small, "Thank you."

"Vance and Emma, you two check out the tunnels while Mia and Leo start with the cast and crew. Denae, you and I will review the investigations into the kids' disappearances. See if we find any suspects or connections to the opera house there."

Emma pushed her coffee cup aside and leaned forward as if to argue, but Jacinda was already staring her down. She swallowed and sat back in her seat.

Before she could change her mind, Leo stood up and gestured to Mia. "Shall we?"

The other agent nodded, and with that, the whole team began moving.

Leo breathed a little easier outside the conference room, leading the way back downstairs. He'd seen in Emma's face that she wanted to be doing the interviews, but her good sense must have kicked in and told her Jacinda had her reasons. Leo would've felt the same in Emma's position, but she'd been too erratic lately. Too prone to snap judgments and little errors.

And based on the way she'd kept her argument to herself, Emma might be annoyed, but she seemed cognizant of that fact.

He didn't know if that made him feel better about her state of mind or worse.

7

Emma and Vance donned shoe covers and gloves before setting off between set pieces and back toward the stairwell Mia had taken down to the tunnels. He'd investigated after her, containing the scene while she awaited an ambulance with Carla, but he seemed reluctant to head back downstairs now.

Cast and crew, having been corralled backstage, began to drift into groups of twos and threes. Emma's every instinct demanded she stay to help Mia and Leo question the theater troupe, but Jacinda would have her head if she did.

"It's like one of those movies about old-time London, you know?" Vance held the door to the stairway open for her. "Dark, dank. You'd expect vampires or a ghost to pop out."

Thankfully, with her mood as sour as it was, Emma didn't even have to rein in the impulse to startle at the word "ghost." She grunted an acknowledgment and led the way down.

At the bottom of the stairwell, a uniformed officer turned on a high-powered flashlight and guided them to the scene, talking as he went. "I've done rotations for VIP security here before…when bigwigs come through, you know…but I've never been down here. Didn't even know these tunnels existed before tonight."

Emma scoffed. "So much for VIP security."

The cop paused in his stride, shook his head, and resumed walking. If Emma's comment had pissed him off, that had not been her intent.

"Stage manager told me just about everyone on the cast and crew has access via keys. Same for maintenance guys who work here. Custodians, cleaning crew, that sort of thing."

"They just hand out keys to these tunnels? For what? I can't imagine anything useful gets stored down here."

"Nah, it's more like nobody ever bothered to change the locks. Backstage key gets you into pretty much any door in the building, including the tunnels."

"So anyone who has a key could be our unsub. Nice."

Vance and Emma paused at the doorway to the room where Carla had been found, standing in a little triangle with the cop and looking inside at the techs gathering whatever evidence they could find. High-powered lighting had been set up to illuminate the dank, gray, claustrophobic interior. They showed every threatening detail of the space.

"Creepy as hell," Vance pulled his jacket tighter, "and we're adults armed with weapons and high-tech lighting."

The cop frowned and handed a second flashlight to Vance, gesturing farther along the tunnel with his other hand. "Other crime scene's just three doors past this one. I'll be at the stairwell 'case anyone else needs an escort down."

"Let's look around." Emma aimed a thumb down the hall to where techs were coming and going from another crime scene. More light filtered from that doorway, along with flashlights that bobbed in the dark. "That's what we're here for, right?"

Vance grimaced but led the way with the light. Emma followed behind him, taking in the tunnels in more detail. No windows. Nothing on the walls. Just a dark, creeping emptiness, which made her feel strangely at home.

She peeked into the second crime scene with Vance, doing her best not to focus for too long on the bodies at the center of it. The child-sized corpses looked even smaller with grown men and women working around them, and Vance kept his distance even more than Emma.

Scattered bits of packing material and what looked like old theater programs spilled from a discarded box in one corner.

"These tunnels are pretty extensive." Vance muttered a curse, looking at the blueprint one of the techs had laid out. It showed the same layout Jacinda had displayed for them in the briefing. "Could take days to search them."

Emma nodded, but she didn't think it would take that long to discover where the killer had been bringing in children. The niche had gone cold around her, and although two different tunnels shot off from it, the little room they were in, lit now by crime scene lighting, directed her to one of the tunnels.

At that entrance, a red-haired girl with white eyes was gazing at her with a confused frown. Her scuffed jeans and happy sweatshirt were betrayed by the odd angle of her neck on her body, leaning to the side, and she swayed a bit on her feet.

I'm glad Mia's not with me. I wouldn't want to tell her Jessica Howard is here.

She gestured to Vance, working to keep her voice light. "Let's go deeper into the tunnels. See what we can find."

He frowned. "We're not really prepared to start mapping—"

One of the techs held up a span of neon-colored rope. "If

you do go, take one end of this so you find your way back here without trouble. 'Til we get it all mapped and lit, can't have Feds disappearing everywhere."

Emma went over and took hold of one end of the rope before Vance could argue. "I'm going. You coming?"

By way of answer, he removed his fancy suit jacket and laid it carefully on a table set up with mostly unused evidence bags and other materials. He made a point of tying the opposite end of the neon rope to a pipe running along the wall at the entrance to the tunnel. His hands worked the knot right beside the ghost girl's red hair, where it brushed against the wall in a spray of curls. Emma bit her tongue to hold back from telling Vance he should respect Jessica's personal space.

Jessica, however, clearly didn't care. Her ghostly form remained swaying where she stood.

As soon as Vance finished tying the rope to his satisfaction, the ghost disappeared. Emma didn't waste any time in leading the way toward what she guessed must be the entrance.

The tunnels were, true to reputation, a maze of darkness, pipes, puddles, rodents, and crumbling brickwork. They found more discarded boxes, some empty, others full of rotten fabric, and, in one case, the remains of what had probably been a grand costume before mold and rodents got to it. Even though the tunnels felt safe enough—Emma had her doubts they were structurally sound—the way their footsteps echoed left her feeling as cold as the Other.

In the presence of techs and crime scenes, she'd been able to embrace the emptiness and ignore Vance's claims that the place was creepier than a horror movie. Pools of illumination from the tech's high-powered lights had put everything into stark relief, as if they'd been on a film set rather than lost below the city.

Now that they'd left the active crime scenes behind, they were forced to maneuver in the darkness with only the little blobs of light offered by their flashlights. Emma imagined ghosts, and spotted Jessica's each time they reached an intersecting tunnel. The red-haired girl would flicker into shape, as if to guide Emma's progress, and vanish the moment she and Vance turned down the tunnel.

As they moved, Emma wondered how many other ghosts must live in the tunnels. She also wondered about the potential for real-life killers who knew how to stay quiet better than the rodents that kept scampering away from their flashlight beams.

Despite the dark and the rats and the fact that they didn't know who, or where, their killer was, Emma's nerves felt numb. If it hadn't been for the occasional flashes of Jessica's ghost, Emma would have followed Vance's entreaties and left the tunnels to their emptiness.

Jessica's red hair glowed ahead of them. At the next corner, their flashlight beam glinted off the *Star Wars* glasses Daniel's ghost wore. They hid his white eyes, but his yellow sneakers, absurdly clean in the dirty tunnels, all but begged her to keep going forward.

Her body was mostly numb with the heavy cold of the Other that came and went, along with the dank chill of the tunnels, but she kept going, speaking only to encourage Vance to continue following her.

She spooled up and then unspooled more of the neon rope as they backtracked from an empty room and followed the passage down the other way. Ahead, Daniel Jackson's yellow sneakers stood glinting at the side of a tunnel.

"Shit. This place is dead-end city." Vance shined his flashlight over what looked like a boarded-up passage. "We're getting nowhere, Emma. Let's head back."

Daniel's ghost bounced on his heels, antsy in death, and

Emma got the impression of a high-strung child practically erupting with energy that had no outlet. He was aching to speak to them but wouldn't.

I see you, she mouthed to him, inching forward with her phone held out, using her flashlight to illuminate the boarded-over passageway. Plywood and nails. And hinges.

"Vance, this is a door."

He stepped closer, playing the light along the edge of the boards. The wood had been nailed together, blockading the door behind it.

Emma gestured for Vance to cover her. He unholstered his gun and braced the weapon across his wrist, keeping the flashlight in his off hand aimed at the doorway. With both of them braced for whatever they'd find, Emma pulled on the door, fully expecting it to open.

It held fast, and another yank offered up the sound of a padlock jangling.

Emma looked to Daniel, but the boy was gone, so she focused on Vance, who wore a surprised little smile. She nodded. "I think we know how our killer's getting in."

8

The Washington Grand Opera House sat at the end of a busy, upscale neighborhood, and I couldn't avoid the smiling faces as I headed back in. Couples coming out of bars, friends hugging each other goodbye and hello. Even a few parents toting around sleeping infants, late as it was. With my hand curled around the extra rope in my pocket, I mustered every ounce of energy I had to hold myself back.

How beautiful it would be to end the facade. To force all these people to face the fact that their lives were miserable, with moments of drunken or misled happiness only hiding the truth from them.

If only I could.

But I knew the reality. I'd be taken down in an instant if I tried to fix this abomination so publicly, on such a large scale.

Better to focus and do each bit of good I could in the already decaying corners of the world.

I avoided the gaze of a smiling drunkard and played my fingers along my trusty rope, the tool that would end that little girl's suffering once and for all. She waited for me ahead, and with the opera house cleared out after the night's performance, I could come and go in peace.

As I give her peace.

She would see me and cower in fear…at first. Eventually, though, she'd realize I was just the Angel of Peace releasing her from a life riddled with misery. It was in those moments of truth that she'd wish for the end.

She's already suffered too much for one so young.

Through my releasing process, the little girl would understand the true horrors of consciousness without distraction, alone in her misery all this time. Watching and feeling her own life drain away, she'd recognize how the pain she might be experiencing, however awful, was nothing compared to the life of suffering she was leaving behind.

It was time to give her the sweet release of death she must be craving, now that she could understand the value of nonexistence.

The cold wind hit me harder as I turned a corner, now just a few blocks from the opera house. I breathed out around my scarf, grounding myself in the cold that made my teeth chatter.

Misery.

As it should be.

Anchored like this, in the frigid cold, I'd be all the more prepared to place my freezing hands and that rope around that little girl's neck, proving to her the futility of life and the bliss of death.

The child in the opera house needed me. If only I'd been able to do this same service for my mother. At least her death had been quick, drowning after slipping on the wet concrete by a pool's edge. My father's death had been a fitting revenge —as he'd been too drunk to save her. He'd wasted away in the juices of his own alcohol addiction, poisoned from the inside.

Of course, my mother had deserved some blame too. Birthing me, birthing any human, was worthy of punishment. Perhaps some considered life a gift, but they were wrong.

Life was a gift I'd neither asked for nor wanted.

At least that girl in the tunnels would never bring children into this miserable world. Killing her was a favor twice over, given that she was a girl who'd grow into a woman capable of bearing new life.

The thought of that warmed me, despite the cold. It had been a long time since I'd felt real pleasure, but when I remembered I was saving her potential children from being born? Well, there was no greater joy.

Not that I could imagine, certainly.

When had I ever felt happiness like when I found that first boy and delivered him to the last mercy of sweet oblivion? The very sensation was as confusing as it was intoxicating.

I made the mistake of licking my lips, feeling the chill seep into the cracks with the wind, and I flinched. Best to get inside as quickly as possible, before I became sick.

My step faltered as I came within sight of the loading bay where employees entered through the back.

The whole area pulsed with flashing lights, police cars, ambulances, and even a fire truck. They covered every square of blacktop. A long line of unmarked cars was parked bumper to bumper, suggesting plainclothes first responders were on scene along with the rest of the circus.

Four uniformed cops milled around the side exit ramp, blocking my usual route into the opera house and the tunnels where I'd provided the miserable, godforsaken children a forever home. Two of the cops talked on phones, probably calling even *more* people into this zoo.

Swallowing, I pulled out my own phone and pretended to

peruse it as I walked forward, glancing up occasionally as I wove around a few onlookers, opera visitors who had chosen to linger and observe. I didn't allow myself to stare. I didn't turn into the back driveway of the opera house, but continued forward as I took in the chaos.

A small part of me protested, screaming for reason. They *couldn't* have found the girl yet. She was bound and gagged, so close to her deliverance. I'd come back to gift it to her. The final bleeding must be complete by now.

If the cops found her, I won't be able to finish my work. I was so close to severing another life from suffering, as the Teachings instruct.

But there was no way anyone could have seen me bring her inside. This chaos had to signify something else. A fire. A fallen backdrop that had crushed some of the insufferable actors or crew.

I continued on my way, wandering like any of the other denizens of the night beginning to emerge from bars in the area. I opened a rideshare app in case one of the cops noticed me. I'd need a good reason to be out here this late.

When I reached the other side of the opera house, I backtracked and came up along the side wall, listening for any sign of what had happened. They barely noticed me, but I heard them.

Talking of a little girl who'd been taken to the hospital. Found in grisly condition. More bodies of children, as if the opera house's tunnels were a morgue.

My instincts suggested I flee, but if I did that, they'd know it was me. Still, I hadn't yet been noticed. I leaned against the wall, wishing I had one of those blasted cigarettes that half of D.C.'s walking puppets smoked at every turn. If the cops saw me, they'd approach, and I'd tell them I was just coming in to get a head start on the next day's cleaning after a full weekend of performance.

My memories and the Teachings! What if they search the building? They'll find it all and know it was me.

I'd have to get inside and move them, hide them somewhere. I was a fool to think I could trust this building. I'd thought there could be no better place to conceal the grand opera of my life's misery, but I'd been wrong.

I couldn't do anything about that now, not with all those cops crawling around the place. But the instant I was back inside, I'd collect everything and move it somewhere safe. Somewhere protected and hidden.

Not home. Not to the place where it all began, no. But somewhere fitting. Perhaps I'll get lucky, and the cops won't search my hiding place.

I knew the instant the thought occurred that I was engaging in folly. Cops searched everything related to a crime. But I still might have time to move my treasured belongings.

I skulked back along the building, keeping to the shadows without allowing my steps to speed or slow. My best bet now was to avoid notice and drift back into the late-night crowds.

Tomorrow, I would come into work, reevaluate, and move forward.

Once I reached the street, I turned away from the opera house and forced deep breaths in and out of my lungs, luxuriating in the cold night.

So what if they'd found the girl? I'd worn gloves and a mask when I was down in the tunnels with her. Children's minds were notoriously imaginative and unreliable anyway. Any description she gave would be monstrous and useless, leaving me to my anonymity.

I'd be okay. I would. And my work was not done.

The tunnels had seemed like the perfect spot, but there were other potential options. Hell, my family's own house had been my own original dungeon. I'd thought the darker, more sepulchral atmosphere of the tunnels more fitting, but perhaps I should've stayed with my initial instincts.

Fate had smiled on me, after all. I saw the police rather than stumbling into a trap they'd laid. That would've been disastrous.

Because I was just getting started.

9

Emma trailed Vance up the stairs, away from the tunnels. He'd been more than ready to leave, and she practically had to speed-walk to keep up with him.

So much the better. Him being ahead of her meant she didn't have to fake having patience for small talk.

Vance headed toward a corner of the theater where Leo and Mia were interviewing two women dressed in black. Stage crew, Emma supposed, but neither appeared capable of passing as a man—presuming the "man who'd said something frightening to Carla" was their unsub—or strong enough to handle getting those children into the tunnels alone.

Finally, Mia left Leo to finish things up and came over to Vance and Emma. Her face still appeared pinched and more withdrawn than normal, but she had some of her color back.

"Emma, you're practically bouncing on your toes." Mia raised an eyebrow pointedly. "I take it you found something?"

Nodding, Emma explained as she kept an eye on the theater personnel roving around the area. "A locked door disguised to appear boarded over. We're going to grab a tool and pry it open. What about you? Any news?"

"No. Everyone we spoke to is horrified, and it all reads genuine to me. These people are freaked out. If our unsub is among them, he should get an award."

Vance had been eyeing the area since they'd come upstairs, but when his gaze came back to Mia, Emma got the impression he hadn't found what he'd been looking for. "What about Mr. Grumpy from earlier?"

Mia shrugged. "We haven't spoken to him yet. I think he just had a long night, and—"

Emma held up a hand to interrupt her. "Who are you two talking about?"

"The stage manager. Ted Fishbourne. Vance and I met him after the performance."

"Bad vibes," Vance said under his breath, leaning toward Emma, "and he might be a little older than I would have guessed based on what our unsub has to be capable of physically, but I wouldn't say it's impossible."

Mia's lips pursed. "He just wanted to go home to bed, and us talking to the performers was keeping that from happening."

"He seemed so grumpy, I bet he left without waiting." Vance pointed at a door opposite where they stood, focusing on Emma. "The guy walked out like a toddler in a huff when the performers wouldn't wrap up our conversation. Sure, he might have been going to an office, but who knows?"

Mia looked like she might protest again, but Emma spoke first. "Even if it's probably nothing, we still want to talk to him. I can do it."

Instead of agreeing and pointing her in the right direction, Mia looked to Vance as if for help. And then she opened her mouth to say something but didn't. Watching her, Emma felt a little stab of annoyance. Even her friends doubted her now…and when it came to interviewing? She bit back a curse and waited for the hammer to fall.

Vance stuffed his hands into his pockets, frowning. "Don't worry about it, Emma. We want to get back to that door anyway, right? Leo and Mia can cover the interviews."

Right. Because I'm too unstable to be depended on. Good for stalking through dark tunnels and breaking down doors, but damn little else.

So be it.

"Promise you'll let us talk to him, okay?" Mia reached out and gripped Emma's arm, squeezing a touch more than she had to. "It's okay. Leo and I've got it covered."

Emma pulled away, but before she could think how to respond beyond simply nodding—she wasn't sure this would be a promise she could keep, after all—Vance whistled under his breath, just loudly enough for her and Mia to turn.

"Look who just walked in." He nodded toward the orchestra pit, where a rumpled, middle-aged man was just heading toward the stairs. He angrily shoved a mop bucket aside from where it had been left too close to a stairwell leading to an upper floor. That done, he made as if to ascend the stairs, but paused on spotting Vance and Mia. Adjusting his glasses, then smoothing down his shirt, he pivoted in their direction.

Emma fell back a few steps as Mia took the lead. "Mr. Fish—"

"You were here earlier, the ones with the VIP passes. Why are you still here?" He glanced between Mia and Vance, unapologetic for cutting Mia off. "What's going on?"

Vance pulled out his ID—unnecessarily, so far as Emma was concerned—then explained what had been found in the broadest details possible. Fishbourne's lined face went a shade gray, then slack. He'd seemed confused, maybe annoyed, when he'd approached. Now he looked like he might vomit.

"I...I can't believe that." He pushed past Emma and took a heavy seat on a stool beside a panel of levers and switches set into the wall. "To think we were all up here, performing and working, while that—"

"Mr. Fishbourne," Mia spoke quietly, coming up beside him and cutting off Emma's direct view, "where did you go after you spoke to us?"

He shrugged. "I went to my office upstairs, to wrap up notes." He indicated the stairwell. "I was tired and wanted to get home as soon as possible."

"Did you know about the tunnels?"

"Yes, of course. Everyone who works here knows about them. They're one of the reasons the stage is so freezing cold when we don't have the stage lights burning our skin off. I haven't been down there in years, though. We used to use them for storage, mostly for costumes or props we had no intention of ever using again. For performances that would never be revived. Rats and who knows what else made quick work of anything that went down there, but nobody cared really. The practice was stopped when the opera's benefactors realized some people will pay good money for an authentic costume."

Emma angled sideways, watching the stage manager fumble for words. Maybe he'd been grumpy earlier, as Vance had said, but now he seemed more pitiful. Not necessarily innocent, but not someone who screamed *suspect* to her either.

"And do you know of anyone who could have done this?"

He released something that might have been a laugh, if harsher, and removed his glasses. He took a cloth from a pocket and began rubbing at them. "Do *this*? No, of course not. If I knew anyone like that and hadn't already reported them for suspicious behavior, I'd be someone you should lock up."

Vance let the statement hang for a touch too long. "And were you home with anyone before you came to the theater before last night's performance? Or over the weekend?"

Fishbourne scowled, but squinted as he aimed his gaze at Vance. Apparently, he really did need his glasses. "I live alone, so I have no alibi for any point this weekend when I wasn't here with everyone else. Beyond being exhausted and half blind, that is. Not exactly killer material. I have a weak ankle that's wanting for an ice pack, too, and having an upstairs office makes that a delight. Do you want a doctor's note?"

"So you'd avoid the stairs," Mia spoke gently, clearly trying to interrupt the grousing at Vance, "but you knew they were there."

Fishbourne nodded, still rubbing at his glasses. "Everyone knows about them."

"Everyone?"

"Yes. Our theater company, and any that rent the hall from us during off-season shows. Actors will go down there to smoke, or to practice in solitude. It's not the greatest place to recite your lines in full costume. You'd ruin the hems with all the muck on the floor. But for early rehearsals, sometimes performers want to go somewhere they can prepare out of sight of anyone else."

Mia pressed him. "So anyone with access to the building, going back years, could conceivably have known about or been in those tunnels."

"Yes, I'd say that's correct."

That left them with far too many names to be of use.

Emma fought the urge to shake the man, to demand he tell them something helpful, when she felt a familiar cold seep through her coat.

Daniel Jackson's ghost stood at the entrance to the

stairwell going up. He hovered around by the mop bucket Fishbourne had shoved out of his way when he entered.

The ghost's face turned toward the stage manager. He said nothing. Maybe he intended Emma to see him as more curious than accusatory, but maybe not.

Emma refocused on Fishbourne, who pursed his lips and nodded as Mia read off some names he'd offered for confirmation. The man didn't seem particularly nervous, but he also wasn't overly interested in being helpful or answering questions.

Of course, it's three in the morning, Emma girl. You being up doesn't mean much, but for this guy?

"And when did you stop using the tunnels for storage?" Vance gazed at the long list of names over Mia's shoulder.

Fishbourne gave his answer to Mia, apparently still annoyed with Vance. "Ten years ago. They were originally used during the Civil War. This was a garrison for Union soldiers, you know. We have a plaque somewhere around here with Abraham Lincoln's signature. It's a bronze casting, of course—"

Mia put a hand up. "That's great, Mr. Fishbourne. Fascinating history. But you were telling us about using them for storage."

"Yes, of course. We stopped using them, like I said. About ten years ago. The tunnels flooded and ruined almost everything. Cost the opera hundreds of thousands of dollars, from what I remember. We started auctioning pieces, and that includes props and small set pieces. Anything we thought someone might pay to own. Nobody trusts the tunnels anymore. All the exits were boarded up or sealed once we didn't need them."

Vance exchanged looks with both Mia and Emma. This was loosely the same story they'd heard from the opera house manager upon arrival. Not so verbatim as to be rehearsed, but consistent.

Handing over his card, Vance told Fishbourne he was free to go for now. "But stay in the area, and please call us if you think of anything that might be useful, no matter how trivial it may seem."

The stage manager huffed and stuck the card into his pocket, doing the same with Mia's and Emma's after they offered them. Fishbourne turned on his heel and headed back past Daniel's hovering ghost.

Leo wandered up, and Vance and Emma took turns filling him in.

"Woulda been nice to have a suspect right off the bat." He nodded at Mia as she approached. "But I can't say I'm surprised. I'm not getting red flags off anyone we've talked to, and none of them have mentioned Ted Fishbourne as being suspicious. I think the words they used most were 'grumpy,' 'irritable,' and 'bad-mannered.'"

"And they'd all know him." Emma spoke quietly, watching the man walk up the stairs leading to his office, favoring his right ankle. "No way for him to go unnoticed, being the stage manager."

Of course, hiding in plain sight is a cliché because it often turns out to be remarkably effective.

"Not remotely." Mia tucked her iPad under one arm, adjusting the coat she wore over her dress. "So are we agreed to just keep an eye on him?"

Emma nodded along with the others. She desperately wanted to talk to Fishbourne on her own, given that Daniel's ghost seemed interested in him. His white eyes remained fixed on the stairwell entrance, as if not wanting to obstruct access to the stairs. But Emma would have to figure out how to approach the stage manager in a way that didn't conflict with Jacinda's orders that she not conduct interviews at all.

Leo gazed around the space. "I think we've talked to everyone. I'm going to track down addresses for the victims' families."

Emma caught Vance's eye, then pointed back toward the stairwell to the tunnels. "Before things wrap up, I want to see what's on the other side of that door."

Mia gave an exaggerated shiver and turned to follow Leo, but Vance pulled his jacket tighter. "I'll ask Fishbourne where we can get a tool for the job."

Emma lagged behind and glanced around for signs of Daniel, but the ghost had disappeared.

Maybe he'd appear in the tunnels and offer some kind of verbal assistance, since it seemed the only interviews Emma could expect to conduct would have to be with their victims.

10

With the help of a crowbar and a hammer, Emma made short work of the lock on the badly hidden door. The padlock's anchor flew away from the doorframe when she wrenched it open, jangling off into the dark.

Vance kicked at the hammer where she'd dropped it. "We could've come at it from the other side and picked—"

Emma turned and glared at him. "You wanted to go wandering out into the D.C. night and find the tunnels from the other side and hope to find our way to the door?"

Suitably chastened, he pulled the door farther open and gestured her into the next phase of tunneling. "Point taken. Ladies first?"

Not bothering to answer, Emma hefted the crowbar and flashlight and moved forward. This part of the tunnel looked much like the areas they'd already passed through. Dark, dank, and with little more than puddles and the occasional bit of pipework to distinguish one patch of light from the next.

Emma bounced the flashlight beam along their path ahead. "Fishbourne said it was a straight shot from the mid-tunnel exit to the storage building, so assuming we found our way to the right exit he was talking about, we should be good to go."

Vance didn't answer, but his footsteps echoed behind hers. Within another hundred feet, they came to a door much like the one that had let them into the tunnels to begin with but without a padlock holding it closed. Emma propped the door open with the crowbar. A light switch obediently flicked upward to illuminate another concrete stairwell, mirroring the one Mia had initially come down.

Not bothering to wait for her partner, Emma sped upward, taking the stairs two at a time.

She should've been tired—she'd had more than her fair share to drink that afternoon, and slept only a few restless, drunken hours before waking again to devour those fried eggs—but the adrenaline of the case pushed her along. One good way to chase away her own demons would be to start hunting down another murderer. And this one, a child killer no less.

She was an FBI agent, for crying out loud. Not a lovesick or grief-sick heroine who couldn't live without a damn man and family to keep her occupied.

At the top of the staircase, a metal exit door opened to reveal a warehouse space. Flats of theatrical scenery approximating a Shakespearean-era tavern leaned up against the wall to the left of the door, and a veritable maze of stage-worn furniture and dollies spread out before them. Emma flicked another light switch, and weak, buzzing fluorescents came to life above them.

Before Emma could decide which direction to head, a lumbering, ponytailed security guard came hurrying around the corner past a flat painted like a London street. "Where the hell did you two—"

"Federal agents," Vance held up his badge, stopping the

man in his tracks, "and you should have heard we were coming."

The guard squinted at them through his thick-framed glasses and came to a slow halt a few feet away. "Yeah, I heard. But I figured you'd come through the front door tonight. Was there waiting for you."

Emma held up her own ID. "Special Agent Emma Last. Apologies. We wanted to get a head start."

The guard nodded and gestured to the side of the door they'd come through. "I get it. I took off the padlock just in case."

Emma looked back and saw a padlock resting on the ground near the door. At about five feet up, metal latching and bolts gave the padlock a home for when it was in use. Locks needed, indeed.

Vance gestured to a couple of couches. "How about we sit down, and you tell us what you can?"

"Yeah, all right." The guard brushed his hand through his long ponytail, and Emma revised his age downward. She'd guessed him to be in his forties, but the nervous gesture made him seem quite a bit younger, as did the shine in his hair. In his thirties, maybe.

"Your name?" Emma took a seat beside Vance, eyeing how easily the guard sat down across from them. No compunction about sitting on the stage furniture, and no worries for how they observed him or who might be watching. Comfortable in the space as well as in his own skin.

"Frankie Wilson. Worked here five years now. Nights only. Lets me get home to my kids and get them off to school."

"Must be hard on a marriage, Mr. Wilson?" Vance smiled, but Emma read the subterfuge in it.

"Not mine. And call me Frankie." He grinned. "Wife

works as a night manager at a D.C. hotel. Her mom and mine take turns getting the kids to bed most nights, but we're there in the mornings and afternoons. Probably spend more time with our kids than most working parents do."

His eyes dimmed, and Emma saw from his glance to the door that he'd suddenly thought back to the children's bodies found there. She met Vance's gaze and knew he'd come to the same conclusion.

"I don't see any security cameras," Emma brought his focus back to them, "but this place is high society. You'd think there'd be cameras all over the place."

Frankie shrugged. "They got plenty in the actual opera house, where the public goes, but not over here. Not much need for them. Being here at night, I go whole weeks without seeing anyone come or go from this space when the house is deep in rehearsals and then putting up a show. Mostly, folks just come through here when they're starting on a new set or costuming a new cast."

"That's it?" Emma glanced back to the stairwell door. "So you'd know if someone were using this area to get in and out of the tunnels?"

"Oh, for sure. Nobody uses that access door unless they're moving smaller set pieces, like the stuff you can carry by hand. Everything else gets taken over by truck from the loading dock outside." Frankie frowned. "That's where our cameras are focused, on the outside doors and windows. Just deterrents really, you know? In case of vandalism, graffiti, stuff like that."

"Looks like there might have been one there." Vance gestured up to what looked to be a piece of plastic dangling from a corner of the ceiling, down the wall from the stairwell door. "Know anything about that? Maybe a camera that was focused on this door we came up through?"

"I, uh…" The guard got to his feet and moved over to the

area where the plastic hung, Emma and Vance following behind him. "There mighta been one there. But the main cameras look out on the doors and windows, like I said. The loading dock. Some of the stuff we get in for props is borrowed or antique, so we can't afford for it to be stolen or for someone to say they delivered it when they didn't."

Emma eyed the hanging plastic, which looked dusty and decades old. Their unsub might not have had to work too hard to get past cameras, after all. Not if he had keys and knew how to avoid security. "Any security footage you could look at? See if there's anything suspicious?"

Still frowning at the plastic bracket hanging off the wall, the guard finally nodded. "Yeah, gimme a few. Should be able to speed through the last few days and see if we've got activity. But like I said, it'll all be outside the building."

"We'll take anything." Emma loosened her coat, glancing around the large space. "In the meantime, you mind if we look around, Frankie?"

"Help yourself. Holler if you need me." With that, the guard walked away, and Emma headed toward a large roll-up door operated by a pulley system. A glance outside showed the loading dock, mostly unlit and with a camera in a corner.

She gestured for Vance to fan out and began exploring, but the guard called out for their attention before two minutes had passed. When they got to him, they found him shaking his head over a bank of monitors set above an old metal desk with two computer towers tucked underneath. A corkboard hung on the wall behind the monitors. Colorful thumbtacks held papers, a calendar, and several ticket stubs in place.

Frankie pointed at a screen showing the loading dock. "That ain't what it's supposed to be." He'd stilled it on footage of an old, Victorian-looking couch being rolled inside.

"It's an ugly couch, I grant you." Vance stared at him,

apparently waiting for the punch line, but then continued. "But I'm guessing that's not what you're telling us."

Scowling, Frankie pointed again at the couch. "I spotted it on the feed from two days back and knew something was up, so I went back further." He scrolled the feed. "Last week, there it is again. And again, the week before."

Emma tapped the screen. "Is that unusual, to have a set piece moved in and out so frequently?"

"That's usual, sure, but that couch got stored away two months ago. I was working day shift when it came in, and I know it hasn't been pulled out since, because it's sitting right over there." He pointed across the space, and Emma just made out the scrolled woodwork of the couch's frame.

She turned back to the monitors. "And this feed you're showing us doesn't match up why?"

"It's from twelve days ago. See the date there?" He pointed at the time stamp on the screen.

Vance ran a hand through his hair. "The explanation for this could be…?"

His question hung in the air for a moment until Frankie shook himself. "Somebody reset the camera to replay old footage instead of recording new. It's been like this for," he scrolled backward through the recording, "looks like since the last week of February. The twenty-fifth."

"You mean…" Emma trailed off, more shocked than she would have been if the facility had simply had no cameras at all. "This camera view has been altered for twenty-one days. And nobody noticed?"

Frankie's pale skin went a shade of red she'd rarely seen, and he sat down heavily in the chair by the desk. "Nobody comes around here. You want the truth, the manager who hired me told me I could sleep the whole night through as long as I woke up if a door rattled, a light came on, or the phone rang. I don't," he looked up fast, eyes wide, "understand me, I don't, Honest Abe. And I was awake on every shift the past three months. I swear."

"But you didn't notice this camera feed had been tampered with."

"We don't watch 'em really. Only time we'd review footage is if something goes wrong, like, if we had a theft or something turned up missing."

"You don't monitor the feeds at all?"

"This place is a dead zone. Nothing happens here, and even though they said I could sleep on the job, I don't. Not unless I'm really beat, but I swear I've been awake every night since New Year's."

Vance put his hands on the desk, edging Emma back a step, and looked Frankie in the eye.

"So what do you do on your shifts? When you're awake?"

"I walk around, glance at the cameras and make sure they're turned on. The little blinking light, you know? If anybody woulda noticed the camera feeds being messed with, it woulda been the daytime guys, because that's when the couch was brought in."

Emma gestured for control of the computer, and Frankie stepped aside. She scrolled through the footage again, checking date and time stamps for the couch's delivery. Sure enough, it came in at two in the afternoon on the twenty-first of January.

"You normally work nights, right, Frankie?"

"Mostly, yeah. Now and then, I cover for someone on day shift if they're taking vacation, or if somebody's out sick. I think that's why I was here that day."

"And what about on the night of February twenty-fifth? The day the camera feed was altered."

Frankie's mouth fell open. "Aw, no. You aren't thinking it was me, are you? I got kids of my own. How could I do something like this?"

Vance put a hand up. "Standard question, Frankie. If you have an alibi, then all's well. So how about it? February twenty-fifth. You worked that night?"

The guy rubbed his brow and squeezed his eyes shut before turning to the desk again. He sifted through the papers tacked to the corkboard, pulled one down, and handed it to Vance. Then he did the same with the calendar.

"I was here that night. On shift from nine in the evening until six the next morning."

"And you didn't notice the feed being changed?"

Frankie's mouth turned down, and his chin shook. "I take my break at two every night I'm here. I know that gives me no alibi, but…" A tear escaped his right eye. "I couldn't do something like that. I swear. They were just kids."

Emma gauged his sincerity, wondering if his tears were genuine. Having cried so many of her own recently, it was hard to accept that anyone else knew what true sadness felt like.

She gripped his shoulder. "Hey, you've given us your best alibi. We'll confirm it if we can. In the meantime, what else can you tell us about the security system? Who else might have accessed it on the night feeds were changed? And would they have been in here with you, maybe during your 'break'?"

"No way. I take my break right here at the desk." He wiped a hand across his face and refocused on the monitors. "No chance anybody could've come in here while I was on shift without me noticing them."

Vance leaned closer to the paused video feed, then glanced at Frankie. "You think you could send us this footage?"

"Do you one better and make you a copy right here." He reached for the desk drawer and lifted out a stack of blank CDs. "Give me about ten minutes to burn this?"

"That'd be great. Thanks."

"You bet. And I'll try to figure out exactly when the feed changed over and who was here when it happened." He frowned at the monitors as if they'd betrayed him. "I'm sick to my stomach over what went on in those tunnels. It takes me all the rest of the night and the next two days straight, I'll do my best and let you know."

They waited quietly and watched him work. That done, he handed Emma the CD in a jewel case.

She patted him on the shoulder and offered her card. "Can you point us to that front door you mentioned?"

Frankie walked them out and even held the door as they departed.

Emma kept pace with Vance on the walk back to the opera house. "You think he knows anything?"

"No. But I wish he did."

She trudged along, the energy she'd felt earlier suddenly draining with each step. Now that the adrenaline had worn off, she could've fallen asleep on the sidewalk if Vance would've let her. "That leaves us with two possibilities. Whoever did this had inside access, or they have an accomplice who works on the inside."

11

Leo and Denae stopped outside the metal detectors, offering the school's security guard a chance to turn the mechanisms off. Instead, he only waved them through. "Machines are broke," he flipped a newspaper page, "so come on in. Principal's office on your right."

"You don't want to check our IDs?" Leo opened his coat to reveal the holster on his hip.

"Maybe find out why two armed adults are here?"

The security guard heaved a sigh and lowered his paper. "Y'all are Feds."

Denae scoffed. "And you don't need to see ID to confirm that. Go on, Mr. Detective."

"I know a cop when I see one." The guard rustled his paper like he'd start reading again but left it on his lap. "No uniforms, no cocky swagger. You're Feds. Principal's office is on the right."

With that, he ducked behind the newspaper again.

Leo led the way, an annoyed set to his shoulders. When he got to the door, he held it open for Denae and spoke under his breath. "Some security guard, huh? No wonder inner-city kids don't trust cops."

Denae wrinkled her nose and scowled. "Leo, these kids have probably never seen a cop doing anything other than arresting or shooting someone they know. That's why they don't trust them."

Leo couldn't help mirroring Denae's scowl. "Schools shouldn't need security guards in the first place. This feels more like a prison than a learning environment."

A frazzled admin assistant glanced up from her desk, freezing as Denae flashed her ID. The assistant dropped her pen, as if on autopilot, and reached for her phone. "I'll call Principal Wexler for you."

Leo tried for the warmest smile he could offer, given the reason for their errand. "We're here about Daniel Jackson. If we could see his teacher also, that would be helpful."

The woman's brow furrowed before she relaxed a touch. Maybe she was relieved they'd come about a missing student versus seeking out one of the students sitting in a classroom on a Monday morning. "I'll send someone to cover for her."

Taking a seat on a bench at the side of the room, Leo eyed some framed articles hanging on the opposite wall. One highlighted the efforts of Jefferson Elementary's principal and teachers when it came to after-school programs and community-building events.

Leo read the headline just loudly enough for Denae to hear. "'Principal and Teachers Organize Backpack Drive That Sees a Thousand Backpacks Full of Supplies Donated for Local School.' It's left to teachers and principals to figure out the basic supplies for these kids. Not like they don't have enough to deal with already."

"Par for the course, Ambrose. Unless you're talking about schools where the lawns are all shiny green and crime is something that happens to other people."

Leo stood as a middle-aged man entered and held out his

hand even before the door closed behind him. Wearing a sweater-vest and khakis, he could have passed for a Black Mr. Rogers if not for the cautious set to his lips that took the place of a smile. Leo couldn't blame him. A school like this probably didn't see Feds showing up for anything other than tragedy and crises.

And here we are, making sure that story keeps getting told.

"I'm the principal of Jefferson Elementary, Joe Wexler, at your service." Hope bled from every word as he continued. "I understand you're here about Daniel Jackson? Have you found him? Is he okay?"

As Leo pulled out his ID, Denae shook the man's hand. "Special Agent Denae Monroe, and this is Special Agent Leo Ambrose. We should speak in private, if we can."

The principal's hands fell to his sides, and he slumped as though a weight had just been placed on his shoulders. "Of course." Pausing at the desk, he asked the woman they'd spoken to before to send in Daniel's teacher as soon as she arrived. He motioned them to a door decorated with crayon drawings of fruits and vegetables.

The office was larger than Leo expected, set up with a conference table and decorated on every side with stuffed koalas. Posters showed koalas surrounded by encouraging statements.

Principal Wexler picked up an oversize plush bear to make another chair available at the conference table. "The school's mascot, so they're everywhere. The kids joke that the green chairs make it look like a jungle in here. Just need some eucalyptus."

Leo sat down across from the principal, giving him a moment to reflect on the collection of stuffed animals, since it seemed like that was what he needed. Clearly, the man knew what was coming. Before he could speak again, though, a heavyset Black woman came flying in the door they'd just shut.

"Did you find Daniel?" Her brown eyes shot between Leo and Denae, mouth still agape with the question. She glanced at the principal and closed the door behind her. "Oh. Oh, no."

"Agents," the principal sighed, "this is Estelle Findlay, Daniel's homeroom teacher."

"I'm sorry to have to tell you this," Leo kept his voice low as Estelle joined them at the small table. "Daniel Jackson's body was recovered overnight."

The principal's eyes went hooded as he slumped in his chair. "It never gets easier, losing a student. And Daniel, of all of them. So small…"

"Had the *Star Wars* movies practically memorized." Mrs. Findlay's voice broke, and she tore her gaze sideways to stare out the window. "He was so creative too. Would write short stories that I swear someone out there would've been proud to publish."

Leo gave them a moment, antsy as he was to press forward. "We're here partly because Daniel's body was found along with that of another little girl."

"From another school," Denae put in.

Leo nodded, acknowledging her statement. "A third child, fortunately, was recovered alive. Also from another school."

Principal Wexler reached sideways and clutched Estelle's hand. "I'm glad at least one child could be saved. We'll help however we can—"

"Without traumatizing the other children." Estelle sat straighter, her dark eyes going a little harder.

Principal Wexler gave a small shrug and straightened in his chair too. "Forgive us. We haven't had the best interactions with law enforcement at our school. As Estelle said, the kids come first."

Nodding, Leo took out his iPad, trying not to think about

the conditions of the campus and the lackluster attitude of the security guard charged with guarding these precious teachers and students. "We appreciate that, I promise. And at this time, I don't think we need to trouble any of your other students with questions."

The principal's shoulders relaxed a touch. "Thank you. These kids don't have the best lives, for the most part. I'd rather they not have to associate school with being interrogated."

Denae shifted in her seat. "We don't normally interrogate children, not without parental—"

"The cops sure do." Estelle scoffed, releasing her supervisor's hand to cross her arms. "You should've seen the way they burst in here after a few unruly boys stole candy from the bodega down the street. Wanted to drag the whole fifth-grade class down to the precinct!"

The principal's lips quirked, as if holding in reluctant amusement. "It wasn't quite that bad, but you'll understand our caution."

Leo nodded, holding back his own smile. If Estelle Findlay wanted to get her defenses up rather than fall apart over a student's death, all the better. Anxious and angry people were often more ready to talk and could reveal information they'd otherwise have kept to themselves.

He placed his iPad on the table, displaying a school picture of Daniel Jackson. "Anything you can tell us about Daniel could be useful. Anything you haven't already shared."

Mr. Wexler gestured to the woman beside him. "Estelle can tell you more, but I'll tell you that Daniel never got sent to my office. Kindergarten through fourth grade, he wasn't ever a student who got into fights or caused trouble. I saw him when I visited classes or the cafeteria or handed out honor roll certificates, and that was about it."

Leo nodded to Estelle to continue. "Did he have a lot of friends? Was he popular?"

"Oh no, not in the slightest." She waved her hand in the air, as if shooing the thought away. "Not that he shouldn't have been…but Daniel was reserved. Quiet."

She broke off, her lips pursing. The principal nodded at her to continue.

"Joe knows I suspected abuse at home. Daniel would come in with cuts and bruises that he blamed on after-school sports, but that boy hated gym. After-school sports, my big ass. Excuse my language, but you know what I mean."

Leo offered a small smile, noting down everything the woman said. "I get it. He wasn't the type. So if you suspected abuse…?"

The principal frowned. "You'd be surprised how difficult it is to act on suspicions when a student isn't making accusations. I called Child Services once when I saw an especially angry bruise on his arm…we're mandated reporters, and of course we act when we feel there is cause. But Daniel never once spoke up or said anything about his parents or any other adult hitting him. Without that, all we have is our suspicions, and it falls to Child Services to follow up with an investigation."

Denae had been nodding along. "And did they?"

"Far as we know, yes. Daniel was back in school the next day, no new marks on him. None that we could see anyway. We both knew something was going on, but we got so many kids here, you know?"

Leo knew. *It was one bruise, and they have hundreds of kids here, some dealing with worse.*

Estelle sighed. "You want the truth, both Joe and I suspected the parents when Daniel went missing, but the news said they both have alibis. And honestly?" She flexed the fingers on one hand, studying her nails and avoiding Leo's gaze. "I'd accuse them of negligence before murder. I could've seen them hurting Daniel, but I don't think they cared enough to commit murder."

Leo caught the principal's eye. "I take it you never received any threats from them or witnessed anything to corroborate your suspicions of abuse?"

Estelle shook her head, eyes on her hands. "He was such a good kid. Loved science fiction. I was devastated when he disappeared."

Principal Wexler hummed along as the teacher spoke. "Like I said, all we had was suspicions. Nothing that'd stand up in court."

Denae crossed one leg over the other. "You said he wasn't popular. Does that mean he had no friends, nobody who could speak to where he'd go after school?"

"No, not really. Daniel was a loner." Estelle sighed, and Leo could see the weight of grief beginning to sink in. "I tried to encourage him to participate more in class, to play with other kids at recess. He preferred staying to himself."

They spent another twenty minutes going through standard questions and attempting to mine out any new facts that might be helpful. Daniel had been such a solitary figure that it was heartbreaking to have so little to go on.

"Principal Wexler, Mrs. Findlay, thank you so much for your time." Leo shot a look to Denae, who nodded her agreement. "If you think of anything that might help us, please reach out. Here's my card."

The principal took both of their cards and left the teacher behind in his office as he ushered them out past the newspaper-reading security guard. At the entrance, he offered the tiniest of nods before turning on his heel and shutting the door firmly behind him, as if to shut out the possibility that they'd sneak back in and give him additional tragic news.

Leo breathed deep and made a beeline for their car, avoiding his instinct to look back. He'd rather not have the reminder of where Daniel had been required to come every day, caring adults notwithstanding.

As they headed back to the SUV, Denae walked in step with him, moving a touch slower than usual. "Makes you wonder about the type who has kids only to leave them with bruises."

Leo swallowed a lump of air. He felt so awful for Daniel, it was difficult to respond at first. "Maybe we'll have more luck with the other parents."

"You look at Jessica's file yet?" Denae raised her eyebrows.

"Don't tell me it's the same." Leo glanced at his partner, frowning.

Denae paused at the door, waiting for him to unlock the vehicle. "More stories from this side of the tracks. I hope you're ready to hear them."

Leo opened the vehicle and climbed in, waiting for Denae to buckle up before starting the engine. "You're telling me it's another case of abuse and neglect with nobody doing anything to save the kid?"

"There you go again, assuming the worst. Okay, yes, it's probably more of the same, but hold off on thinking, 'Nobody did anything.'"

"What should I be thinking? You still haven't told me what's in the file."

Denae waited a few breaths before answering. "Troublemaking little girl acting out to get her mom's attention, if you believe a neighbor's complaint. But it did lead to a drunk-and-disorderly for the mother. She and the father aren't on the best of terms, and she had one too many after an angry phone call. Jessica went to a neighbor for help with her homework, the neighbor called the cops when Mom came over to 'get her daughter back.'"

Leo couldn't decide between stomping on the accelerator or pulling over and calling it a day.

This is going to be one hell of a depressing case.

12

Mia tapped the steering wheel as she waited for a tow truck to pull into traffic. She bit back a sigh and glanced at Vance, who was fiddling with his phone. "You mind looking up the police reports on Daniel Jackson and Jessica Howard?"

Vance pocketed his phone and reached for his iPad. "I gotcha." After tapping the device a few times, he started reading from the reports. "Looks like police conducted initial searches, but nothing turned up. Both families live below the poverty line, but all the parents had alibis, and no other people had regular access to the homes or interactions with the missing children. No siblings, no live-in roommates or grandparents, etcetera, etcetera. Cases were all but forgotten, they were so cold."

Mia blinked. "But the kids were still missing—"

"As of *weeks* ago." Vance reached sideways and rested a hand on her shoulder. "You know the first forty-eight hours are where the investigation happens. If no leads pan out after that, chances are that child isn't coming back. Even if they are still alive."

Mia wanted to argue, but instead, she only gripped the

steering wheel tighter. "It's only been a few weeks. It makes me sick that they'd give up like that, even without a suspect."

"These are poor kids we're talking about, Mia. And parents who barely have what it takes to get by themselves. Daniel and Carla were minorities. They don't get the same kind of attention as rich white kids who go missing. Our killer picked the right victims so he could skate under the radar."

"I don't know how to respond to that." Mia realized the SUV was wavering between lanes, nerves had so taken over her system. "It's not okay."

"No argument from me there, babe."

Vance went silent, and Mia focused on driving, fighting back an urge to scream at the world. She regretted asking him to look up the reports to begin with.

Across town, the GPS led them to a run-down apartment complex marred by peeling paint and abandoned furniture moldering along the curbside. Gang tags and graffiti shrouded every wall and boarded-over window in sight. Mia recognized the big, bubble-like tag representing the Powders gang that had dominated D.C. for a few years now. She noted a less familiar red-and-blue, diamond-shaped tag overlaid the Powders' symbol.

Mia pointed it out and Vance grunted. "That's the Disciples. New gang moving in. That'll be fun soon."

Mia slowed to peer more closely at one of the Disciples' signs—a blue, triangle-shaped sign with a red *D* above it. The symbol looked more like a child's version of a road sign than anything meant to indicate gang activity.

She pulled into a small lot and parked beside a car with two teenage boys sitting on the hood. They traded a cigarette back and forth, at a time of day when they should've been in school. The youths took one look at Mia and Vance inside their vehicle and hopped down to trot off down the street.

"Afraid we'll take them back to school?" Vance nudged her elbow.

She frowned. "Or jail."

Vance gave her shoulder a squeeze before getting out and heading toward the Alvarezes' apartment, which faced the parking lot.

He had a fist raised to knock when the door flew open. A short, athletic woman froze at the sight of them, one hand on the door and one on an oversize purse. "Mrs. Alvarez?"

"I, uh, yeah." The woman glanced between them. Bags showed beneath her eyes. "You're here about Carla?"

Mia showed her ID, leaving it open until the woman nodded, indicating she'd examined it well enough. "We are. Do you have a minute?"

"Just a minute." She stepped forward, pulling her door shut behind her and locking it as she spoke. "I just came home to get fresh clothes for Carla. The docs are going to let her come home today, but her clothes were ruined…"

When the woman trailed off, Mia nodded that she understood. "Mrs. Alvarez, I…I was the one who found her. I'm so sorry for—"

Mrs. Alvarez had her arms around Mia before she could get another word out, squeezing her so tight she thought a rib might crack. "Thank you! Thank you, thank you, thank you…" She trailed off as sobs overtook her, and she shook, loosening her grip and slumping against Mia's chest.

Mia held the woman in an embrace while Vance looked on.

With sobs still shaking her, Mrs. Alvarez slowly pulled away and straightened, wiping at her cheeks. Mia wished she could hold the woman forever, to tell her she would never have to worry about something like this happening again.

No parent should ever have to endure this kind of torture. Not ever.

"Mrs. Alvarez—"

"Call me Marta." She gathered herself, taking an extra beat to stifle her sobs and resettle the big bag on her shoulder. Mia glimpsed a neon-green shirt poking from the top now. Gear that was bright enough to bring a smile or grimace to any child's face. "I don't think I could live without her. I don't know what I'd do. I was out of my mind with worry. To think of where she was…"

"Don't think about it." Vance held the woman's gaze. "Just don't. You have her back now, and we're going to catch the guy who took her. Okay?"

Mia fought back a groan. She agreed with him—she did—but she hated making promises like that, especially to parents. "Mrs. Alvarez…Marta…what can you tell us about your daughter?"

"She's a good girl." Marta leaned back against her door, eyes going a little distant. "I work every day, trying to take care of medical bills and keep a roof over our heads, and she has been so good. My Carla is a champion. And you know what she has to put up with at school, the bullies. Those mean children, and at just ten years old. How can a child that young be expected to endure such torment, and from her friends?"

Mia and Vance traded a look, and he brought out his iPad to take notes. "What kind of bullying are we talking about?"

"Life hasn't been easy on her lately, even before this…*this* happened. The doctors gave her a brace, to make her back grow straighter. And the first day, her classmates called her names and teased her relentlessly. They had to call me from work, and my manager was not happy to have me leaving in the middle of my shift. Carla refused to go to class one day and just walked away from the school."

"Did she come home? Where did she go?"

"The security officer went after her, and they called the

police. I got a phone call from a truancy officer. For my Carla. Can you imagine, a girl so good, who works so hard at school. She always got As on tests, every time. Until the brace."

"Her grades suffered?"

"Suffered. Yes, from As to Cs, but I don't blame her. It's because of the bullies, the children she would play with before the brace. Now they're like enemies, and she did nothing to them!"

Vance was taking diligent notes as Marta spoke. "She was struggling with bullying from her peers. Did she ever mention adults making comments?"

"No. Never. The school would've heard from me if she'd told me anything like that. If one of those teachers…" Marta's face scrunched up in an angry scowl. "I'm not making a threat, but I tell you, that school would not be the same after I was done."

Mia nodded, acknowledging a parent's devotion to protecting her only child. "So you don't know of any harassment Carla may've suffered beyond what happened at school?"

"She hasn't been bothered by anyone around the neighborhood. Not until Friday. I'm sorry, I need to get back to her."

"Here's my card." Mia pressed it into the woman's hand, and Vance did the same, adding, "Call or email anytime. If you think of anything, or if Carla remembers anything—"

"I will." The woman dug out her wallet and slipped the cards in between a few bills. "Thank you."

Mia stepped aside, allowing her to pass. She headed over to the beat-up little Honda that the teen boys had been sitting on.

Vance moved back toward the SUV. "Rare to give out our cards and think someone'll actually call."

"I think she will too. She breaks the mold of other parents." Hand on the vehicle door, she stilled and met Vance's gaze over the roof. "Do you see any pattern here? Anything that ties the three victims together? Other than poverty, I'm not sure we can point to a connection yet."

Vance drummed his hands on the roof. "You're saying you think they got picked by our unsub because of their circumstances? I thought we already determined that, but I guess it doesn't hurt to confirm a hypothesis."

"Yeah, you're right. We knew that. I just want so badly to know where this guy is and stop him before he hurts another child."

"You and me both."

As Mia got the SUV started, Vance pulled out his phone. "I'll see if Jacinda has an update for us."

Muffled voices came over the phone while Mia wheeled them out of the small lot. Vance put the call on speaker as they pulled onto the road.

"Not much to report. The kids didn't come home when the parents expected them. Alibis all around." Jacinda sighed. "But these parents are struggling. I found Jessica's mom drunk at half past eight—"

"In the *morning*?" Vance's eyebrows shot up. "You gotta be kidding. Please tell me you're kidding."

"Wish I was. Two bottles of white wine gone when I arrived."

Mia bit her lip, her heart clenching at the thought of the pain closure would bring to those parents from now on. "After losing a kid, I'm not surprised. I'd have gone through three bottles."

Vance reached out and rubbed her shoulder. "What about Daniel Jackson?"

"His parents are dealing with a domestic violence issue, which I can only imagine isn't helping investigators looking into their son's death. I'm headed to the courthouse now to talk to them."

Vance related what they'd seen and heard from Marta Alvarez, which was at least less depressing than what Jacinda had found. Of the three kids, it seemed like the one with the best support system had been the one to survive. That was something, maybe.

Over the speaker, Jacinda kept talking, but the update was mostly relaying nonstarters. Local uniforms were looking into suppliers of medicinal leeches that might match the type found on Carla's arm. Any number of medical professionals might have access to them through work in hospitals, plastic surgery centers, or certain therapeutic clinics. Even so, the list of possibilities was too long to be helpful. Their unsub could've just collected them himself, swiped them, or bought them under the counter from a medical supplier or with a fake license online.

Mia's gaze caught on a toddler kicking the back of his mom's seat in the next car over. The mother just kept driving, mouth moving as if to try to calm her child, but without any apparent anger. Just regular frustration. A normal day in the car, then.

With moisture stinging her eyes, Mia tore her focus back to the road. Parents and kids survived life in the city every day. Maybe she'd be a parent herself one day, or maybe she wouldn't. For now, she had a job to do for Marta Alvarez, for her daughter, and for the other kids with no one to care about their fates.

13

Emma hadn't enjoyed watching her colleagues buddy up and head off to interviews without her. At least that left her free to explore the tunnels alone. Flashlight in hand, she'd gone back down and set out to see what else she might find in the darkness below the opera house.

Technically, she wasn't supposed to be doing that, because Jacinda had insisted on a buddy system for any work done belowground. But Emma wasn't about to pass up the opportunity to speak with Daniel's or Jessica's ghosts. Assuming they chose to appear and decided to speak instead of just standing around near doorways.

At this point, I'd take a silent ghost over palling around with Vance down here.

On their walk back from the storage facility, he'd been unrelentingly positive they'd find their unsub. His attitude was grating.

The world wasn't all sunshine and flowers. It also held space for sadness and heartbreak. Space for unsolved mysteries and unfair situations. Who could be so naive as to insist they'd find the man who killed Daniel and Jessica. Who would've killed Carla if Mia hadn't been lucky enough to hear her cries?

Emma turned a corner and found herself in a hallway she hadn't visited before. At least, she didn't recognize any of the bricks or mold stains.

You very well could've been here before and just didn't notice the details, Emma girl. Your head isn't in the game right now, and you know it.

Emma kept moving forward, flashlight out to illuminate the way. The hall ended at a *T* intersection. She debated which way to go. The cold began seeping into Emma with more insistence, to the extent that she even looked around to assure herself no ghosts were shimmering into view somewhere.

It was just the atmosphere of the tunnels. Labyrinthine and cold and dark—even with pockets of light built up around the crime scenes and turns and stairwell entrances—the area was as welcoming as a grave site.

Fitting, Emma girl, but not remotely funny.

With her luck, she'd wander in circles in the cold, waiting for ghosts, and they'd only deign to show their presence when she was in the company of the living again. She'd just about scream if that happened. Instead, she backtracked until she spotted the uniformed officer monitoring the stairwell door.

With nothing but a hand waved in greeting, Emma bypassed him and trudged up the stairs.

As much as she liked solitude, Emma knew she shouldn't be lingering belowground alone. Jacinda had implemented the buddy system for a reason, and it wasn't just to *"watch Emma to make sure she's okay."* Getting lost or injured were still possibilities they had to consider.

Emma strolled through the backstage area, hoping to find Ted Fishbourne again. She saw no one other than a few members of the theater company meandering between the stage curtains. As she made her way around, she acknowledged people with nods or waves as she passed them. Near the greenroom, she spotted the two costars of *Tristan und Isolde*, Jason Engelson and Layla Simon.

Both wore far less regal attire than the costumes they'd had on last night. Jason was in a polo under a shabby, flannel shirt with jeans, and Layla wore a threadbare sweater over loose-fitting slacks. They sat together in some chairs near the prop table, playing their voices off one another in some sort of strange vocal warm-up. Emma listened for a few moments unnoticed, then approached when Layla happened to glance her way and made eye contact.

Restless. Waiting for news. I can't blame them for that.

Emma waved as she walked up, flashing her ID in case they hadn't noticed her the night before. "Mr. Engelson, Ms. Simon, mind if we have a word?"

Layla sat up with a fast smile, but Jason frowned and looked her up and down as if she reeked of the damp mustiness of the tunnels. "We already told your colleagues everything we could last night. What else do you want from us?"

Pulling up the lone chair that remained empty, Emma perched in front of them and tried for a friendly smile. "Nothing but information, I promise. Sometimes, you don't know what could be helpful, and that's where my job comes in. Your specialty is opera. Mine is crime."

"You mean your specialty is corniness." Jason stared at her as if waiting for her to challenge him, but she only held tight to the smile she'd scrounged up on her approach. The man was a grumpy actor who'd likely gotten less sleep than she had. She could be patient.

"Jason, be nice." Layla swatted him with her script and then looked back to Emma. "We're all on edge. The idea of those kids tied up down there while we were all playacting a tragedy? It's hideous."

When the actress shivered, Jason put one hand out to grip hers, raising Emma's estimation of the man just a touch. He glanced back at her. "She's right. I'm sorry."

"That's all right. It's understandable." Emma made a point of looking around before leaning forward. "What I'd like to ask you about is your stage manager, Ted Fishbourne. Can you tell me anything about him? And do you know if he's around?"

Jason's eyes widened a touch. "Is he a suspect?"

"We want to cover all bases, and from what I've heard, the stage manager knows everything that happens under the theater roof." Emma flipped open the cover on her iPad and laid the device on her lap, hoping for something that would be worth noting down. "So that said, what can you tell me?"

The costars looked at each other, but then Layla shrugged and turned back to Emma. "He's a professional. Good at his job. I'm sure he's around only because he has to be. But I admit, I've never been a fan. He does do a good job of running things, but he's also pretty rude. Cold sometimes. A little too…I don't know. Dispassionate, maybe?"

Emma nodded as if she understood. "And you work in a job where passion is expected."

Frowning, Jason shifted in his chair. "You have to be devoted to make a life doing theater work, and that usually means passion. Devotion. Unending studying. I've seen stage managers who were ready to chew through brick walls when a roll of gaffer's tape went missing. Ted would probably just yawn and wave it off as if it were nothing."

"And would it be? I don't know what gaffer tape is for."

Jason threw his hands in the air and groaned.

Layla cut in with a reply. "It has a lot of uses, mostly to

hold down cables or other trip hazards, or for when we run out of spike tape."

Emma hadn't wanted a crash course in stage work, but she was getting one. "Spike tape…does what it sounds like?"

Jason leaned forward, elbows on his knees and palms together. He gave her a patronizing grin. "For spiking where set pieces will be placed. Small *l*'s or *s*'s on the stage mark where a corner should go, so the crew can quickly change over a scene. This business is about time, urgency, and precision."

Emma lifted an eyebrow. "You certainly sound passionate enough to work in theater. Does that passion translate to other activities?"

"What are you implying?"

Layla put her hands out between them, as if separating boxers who'd gotten tangled up.

"Jason, we're all a little tense. Let's just calm down and let Agent Last conduct her interview so we can get back to rehearsing."

"Thank you, Ms. Simon. I do have some other questions, but they shouldn't take long." In all honesty, Emma didn't have any other questions, and she'd been explicitly told not to interview anyone to begin with. But she wasn't about to let the opportunity slip by.

"Mr. Engelson, Ms. Simon, is there anything else you can tell me about Ted Fishbourne, anything you haven't thought to mention yet? Maybe our conversation about tape and spikes shook something loose?"

Jason grunted, meeting Emma's eyes. "Did you know *Tristan und Isolde* is four-and-a-half hours long?"

"You're joking." Emma laughed, momentarily shaken by the abruptness of his question. "Four hours? Seriously?"

"Yes, *seriously*." Jason waved around the stage area. "And the amount of money and time that goes into a production like this is hard for someone to imagine if they haven't been involved directly in something similar. So when Layla and I say that we're not sure why Ted's in the job, at least at this point in his life when he seems bored with it, we're not just blowing smoke up your ass, I promise."

Right. But you could be trying to shake me off your ass, Mr. Engelson, or just playing out a grudge.

Layla frowned at him, but he only shrugged, and Emma decided to let him keep on going. To dig his own grave or someone else's.

"Well, it's true. If the man's done with theater, he should let it go. Leave all of us alone rather than browbeating us into meeting his needs and holding to his schedules all the time. He knows we work hard and hold ourselves to a high standard, or he ought to." Jason paused there, glancing back at the entryway to the tunnels before he met Emma's gaze once more. "And besides, Ted gives me the creeps. Just like those damn tunnels." He dropped his script to the ground as if to put a period on the discussion.

Emma waited for him to continue and pressed when he didn't. "Has Ted ever done anything strange, or suspicious, to make you feel that way?"

Jason frowned, but ultimately shook his head. "No, I can't say he has. Just…more of a general vibe."

Well, that's disappointing. And I'm not as likely to trust a vibe as much as the Other when it comes right down to it.

"And do you know anything about his personal life?" Emma glanced around once more, willing the stage manager to refrain from appearing. "Anything about how he feels about kids, perhaps?"

Layla paled. "No, but I can't imagine he'd…" She trailed off, looking helplessly to Jason even as she continued. "I mean, I don't think he's married. I can't imagine he has kids, or I'd assume we'd have heard about it. He's just private. A loner."

Being a loner seemed to be a theme of this case, but even as Emma waited for a punch line, she could tell the actress was done talking, and that bothered Emma more than she hoped her face revealed.

Weren't actors supposed to have good instincts? A feel for people and psychology? They had to, in order to be good at their jobs, and this was a professional theater, not some unfunded community outfit running on bake sales and donations. They had benefactors, a board, and fundraising dinners with auctions.

Jason Engelson and Layla Simon were making real money off their talent—opera was their livelihood—which meant they knew what they were doing. They had instincts they worked from.

Their disapproval of Ted Fishbourne had to count for something. Vance didn't care for the man, either, and he'd remained more grumpy than sympathetic when dead children had been discovered virtually beneath his stage.

Seeming to read Emma's mind, Layla Simmons leaned forward and spoke quietly. "Agent Last, we may not like Ted, but there's no way he'd be capable of something so horrible. We've worked with him every day for months. Sometimes, for sixteen-hour days. We'd *know*."

Emma resisted reminding her that Ted Bundy's family probably felt the same way. Everyone who lived and worked near a criminal—well, almost everyone—eventually fell back on saying they *should* have known something.

Survivor's guilt manifested in myriad ways, but Emma didn't see the point in attempting to convince Layla Simmons of that fact.

"You said he's probably around here right now since he always is." Emma met Jason's stare. "Where would he be?"

"His office." He pointed stage right, to the stairs and a side exit. "Go through that exit, and you'll find a stairwell just a few doors up toward the lobby. Third floor. It's all conference rooms and offices up there. He's in the last room on the right. Big, messy office. You can't miss it."

Emma smiled and held out her hand, shaking each of theirs in turn. She stood so quickly that she set the chair she'd occupied rattling, and it made Layla jump. But they'd have to understand she was in a hurry.

Turning to head toward Fishbourne's office, Emma was met not by an open path, but by the accusing stare of none other than Special Agent Leo Ambrose.

14

Emma stilled at the sight of Leo, breath catching in her throat. But realistically, what did it matter?

He'd lied for her before, when he'd hidden the fact that she'd known their last unsub's gun was empty and shot at Adam Cleaver anyway. If he'd protect her secret when it came to something like that, he'd have no reason to tattle on her about talking to a couple of opera stars who weren't even serious suspects at this stage. No more than anybody else was anyway.

New resolve in her step, she headed for the stairs down to the pit, working on ignoring the fact that Leo was making a beeline to cut her off.

"Emma, I thought you were downstairs in the tunnels." Despite the man's charm, suspicion radiated from him. "Investigating the underground network in case there's more evidence to be found down there, even though Jacinda explicitly told us not to do that without a partner. Buddy system, remember?"

Emma stepped pointedly around him, taking the stairs into the orchestra pit. She didn't pause when his fast steps followed her. "And I thought you were with Denae," she spoke without turning to face him, "at Daniel's school."

"We came back to check in with Jacinda, but she headed back to the Bureau to meet up with Mia and Vance. Hey…" He caught her elbow as she reached the exit door that the opera performers had pointed out, pulling her around to face him. "What's going on?"

"Fishbourne. That's what."

His forehead lined with confusion. "The stage manager? We talked to him last night—"

"And I want to talk to him myself." She yanked her elbow away from Leo's grip, and he had the grace to look embarrassed at having held on so long.

Leo leaned closer. "What more is there to ask him, Emma?"

She turned away without trying to explain herself. What could she really say…that a ghost had been acting in a way that made her suspect Fishbourne's involvement? "I have my own questions, Leo."

"And Jacinda told you not to ask them. Right?" He caught up and reached ahead of her to grab the handle of the exit door, pulling it open for the two of them. "If you're going to break the rules, fine. But at least let me tag along so I can cover for you in case it gets back to Jacinda."

As they headed down the hallway, Leo told her about the meeting he and Denae had at Daniel's school.

"That school…I can't believe we have places like that in this country. How is it possible that we have so much wealth, and kids are still being sent to a school that looks more like a prison?"

Emma paused. "Do you think our unsub is picking these kids because of where they come from?"

"Yes." Leo sighed, running one hand up and down the banister beside them as if to quiet his nerves. "I do. So does

Denae, and it makes sense. They're already on the fringes, so they're easier targets. Obvious ones, even."

Thinking of how thin Daniel's ghost had been, how malnourished he'd looked, and then considering the pictures she'd seen of the other victims, Emma had to gather herself before she could meet Leo's eye. Her partner looked exhausted—more so than could be excused by a poor night's sleep.

Emma turned on her heel and continued up the stairs. "Come on if you're coming."

Leo followed behind her, and Emma fought down her sorrow in favor of a mask to show Fishbourne. If he was their unsub, better he see an objective agent.

She knocked hard on the door, and when the stage manager told them to enter, she did so quickly, not giving him time to change his mind. He sat behind a large desk with stacked trays for paperwork, marked *Incoming* and *Outgoing*.

"Mr. Fishbourne, I'm not sure we met formally. I'm Special Agent Emma Last."

He nodded as she sat in the chair in front of his desk.

Leo remained standing behind her.

"Make yourselves comfortable, I guess. How can I help you?"

Emma let the question hang in the air, noting the way Fishbourne filled the silence first by fidgeting with his glasses and then brushing his unruly hair back.

Trying to channel a bit of her partner's charm, Emma leaned forward and held Ted Fishbourne's eye. "Ted, do you have any experience working with or around children?"

He paused, paled, and then scrunched up his nose. "No."

"In all your years in theater, you've never worked community theater?"

Fishbourne sat back in his seat and glanced warily up ay Leo before answering. "I was an assistant stage manager for a production of *Footloose* once. High school students, with a few who'd recently graduated. It was a summer performance as part of a festival to support aspiring actors."

Emma held his gaze, waiting for him to reveal more. When he didn't, she tried another approach. "How would you describe the experience? Was it enjoyable?"

"Enjoyable?" He turned to Leo. "I'm sorry...do you have any questions for me, sir?"

This jerk's talking over me. And not exactly being subtle about it.

Emma placed her hands on the stage manager's desk and leaned forward. "When was the last time you saw kids in your opera house, Mr. Fishbourne? How did you feel about it?"

"Special Agent Ambrose, I believe it is?" Fishbourne narrowed his eyes above her. "Do you have any questions?"

Emma slammed one hand on his desk and ignored the soft "Dang it" Leo let slip behind her. Ted was looking at her again, and that was what she'd wanted.

"And are you a happy person, Ted?"

"What..." His eyes shot between her and Leo again, betraying his nerves. "That's none of your business. And I don't know what kind of question—"

Leo shifted behind her. "Sir, I'm very sorry." His hand came down on Emma's shoulder, squeezing in a way that suggested he'd clamp a hand over her mouth next. "Agent Last is pursuing a particular line of investigative work, and sometimes that means we're forced to ask some questions that appear improper. We won't bother you again."

Emma allowed herself to be pulled from the office and couldn't help flinching back against the wall when Leo all but slammed Fishbourne's door and whirled on her, eyes narrowed. "What the hell was that?"

"Our instincts match up on this—"

Leo scowled at her, all of his charm having run out along with his patience. "This isn't about instincts. This is about—"

"An unsub!" Emma stalked back toward the stairwell, knowing he'd follow. "It's about our killer targeting kids born into poverty. It's like he wants to put them out of their misery."

"What makes you say that?"

She turned back to him when she reached the door, surprised to find that he'd stopped a few paces behind her. A big part of her suggested she lie, but she found herself unable to say anything short of the truth.

Whether it was the fact that they were investigating murdered children, or because one of her colleagues had refused to let her pretend any longer, Emma finally let the tears fall. She cried and slumped against the wall, avoiding Leo's eyes.

Crying in front of someone else, for the first time in a long time, felt so good she was afraid she might not ever stop.

"He's dead, Leo. Oren is dead. He's gone, and he's never coming back, and there's nothing I can do to change that. I couldn't even stop it from happening. Dammit!"

His hands rested on her shoulders, and she forced herself to meet his gaze. She'd expected to find him smirking or wearing an expression that said, *Grow up—you're a federal agent.*

Instead, his dark-brown eyes met hers with sincere curiosity. Sympathy too. "Emma, what makes you so sure our unsub is trying to put these kids out of their misery?"

Still crying and wiping at her eyes, she swallowed the retort that had been on the edge of her tongue. Instead, she said the one thing she knew she probably shouldn't, but that she'd been desperate to give voice to. "Maybe it's a feeling I can relate to. Feeling so miserable that it's all I can see in the world. It's all I can feel, every morning when I wake up. Every night when I lie down to sleep."

Leo's lips thinned, and he deflated a touch. "Emma, things are rough for you right now…" He held a hand up, stopping her before she could argue. "But they'll get better. Trust me. I know what you mean when you say you can't change what happened, and you couldn't stop it from happening in the first place. You feel helpless, and you're afraid you'll always feel that way."

Hearing him put those feelings into words gave Emma something to hold onto, something firm and real. She stood away from the wall, straightening up as Leo's hands fell away from her shoulders.

"You're right, Leo. I'm acting like an idiot."

"No, you're acting like someone who's grieving. And, like it or not, there's no schedule or timeline for when that's going to change. It'll come, and it'll go. Meanwhile, Emma… you have to back off. This won't end well if you keep charging ahead, going against Jacinda's orders. You're being reckless. If Jacinda has to sit you down one more time, I'm afraid that'll be the end for you. I don't want to see you jeopardize your job."

His voice had gone soft at the end of that statement. Too soft for Emma to pretend he wasn't seriously worried.

She didn't want anyone worrying about her. Least of all Leo. Yet here he was, refusing to let her wallow or rage or whatever it was she'd been doing these past few weeks. "I'll be more careful. I get it. I do, seriously. And thank you."

He took a step back, measuring her or deciding whether he believed her. Either way, Emma knew their conversation had reached a conclusion. She gestured toward the door leading downstairs.

In the stairwell, Leo picked up the conversation that got

them upstairs in the first place. "So what really got you thinking about Fishbourne?"

"The actors said something about him being bored here, like he had no love for the job. And that didn't add up with a life of theater work. Maybe I just needed someone to yell at who wasn't me."

"Sounds like you were following a hunch. We both know that isn't good enough."

She shrugged, not bothering to answer. Leo could be as frustrated or concerned as he wanted. There was no way she'd let a ghost go unavenged only because she didn't have the evidence to toe every legal line perfectly.

If there was one thing the Other was good for, it was helping her find murderers. Maybe the ghosts who communicated with her weren't the most articulate bunch, often causing more frustration than satisfaction, but the end results were the same.

They caught their unsubs because the denizens of the Other wanted Emma to succeed. Even the ones who didn't seem to care for her, like the grumpy yogi in Oren's studio. He was instrumental in helping Emma catch Oren's killer.

No matter how she complained to Mia about it or lost sleep over it, the ghosts from the Other had helped her solve cases.

I won't let that benefit fall by the wayside just to avoid raising a fucking eyebrow or two.

15

Emma paced around her kitchen, flipping open drawers and cupboards and cabinets. Aside from bacon and eggs, her fridge didn't hold much of anything.

When was the last time you sat down and made yourself a proper meal, Emma girl?

Her phone buzzed and saved her the trouble of deciding between going out for a burger or calling her favorite Chinese place for delivery. Mia's perky face graced the screen. Emma almost ignored the call.

Leo's logical words of sympathy came back to her as Mia's ringtone continued to jingle the phone. Before she could second-guess herself, she swiped to accept the call.

"Hey, Mia, what's up?"

"Dinner?" Mia paused only briefly, then rushed on before Emma could decline. "I know you, Emma Last, and I bet you're sitting there looking at takeout menus with an empty fridge behind you. Am I right? You don't have to answer that…just come out with me instead. Just the two of us, like old times."

Emma looked at the junk drawer she'd left hanging open, a spray of takeout menus sticking up.

"I'm not exactly the best dinner company right now. I might ruin your appetite."

"I doubt it. C'mon. Please. I'm not in the mood to eat by myself, and Vance has a family thing that I do *not* want to deal with. You'll be doing me a favor. I'll even pay."

Emma's lips quirked in the tiniest of smiles. "Only if we do Italian."

❄

With their orders placed, Emma and Mia took turns dipping freshly warmed bread into the restaurant's house-made mix of oil, herbs, and garlic. Mia washed down a bite with a sip of pinot grigio, then asked the question Emma had been dreading.

"So seriously, how are you doing?"

Emma smooshed her bread into the oil and herb mixture, virtually soaking it. "I'm fine."

More than fine, if they keep this bread coming and I manage to change the subject.

"Emma..."

Emma took a long drink of wine, meeting her friend's eyes and seeing that Mia was not going to let her get away with it this time. Maybe she and Leo had decided to provide tag team counseling. Or maybe her friend was just tired of being frozen out of her life. But Emma knew she wasn't ready to melt all the ice and let the flood start up again.

"I'm...okay, Mia. I really am. I'm grieving, but I'm doing okay."

"I know that's not the case." Mia reached across the table but didn't touch Emma's hand. "Your boyfriend just died, so it's more than okay not to be *okay*."

"I just need to buckle down." Avoiding Mia's gaze, Emma let some of the oil dribble off her soaked bread. "I'll get to feeling better eventually. It's not something I can put on the calendar. I just need to let the process happen. That's all there is to it."

Mia pursed her lips, observing Emma as she lifted her glass, taking a more reasonably sized sip this time. "You need to *feel your feelings* is what you need to do, and that takes time, sure. But it also takes self-care. Really, maybe some more time away from work would be better? You could visit Keaton and—"

"How are things going with Vance?" Emma forced a smile, praying Mia would take the point.

Mia opened her mouth like she might argue, then shook her head in defeat. "We're good. He's just got some family drama to deal with...nothing I need to be involved in. So I figured it was a good time for us to catch up."

Emma had been distracted by some shrimp primavera being delivered to the next table, but something in her friend's voice made her refocus on the woman sitting across from her. She eyed her, sipping her wine. "But?"

"You're too damn perceptive, you know that?" Mia sighed, glancing sideways at the same delicious-smelling dish that had distracted Emma. The man eating it splattered sauce across the table as a shrimp fell from his fork, and Mia looked back to Emma just as a chuckle escaped her. "The thing is...I really do like him, but he's almost too nice. Does that make sense?"

Emma barely held herself back from reminding Mia that she herself had sometimes complained about people saying the same thing about her. *Talk about a way of being unhelpful.* "What do you mean? Like, in general, or—"

"You know what?" Mia shook her head, patting her lips with a napkin. "No. Me and Vance are good. It's not an emergency." She reached over and gripped Emma's hand before she could bring her wineglass back to her lips yet again. "Emma, darling, you are the emergency tonight. I know you're deflecting, but you're the one suffering."

Pulling away just firmly enough to make sure her friend understood the gesture, Emma focused on enjoying another sip. Maybe it wasn't too late to get her meal to go.

"Emma, come on. I know you feel like Oren's death is your fault."

Yeah, Emma girl, you should not have come out tonight.

She finished her glass and forced herself to meet Mia's gaze. "I do not—"

"Remember who you're talking to?" Mia gripped her hand before Emma could use it to wave at the server. "I know you're feeling survivor's guilt. I know it."

Emma opened her mouth to lie, but her mouth was too dry. She felt herself tearing up again, but a restaurant was not the place to have another breakdown like she did with Leo. Still, she couldn't look away from Mia.

She lost Chris. If there's anyone who'll truly understand, it's her.

Something in her expression must have clued Mia into what Emma was thinking. The other woman gave a tight nod. "You know the last thing Chris said to me before…" Mia swallowed, almost choking on the words before she could continue. "Before he shot himself? Do you remember? He said, and I quote, 'You're gonna do great things, Agent Logan. I'm sure of it.' Do you have any idea how that made me feel?"

Emma swallowed, hard. She couldn't speak, so she only shook her head.

"Survivor's guilt, Emma. I felt like I should've been able to stop him. Like we'd been together all that time, and I'd failed him because I'd been too busy saving everyone else. I felt like I should've known something was up, that he was breaking bad on us, helping people who actively wanted to hurt or kill all of us."

"Mia, there's no way you could've known that about him. He'd been working a long game since before—"

"I know. I know that, and it still eats at my heart every time I think about what he said. His literal last words, and they were directed at me, to my face, before he ended his own life. I can't even console myself thinking about where he might be now."

"Mia, that's…" Emma had wanted to say that what happened in the afterlife wasn't something anybody could know for certain until they experienced it, but she knew better than to challenge her friend on something so personal. "Mia, I don't know if I've said it before or enough, but I'm sorry about what happened with Chris. I wish I could've done something. I think we all do. Well, except for Leo and Jacinda, I guess…"

Mia allowed a slight laugh to escape before her lips closed in a thin line. She sipped her wine. "I'm sure if they'd known Chris, they'd feel the same way. But you're not getting off that easy. We're here because you're the one with the fresh wound, and you're still bleeding everywhere you go. Chris—"

"Wasn't your fault."

"I know. I knew that then, even though I couldn't admit it, and I know you're thinking the same thing about Oren. But there's a difference between thinking something and knowing something. There's a difference between saying you're fine and actually feeling that way. You have to get there, for yourself, or you'll drown in guilt. And I won't let that happen."

The angry demands of Emma's stomach were a long-gone memory now as emotion began boiling up.

"I want to hear you say it. Say that you know it's not your fault." Mia was insistent.

Emma licked her lips. The words should've come easily—she knew Oren's death wasn't her fault, logically—but her mouth wouldn't move. She couldn't even get his name out of her chest and onto her tongue.

Mia popped up from her chair and came around the table, leaning over to wrap her friend in a tight hug. She whispered through her hair, bringing tears up to sting Emma's eyes. Diners nearby paused their conversations. Forks and knives stopped clicking against plates. Mia's words vibrated against Emma's cheek.

"Death in the family. She's having a hard time."

The other diners murmured words of sympathy before digging back into their meals. Emma let the tears fall more freely while her friend kept her wrapped up, comforted and secure.

"You'll get there, Emma. Just keep trying, okay? Promise me that. You have to keep trying."

Nodding into her shoulder, Emma swallowed down the sobs and gripped her back. "You're a good friend, Mia. Thank you."

Mia went back to her side of the table as their dishes were delivered. Emma stared down at a gorgeous plate of flounder Mediterranean, perfectly seasoned and accompanied by a mountain of basil mashed potatoes, a few fresh spears of asparagus, and a side of tomato slices layered with fresh mozzarella and oil.

The meal should've made her mouth water. Should've made her stomach stand at attention like a starving dog.

Instead, she could only force a smile as Mia dug into her chicken piccata and fried zucchini planks, giving mouth service to how delicious the meal looked.

Emma's hunger had deserted her.

Mia was a good friend, it was true, but she was also a

fellow agent. One who'd just seen the very depths of her sorrow.

She reached a hand over, and Mia extended hers. Emma gripped it like a lifeline rather than digging into her meal. Because the truth of the matter was painfully obvious. She needed friends to help her through this. Friends she could show weakness to, if needed, and who'd pull her back from the ledge of grief and despair.

Right now, Mia Logan was in that particular hot seat, but the smile on her face told Emma it was exactly where her friend wanted to be.

She released Mia's hand and returned her smile. "*Bon appétit.*"

Emma lifted her fork and sank it into the fish, pulling away a bite that, for the first time in what felt like forever, actually had her excited about eating.

16

By the time Emma sat down in her Prius with a full belly and a reminder of what good friends she had, she was more than ready to continue the evening. She almost suggested a night of watching movies with margaritas at her place, but Mia begged off, saying she needed to get home and into bed.

Emma was briefly tempted to do the same, but how could she try to sleep this early with a child killer on the loose? If she went home, she'd only be staring at the ceiling, wondering where the unsub might be.

And how long we have until he kills again.

She was already close to the opera house. Before Emma could rethink the impulse, she turned a corner and followed the street to the next block. The building was still an active crime scene, and local PD would be there to approve her entry. All she had to do was flash her badge.

Up ahead, the opera house stood proudly above neighboring storefronts and boutiques in the upscale neighborhood. The street was quiet, but that wasn't surprising for a Monday evening.

Emma already had a plan for where she'd veer off in the tunnels. Some of the spaces nearer the entrance into the storage building had barely been skimmed due to time constraints. An extra pair of eyes there couldn't hurt.

She pulled into the employee parking lot and quickly shut off her headlights as Ted Fishbourne emerged from the building.

Head down, hands in his pockets, he all but stalked toward a clump of parked cars.

Emma sank down in her seat a bit, hoping he wouldn't notice the odd car out among what must be more familiar vehicles. He never reached her Prius, though. In the first row of the lot, he climbed into a newish Toyota without even looking around.

Maybe the first unsuspicious thing I've seen him do. Criminals watch their backs.

Emma took her time pulling out and following him away from the opera house. His route carried him into a neighborhood that looked just like a hundred others in D.C. Overpriced houses that were slightly run-down and cramped together with small yards. A few couples were out walking dogs, but it was an otherwise sleepy section of the city. Just when she'd decided he must be going home, he turned off into the parking lot for a park and children's playground.

The park and play equipment sat at the edge of the neighborhood, and Emma brought her Prius to a stop a row back from him and a few spaces to the left. It was a spot that gave her an oblique view of his vehicle. Her hand wandered to her gun and settled there.

Fishbourne wasn't getting out of his car.

Through his windshield, he had a view of the play structures and two kids who chased each other around while two women sat nearby laughing at the children's antics. With the sun less than an hour away from setting, they seemed to be enjoying the cool evening.

Fishbourne settled back in his seat, observing, with his hands resting on top of his steering wheel.

For a moment, Emma wondered if he might have kids after all. Maybe one of those women was his wife, or maybe an ex with her friend or new partner. If that were the case, Fishbourne could be waiting for a custody exchange. The longer Emma watched him, the more she hoped he did, in fact, have a legitimate reason for being there. The alternative wasn't something she wanted to consider.

But nobody on the playground glanced Fishbourne's way with more than casual curiosity.

She noted they'd now been in the park for a good ten minutes, and he'd done nothing but sit in his car, motionless. Emma pulled out her phone and snapped some pictures, making sure to get Fishbourne's license plate. When he finally pulled out of his spot five minutes later, she snapped some close-up shots, including a clear one of his profile, just for good measure.

Back on the road and following him once more, Emma wondered if she'd been wrong about him. He was still alone, but maybe that playground had been too busy for him. Especially if he was accustomed to snatching kids on their way home from school or extracurricular activities while they walked alone.

Or maybe he'd decided not to take anyone tonight because the opera house was still crawling with law enforcement.

And maybe he had alarm bells going off in his head. Just like your alarm bells, Emma girl.

Fishbourne left the neighborhood, and Emma followed him onto a main road lined with restaurants and other small businesses. He pulled into a strip mall, and she managed to park on the side of the street just past him. It was all she could do not to roll her eyes when he entered a toy shop. Was he planning on luring kids into his car like the proverbial bad man with candy in a van?

She took more pictures when he came out with a bag of what she had to assume were toys, and then she followed him away from the strip mall.

She'd been following him so carefully, intent on keeping her distance while also keeping him in sight, that the appearance of Oren's studio took her totally by surprise.

A real estate agent's sign in the window announced the space was available for lease.

Emma wasn't prepared for the sight. She slammed on the brakes, coming to a halt in the middle of the street. A car honked and swerved to avoid rear-ending her.

She didn't bother waving an apology.

After the shooting, Oren's students had left cards, flowers, and crosses outside the studio. Emma had laughed at the absurdity at first, then cried, adding a giant bouquet to the bunch herself. She'd returned twice more just to stare at the collected items memorializing the man she'd come to believe would always be there.

More cars honked, but Emma's hands and feet were frozen. Tears drizzled down her face even as she laughed through her sobs. Oren was supposed to have been her new family.

A man banged on her window with his fist. "What the hell are you doing, lady? You're blocking the street!"

His big red truck sat behind her, wide and accusing. He couldn't have swerved to either side to get by.

Sorry, Emma mouthed as the wide-eyed driver backed up a step.

"You okay, lady?"

She nodded and took her foot off the brake, coasting away from him before accelerating to a normal driving speed. She was almost halfway down the block when she realized she'd lost Ted Fishbourne.

He's long gone by now. She glanced in both directions when she got to the light. His Toyota was nowhere in sight.

She returned to the park, but all she found were the two now very tired-looking women literally dragging the flailing children away from the playground.

Instead of waiting to see if Fishbourne would return, Emma pulled up his home address and headed there. The house was several streets away, and traffic was clear enough that she made the trip in good time. Much good it did her, though. His vehicle wasn't in the drive or parked on the street.

She parked two houses down and waited.

And waited and waited some more.

After two hours, Emma's eyes drooped. She'd slept on and off through the day and night yesterday, but drunken, tequila-fueled sleep wasn't nearly the same thing as a good night's rest. It might only be around nine at night, but her body was already done. Maybe that glass of wine and big dinner had done their work too.

She took one more swing by the opera house and the storage building she and Vance had visited, just to make sure his vehicle hadn't reappeared. The only cars in either lot were local PD patrol vehicles. Taking that as her sign, Emma headed home.

The Other had mostly been leaving her alone lately, and tonight was no different. She made it into her apartment without any ghostly intrusions and settled down in bed with a bowl of plantain chips and a tall glass of water. As well as her laptop.

Going by the opera house had woken her up a bit, and she intended to make use of the energy.

A quick review of the photos associated with the case offered no new insights, so she began digging into Fishbourne. Unfortunately, he had almost no digital presence. No apparent social media. Even the opera house's accounts showed no likes, shares, or follows that might've been him, unless he'd used a fake handle. Emma put a mental check mark next to "social media" for Ted Fishbourne.

She kept digging but came up with two handfuls of empty and a side helping of not a damn thing. The man had no criminal record, no priors of any kind. Not even a mention of harassment, stalking, or being a Peeping Tom.

The best she'd done was ascertain Ted Fishbourne was the only adult resident living in his home, where he'd lived for eight years, and no other adults or children were associated with that address in city records.

With a frustrated grunt, she slammed her laptop closed and shoved it onto the nearby nightstand, nearly spilling her water.

This didn't mean she'd be giving up on pursuing him. Not by a long shot. He must have bought those toys for some particular reason, and if he didn't have kids of his own, what was it?

People didn't go to a shop and buy brand-new toys for a theater performance, and that would be a prop manager's job anyway. And if he had nieces or nephews, wouldn't he have mentioned them when they'd asked him how he felt about kids?

Most people would've.

One way or another, Emma would not allow rules and regulations to get in the way of her helping to save the lives of future victims. She was determined to make sure

Fishbourne—or whoever their unsub might be—did not lay his hands on another child.

She hadn't been able to save Oren, but she would save someone. Maybe that wouldn't cure her grief, but it would be a damn good start.

17

Despite the price of gas, I rarely tired of driving the D.C. streets. That was where I did my best dreaming. The miserable faces I passed were like so many flowers, all waving steadily to the rhythms of the day, and each of them ignorant of their eventual fate. They would all fade, wilt, and wither.

Most of all, they would suffer, because that was the only true constant in life.

I had known this all along, but it wasn't until I found the Teachings that I came to fully understand.

Thankfully, the police had not yet searched my area at the opera house when I went into work today. I managed to secure the Teachings in the tunnels, where they'd already been searched.

The remains had been found, of course, but no connection had been made to me or my possessions.

My work can continue, and more people can be delivered from their misery. The Teachings are safely hidden away.

I recited from the Teachings as I drove.

"People, the inhabitants of human civilization, are as

unnecessary as they are cruel. In their attempts at finding joy, every person on the planet unfailingly ensures someone else will suffer, whether willfully or by accident.

"*The only proper course of action is to ensure people cease to exist. And such an effort should begin with those who will foster future generations of people predisposed to unconscious malevolence.*"

People.

I spat the word in my thoughts. God, how I hated human beings.

And yet, I enjoyed imagining their stories, the pretending they did to make their lives bearable.

At a stoplight, I drummed my fingers against the steering wheel as a man in a suit walked with the pedestrian sign, frowning into thin air with his phone clamped to his ear. I bet his boss was belittling him. Demanding he come back to work, even though it was coming up on nine thirty at night. The man probably felt stuck in his job, unable to break away, and with a miserable family at home that he felt duty bound to support, even though he hated them.

My foot feathered against the gas pedal, thinking how it would feel to run him over, to release him from his pain. I lifted my foot away, waiting until the path was clear before continuing. Better to stick to my mission.

A raw, animalistic yawn broke from my throat as I pressed the gas pedal to move through the next green light—carefully, looking both ways since I *had* a care in the world.

How funny, to realize I didn't want to be erased, even after all I'd been through. I did have purpose now, much as that conflicted with the assumptions that had led me down this path, to kill as if I had no future, no reason for remaining in this world. No reason to exist.

The thought carried me forward, until I landed at the same little playground I'd scouted the night before. In an instant, I found the same boy I'd discovered then. The area was up against a sound barrier fronting the highway. To the side, a battered and fire-damaged apartment complex sat empty and dark. It was the very reason the playground existed in this particular spot, and the reason I'd likely go unseen, just like the boy would.

I parked, grabbed the cold cans of soda I picked up at a gas station, and left behind the safety of my car. The boy sat with a backpack on his lap, kicking his legs beneath the single picnic table in the park. He looked up as I headed his way but didn't flee. He only pulled his hat down, covering his dirt-stained brow, and wrapped his arms around his backpack, holding it tightly against his chubby middle.

"Late for you to be out here alone, isn't it?" I stopped a few feet away, pulled one soda from my plastic bag, and opened it. Taking a sip, I noticed how he watched me. Greedily.

"What's it to you?" His gaze remained fixed on my soda can.

I gestured with my bag. "I have an extra. They were two for one. Want it?"

"You serious?" He frowned and glanced back behind me, toward the parking lot that was empty but for my car. "You like a snatcher or something?"

I chuckled, this time keeping my voice even and warm, and I was surprised by how little effort it took to perform the act.

"A snatcher? Is that something you saw in a movie? Nobody snatches children. Not really."

"My mom says they do. She says to watch for snatchers when I'm waiting for her out here."

For a moment, I was startled, worried the boy's mother was nearby, perhaps a prostitute working in one of the apartments across the street. "Where's your mom, then?"

"She's at work, at the diner."

"The diner?" I suspected that was merely a story she'd told the boy. No doubt she was on her back or dancing at the bar a few blocks away. I guessed her to be the type who would leave the stage wearing less than she had on at the start of her show.

"Can I have that soda, mister?"

The can was in his hand in a moment, and I asked the next natural question. "Why are you out here waiting for your mom instead of at a friend's?"

He shook his head, taking a loud gulp. "Don't have any. Don't need any either."

"Why don't you go home, then? Aren't you cold out here?"

I knew he was. Even in late March, a D.C. night was no joke.

He shrugged, taking a long drink of the soda. "Can't. Neighbor's been threatening to call the cops on Mom leaving me home alone all the time."

"Your mom works a lot?"

"All the time, but she says we need the money. I'll meet her outside our place right after she gets off at eleven."

"I can relate to that." Moving slowly, I settled on the opposite side of the picnic table from the boy. "Plenty of times when I was your age, I had to be somewhere other than home, even though that wasn't what I wanted."

The boy grunted and drank down more of his soda. He looked overfed, and I guessed his mother only gave him junk food. Preservatives and sugar. She probably wanted him miserable and overweight so he'd have no friends and depend only on her, horrible woman that she must be.

"Say," I waved off down the road, toward nowhere, "are you hungry? I pulled in here 'cause I saw you and thought you might want that extra soda, but I was really on my way to get something to eat. Let's head to the diner where your mom works."

Even in the dim light from the streetlamps, I saw the kid's eyes light up, but not with surprise or glee as I'd hoped. He was afraid now. "The diner's, like, a mile away or something. You sure you're not a snatcher?"

I laughed. "If I was, wouldn't I have snatched you already? There's nobody out here to see me do it."

He leaned back from the table, clutching at his backpack as he turned in his seat. Quickly, I put my hands up as if in surrender.

"I swear I'm not a snatcher. Seriously. I'm just a guy who's hungry and remembers what it was like to be a lonely kid. Let me help you have it better than I did. I'll take you to your mom's diner, and she can drive you back home when her shift ends."

"She takes the bus home and only has a pass for herself."

"Well, I'll give her money for your fare. How does that sound? I'm really craving a cup of coffee and some pecan pie right now. I'll buy you a slice too. I'm Linden, by the way."

He'd leaned forward as I spoke, and now smiled. I had him.

"I'm Tom. And, yeah, sure. I could go for some pie."

I grinned at him, standing up. "Come on and follow me."

Walking back toward my car, I heard and felt him at my back. Coming along behind me like a loyal puppy on a leash. And the fact that I wasn't even looking at him meant he'd trust me all the more. In another minute or two, I'd have him in my car. The chloroform-soaked rag tucked between my seat and the door, ready and waiting, would have him out in another minute.

I glanced around to make sure nobody was following us, but this was the perfect location. Nobody around, and with a condemned building on one side, the empty park at our backs, and the highway barrier to the other side, the main vantage points were the empty street and the rows of apartments, all with darkened windows or showing the flickering of television sets here and there inside.

We were safe as could be from prying eyes. If anyone did pass by, I'd just look like a man dragging his son back home after a night on a basketball court. Innocent as could be.

There'd be no opera house for this sad child, though. No, I'd take him back to the basement I'd spent so much involuntary time in as a child. Nobody would stumble upon my work this time.

I opened up the passenger side door and left it open, going around to the driver's side. He swung his backpack into the footwell and closed the door. His seat belt clicked even as I settled in my own seat, and I grinned.

Maybe I'd go back to the opera house myself once I had this boy settled in at home. I tended to spend even my nights off there, and an alibi tonight might come in handy.

18

Leo worked not to wince after sipping his coffee—which he'd made himself—and watched Denae scan through email to make sure they hadn't missed any updates overnight. Sitting at her desk in the VCU, she practically purred over the brew he'd forced the break room's coffee maker to deliver.

She pushed back from her computer and shook her head. "Nothing new. The cops are still mapping the tunnel system, but there's no new evidence showing up in the files."

Leo allowed his gaze to linger on the smiling school photos of their first victims, Jessica Howard and Daniel Jackson, now showing on Denae's screen since she'd closed her email window. "I can't stop thinking about them. They had the hardest lives already, and to end up…how can you be so nonchalant about this?"

As if confused, she scrunched her brow. Leo knew her to be cool as a cucumber, but the apathy underscoring her reaction jarred him. She scowled as he kept staring at her, waiting for an answer to his question. "It bothers me. Trust me. But poverty isn't new for me. I grew up poor and Black. This isn't anything I haven't seen before."

"Yeah, but you had a supportive family—"

"Full of adults who were working two or three jobs to make ends meet. Just like Carla's mom is doing, and probably Daniel's and Jessica's were too. Yes, there was probably some abuse in Daniel's life, and yes, it looks like there's some alcoholism with Jessica's mom. But maybe it was also three adults doing everything they knew how to do. They were trying to raise a kid and had next to nothing to work with while doing it." She shook her head at him, like he should've known better than to think otherwise.

He probably should have, come to think of it. "Life's tough."

She scoffed. "Ya think?"

He forced down a swallow of coffee. "But you grew up okay. You managed."

"And for every story like mine, there's a hundred others that go the other way. I knew kids like them growing up." She eyed him, watching the statement sink in.

"I'm sorry, Denae. I didn't know you—"

"My best friend got jumped into a gang when he was nine. Nine years old, and he's being told by the street that he's got one way to live and one way to die."

Shit.

"Denae, I'm sorry—"

She waved at him, refocusing on her computer. "Don't sweat it. You didn't know because it's not something I talk about. You can understand why."

Leo mentally kicked himself. It was hard enough to be a woman in a male-dominated profession like law enforcement. Denae was also a Black woman with a close friend with a history of gang involvement. She must've been fielding questions and doing her best to ignore her colleague's snide comments for the better part of her career.

"It's horrifying when you first see this stuff." Denae pushed some curls behind her ears. "So yeah, I get that you're upset. But when you grow up knowing about that one kid whose parents probably spent their last dollars on vodka instead of milk, or the one who always had some kind of excuse for why they had a black eye or a busted lip…and let me be clear, those were special cases…you develop a thick skin."

"I can't imagine…" Words failed.

She lifted a shoulder. "Don't get me wrong. That wasn't the rule, not by a long shot. Most families I knew worked hard, did everything they could for their kids. And the kids worked hard, too, because we had to. Life's tough, like you said. But honestly, if it wasn't for the actual kidnapping and killing these kids with leeches, it's just another Tuesday in the hood."

Leo didn't know what to say to that, so he didn't try. He was about to gesture to Denae's empty cup and offer to get her some more coffee when Emma pushed through the glass doors at the side of the VCU's offices. She made a beeline straight toward the team's bullpen, calling out a hello as she did.

Emma dropped her bag at her desk and pulled out her phone without removing her coat, crossing to stand in front of Denae's desk and the two of them. "You won't believe what I found."

Leo blinked and traded a glance with Denae. His work partner and girlfriend looked about as taken aback as he felt, despite knowing Emma's preference for night owl investigating, a preference he had shared with her on their first two cases. Still, this wasn't the same Agent Last he'd met back then. "Emma, you should've been sleeping."

"Uh-uh." Emma pushed her phone in front of his face, displaying images of a man sitting in his car at a playground.

She rushed into a summary of what Ted Fishbourne had been doing the night before, but Leo could barely take it in. Her eyes were red, her mannerisms all but manic.

"Who sits at a park? Like that? Alone? Nobody!" Emma smacked the desk hard enough to make the pages of a notebook feather in the air, but no one seemed to notice. "And then he went to a fucking toy store. That must be how he's picked up kids. Even if they were smart, they could have been lured in by expensive toys. Robots, superhero figures, whatever. Something shiny they'd been wishing for and never had the luxury to own. Why else would he go to a toy store?"

Emma had begun punching at her phone, speaking as she did and acting like after-hours pictures of a man in a park were a smoking gun.

Leo almost felt sick seeing it. And the way Emma practically fumbled her own phone as she pushed it in front of Denae's face didn't make him feel any better about her current state of mind. She hadn't slept, and now that he thought about it, she looked a lot slimmer too.

I wonder if she even ate breakfast.

Denae stood, holding Emma's phone, viewing the images from a better distance, but Leo could see she wasn't any more impressed than he was. Just worried.

"Emma, these pictures could mean anything. Maybe he's buying toys to donate. Presents for a friend's kid or baby shower. You have no way of knowing—"

"He was at a park!" Emma's eyes were wide, her voice a touch too loud. "He was watching kids play! What more do you need to be convinced it must be him?"

"Evidence?" Denae raised an eyebrow, and Leo stepped

between them before Emma could throw a curse—or something else—at Denae.

"Emma, what Denae's saying is that, yeah, this sounds bad, but it's not enough. He could have a kid, but I'm sure you checked. A niece, then. Nephew. Neighbor kid's birthday coming up." He waited for that to sink in, but Emma only glared at him. "And you shouldn't have been pursuing this guy alone and without good cause—"

"It was my time!" She snapped out a hand and grabbed her phone back from Denae, shifting her gaze between them. "I didn't confront anyone, so what's the big deal?"

Leo glanced at Denae, feeling about as helpless as he ever had. Emma wasn't sleeping, and she practically vibrated with energy and anger right now. He met her eyes, trying to keep his voice low and calm as he responded. "Emma, what we talked about the other day. About grieving. It's a cycle, but it doesn't follow a predictable pattern. You were fine yesterday, briefly. Now you're angry, and you're looking for something to hit, something you can force to change, because you can't change the one thing you wish you could."

The fury boiling off her nearly put him back a step, but Leo held his ground. He'd committed to seeing Emma through this, whatever it might cost him in the short term, and he wasn't giving up on her.

If he didn't speak up and she ended up going off the deep end or checking out entirely, he couldn't live with himself, knowing all it might've taken was one more kind word from a friend.

"Emma, I know you don't want to be hearing it right now. But…we're worried about you."

Denae echoed agreement, and for a second, Leo thought Emma might either explode or clock him across the jaw, but he was saved by the SSA's voice calling out from the conference room.

"Briefing room, everyone, now!" When Mia poked her head out from the break room, Vance right behind her, Jacinda waved them forward in a hurry-up gesture. "Come on. Everyone, now. We have another disappearance."

Emma glared at him. "I told you he was trawling for a victim." Before he could reply, she pushed past him.

Leo couldn't look at Denae, knowing the concern on her face would echo his. He could only follow Emma. Maybe they'd hoped for an update or break in the case to come overnight, but not through another disappearance.

When everyone was seated around the conference table, Jacinda directed their attention to the screen and pulled up a picture. A short, brown-haired boy with freckles and a cautious smile stared back at them from a partially rusted bicycle.

"Meet Tommy Grant, a twelve-year-old latchkey kid." Jacinda punched some buttons, and more pictures of the boy showed up on the screen, one of them with him standing by the side of a grinning woman in a server's uniform from a local diner. "His mom got back from work last night, and he wasn't waiting for her outside the apartment like he usually does."

Leo put up a hand. "I'm sorry, a latchkey kid is waiting to be let inside?"

"Neighbors have a track record of calling the cops because Tommy's mom leaves him home alone almost every night."

"He's twelve. How is that a problem?"

"The neighbors apparently take a strict view of childhood neglect. Tommy's mother assures us he's always had three square meals a day and that she just got tired of dealing with, her words, 'Nosy Norman and Nellie Next Door,' so she arranged with her son to wait for her to come home. Responding PD said they saw a clean bedroom, all the indications of a normal and healthy home in which to raise a child. The neighbors have a bug up their butt for some reason, and PD knows this."

"So—"

Jacinda put up a hand to forestall further questions. "Let me finish, Leo. Please."

"Sorry, Jacinda."

"As I was saying, Tommy Grant's mother, Stephanie, was instantly concerned by his absence. He's always where he's supposed to be, at the park beside the apartment building—"

Emma stood up fast enough that the chair she'd been sitting in hit the wall behind her. Mia jumped in her seat, but Emma took no notice. She pushed her phone into Jacinda's face and restated everything she'd said to Leo and Denae just a few minutes before.

Jacinda might look poker-faced to everyone else in the room, but Leo had worked with her longer than anyone. He knew anger boiling under the surface when he saw it.

"Okay, Emma, we'll look into it. Now, if you'll take a seat, I'll complete the briefing." Jacinda turned back to the screen.

Emma dropped her phone on the table with a *thud* and raised her voice. "Are you kidding me? We need to look into Fishbourne now! This kid could die if we don't move quickly enough—"

Turning back to her, fast as a spinning top on her high heels, Jacinda stared her down hard enough that Emma froze mid-word. "I said, we will look into it. Meanwhile, Special Agent Last, I believe you should consider going home for the day." She turned to the table and met Leo's eye. "You and Denae, spend the morning looking into Fishbourne. Mia and Vance, talk to Stephanie Grant and see what you can find out."

Emma's face had gone bright red, and Leo had to look

away. Beside him, Denae wore a sour grimace on her face, like she felt seasick, and he couldn't blame her.

Jacinda spoke over Emma's protests that she ought to be involved in the interviewing. "Everyone dismissed. Emma, stay behind, please."

Leo jerked his chin at the door when Denae seemed frozen in place even after Mia and Vance rose to leave. Finally, she took the hint, and he held the door open for her.

He glanced back once to see Emma leaned against the wall with her arms crossed, staring down at the carpet. Defeat didn't suit her—he'd have felt more comfortable if she were still indignant and protesting.

Emma was drowning in survivor's guilt and flailing for a rescue she didn't know how to accept.

He'd done what he knew how to do—he'd thrown the lifeline her way. And he'd hold onto his end like he promised. He only hoped Emma would grab hers before it was too late.

19

Emma leaned against the wall, breathing deeply, waiting for her colleagues to leave her and Jacinda alone in the conference room. She could *not* explode with indignation. This wasn't the time. She had to find a way to get herself under control and convince the woman that she was the one who should be following up leads on Fishbourne and this missing child.

I need this. I need to do something, to help someone.
I need a fucking win.

When the door finally shut behind Leo and Denae—which felt like minutes, not seconds—Emma immediately focused on Jacinda and began talking before the SSA had a chance. "I made the discovery, Jacinda. I'm the one who followed Fishbourne and got that lead, so I should follow up on it. Leo and Denae must have other leads to follow."

Jacinda's lips were pursed. She smoothed her hair back without speaking, perching on the edge of the table as if daring Emma to continue.

Emma knew she shouldn't. Jacinda's silence was just

another form of interrogation, offering Emma the space to dig herself a deeper grave.

So she dug. "Look, I know you don't want me going off by myself. I get it. But this was after work when everyone else was off the clock, and I still had energy."

Jacinda nodded, still quiet.

"I didn't confront him. I didn't follow him into the toy shop or demand to see what he bought. It was just me, and I lost him, and I went to home to investigate on my laptop—"

"How long did you follow him?"

"A few hours, I didn't, um...I didn't track."

"What time did you go to sleep?"

Emma froze. "What?"

Jacinda sighed and stood straight, holding Emma's gaze. "What time did you fall asleep, Emma?"

Of all the things Jacinda might've asked, Emma's bedtime was the last thing she expected to be called on.

"I...I think about eleven. Maybe midnight."

Jacinda held her gaze, her eyes level and face expressionless. "Emma, I don't know how much sleep you got the night before last, or how much you actually slept last night. But right now? Right now, your eyes are red-rimmed, and your energy is manic. Like you're running on adrenaline and caffeine, not natural rest. So again, I'm asking you, what time did you fall asleep? You went home and continued your investigation of Fishbourne via your computer, you already said, and that was after following him."

Emma swallowed, thinking back to how she'd tossed and turned after sleeping for only a few hours, staring at her ceiling and fighting the urge to come into the office hours early. She'd finally drifted off again only an hour or so before her alarm had sounded.

"What time did you fall asleep? How are you sleeping in general?"

Emma took a deep breath, steeling herself to avoid sounding defensive. "I'm sleeping fine."

Jacinda gazed at her for another few seconds, then shrugged. "Okay, then. It's not like you to lose a tail. What happened? Where and when?"

Mouth drying, Emma fought to keep her voice even. "The evening traffic got heavy. I was following him, and we were in the area of the toy shop over on Seventh Street, but...I just lost him." She shrugged, unable to go on.

No chance was she telling Jacinda that a wall of grief and guilt had knocked her for a loop when she'd passed the Yoga Map.

"Aside from sleep, then, how are you doing?"

"I'm doing fine. I'm trying to do my job. What is this?"

"How are you doing when it comes to dealing with losing Oren?"

"What?" Emma stared, wishing she'd heard wrong. *She's asking this now?* "We have a kid to save. What the hell does that matter?"

Jacinda pulled out one of the conference table chairs. "Sit down."

"I'd rather stand."

Eyes narrowing, Jacinda leaned back against the wall and stared at Emma. "I'm worried about you. So is the rest of the team. You mentioned Seventh Street. That's right by the yoga studio, isn't it?"

Emma just caught herself from nodding, remaining frozen. She couldn't believe Jacinda had seen through her so easily.

"I'm thinking that's what happened. You realized how close you were to the studio, maybe even passed it, and that distracted you. I may be wrong, but even if I am, you're not yourself. I think you need to take some time off and really process what happened to Oren. See a therapist."

"That's absurd, and you know it!" Anger bubbled up Emma's throat, and she felt herself bouncing on the balls of her feet, energy aching to get out. Aching to *strike out*. "I'm fine, Jacinda. I just need everyone to stop worrying about me and let me work!"

Jacinda frowned and turned back to the table, gently shutting her laptop as she spoke. "Well, it doesn't seem that way to me, Emma. That's all I can tell you, and I hope that means something. I'm not going to mandate it…not right now…but I do believe a break would really benefit you, and I hope you'll consider it before I'm forced to make my recommendation mandatory and official."

Emma pulled a deep breath into her lungs, fighting to calm down. Jacinda wasn't going to force her to take a break. That was the takeaway from this conversation.

Knowing what was expected, meaningful or not, Emma lowered her voice. And she lied. "I'll consider what you've said, Jacinda, but not yet."

Jacinda slid her laptop under her arm along with her folders, then gestured for Emma to walk with her toward the door. "All right. If that's how you feel, head back to the opera house and see if you can dig anything else up. We still don't know who interfered with that security footage at the storage building. Start there."

Emma opened her mouth to protest, but Jacinda held up a hand to stop her as they reached the door.

"Uh-uh. You don't want to take a break, fine, but you play by my rules. No more talking to witnesses and suspects. If you decide that's not good enough for you and rethink that break I suggested, then you can back off the case at any moment and I'll support it, no questions asked. Pay remains in place, too, though I don't think that's what's stopping you."

Reluctantly, Emma nodded. "Okay. Fair enough."

Jacinda led the way out of the conference room, and

Emma beelined toward her desk. Before she could get there, though, Leo stepped in front of her.

Emma was tempted to kick him in the shin, or punch him, but instead she only pushed past him. "I'm *fine*." She picked up her bag from beside her desk and turned to face him, walking backward toward the door. "Don't screw this up, okay? Looking into Fishbourne, I mean. He's involved somehow, and apparently Jacinda wants you and Denae on it instead of me. So I'm telling you, don't screw it up. Understood?"

Leo's eyes went wide. For once, the charmer was lost for words. The hurt in his eyes couldn't have broadcast his feelings more clearly if he'd pulled out a billboard.

Shit, that was harsh.

A pit of bitterness opened up in Emma's empty stomach, sloshing around the coffee she'd already downed, and she whirled away from him. He hadn't deserved that sort of rudeness and disrespect.

At the door, she held it open for an extra minute and forced herself to look back at him. "I'm sorry. I'm sure you'll do fine."

Before he could answer, she dropped the door and hurried toward the elevator. Both of them had their assignments, and she'd said more than enough.

20

Leo raised his fist but hesitated to knock on Ted Fishbourne's office door. Replaying Emma's performance from yesterday, he couldn't help imagining the man's reaction to having him and Denae on his proverbial doorstep yet again.

He muttered under his breath. "Prepare yourself."

And then, before Denae could ask, he knocked.

"Come in!"

Leo stepped in first, and the middle-aged man actually rolled his eyes, dropping a red pen down on the papers he'd been marking.

"Mr. Fish—"

"I know who I am, Agent Ambrose. What do you want?"

Leo could practically feel Denae's eyes widening, the way she came to an abrupt halt beside him. He moved forward and took the seat Emma had occupied the day before. "I don't believe you've met my colleague, Special Agent Denae Monroe. We're here—"

"Here to ask me some real questions?" Fishbourne picked up his red pen and drummed it on his desk. "Or do you want to go over my college years this time, my early work as an understudy with a Shakespearean troupe, perhaps?"

We deserved that.

Leo held his smile in place by force. "I'm sorry about yesterday, Mr. Fishbourne. It was a difficult day for everyone, I realize. But we do have some more questions."

The man all but twitched with annoyance, but he finally dropped his pen again and nodded. "So be it. If it'll get you out of my hair, get on with it."

Denae held out her phone, displaying the picture of him sitting in the park. "One of our agents tailed you last night and witnessed some suspicious activity we have to ask you about. What were you doing visiting a local park—"

"One of your agents *what?*" Fishbourne glared at Denae, mouth partially open in shock, then turned to Leo. "Are all the women you work with unable to exhibit any decorum? What right did your team have to tail me?"

"*Sir.*" Leo held up a single hand, channeling every bit of authority and silencing power his yaya had once wielded over him. The way this man had just talked about Denae and Emma, it wasn't difficult. *Talk about chauvinists showing their true colors.* "We're investigating two deaths and four kidnappings. Of *children*. So again, I'm going to ask you, what were you doing visiting a local park to watch children play? You said before that you don't have any children yourself."

Flushing pink, the stage manager sighed and sat back in his seat. Shaking his head, he suddenly looked shockingly tired. Not defensive, which alone made Leo wonder whether Emma simply had the man all wrong. "I wasn't watching children play at all. I simply didn't feel like going home to an empty, depressing house yet."

Leo waited, holding the stage manager's gaze until he shifted in his seat.

"I wanted to be near people. Without having to walk

around a damn shopping center or spend money at a restaurant. And there were more than just children in that park. You might think it's an odd thing to do, but you'd be surprised what works to fight off depression." Fishbourne raised one hand to rub his eyes in the way of a man decades older, then glanced between the agents again. "At least for me. Perhaps the two of you would go to a shooting range or tail innocent people viewing horror movies rather than anything so pedestrian."

Denae huffed. "And what about the toy store you visited after?"

"The toy…" The man's eyes widened, and he leaned forward. "Are you saying I'm not allowed to have hobbies? Really now? Toy stores sell all sorts of things for adults. Do you think they advertise thousand-piece jigsaw puzzles for your average toddler?"

Leo remained quiet for a few seconds, letting the man calm himself. "Sir," he channeled his inner yaya again, "were you there for jigsaw puzzles?"

Fishbourne frowned at him and spoke more quietly when he answered. "I'm building a model train set in my house and was picking up some new pieces. I'd special-ordered them. When a notification came in that they were there, I left the park to get them."

Denae gestured at the man's wallet, which lay on the corner of his desk. "Do you have the receipt?"

"It's at home." The stage manager wrinkled his nose, as if fighting a bad smell, but then he sighed and picked up his phone. "But I do have some pictures."

Leo took the man's proffered phone and found himself looking at an elaborate train set, which rivaled most he'd seen in movies, let alone real life. The set seemed to take up most of a basement. One of the most recent pictures showed a brand-new caboose and railway crossing, still in their boxes, along with some scale-model trees and horses.

"I haven't set up the new pieces yet, but I took pictures to show the people in the train hobbyist group I belong to online." Fishbourne grabbed his phone back from Leo as soon as it was held out to him. "Does that suffice? Or would you like to come by my house this evening and take pictures of the receipt?"

Leo glanced at Denae, whose tight expression seemed more annoyed than suspicious. At this point, he rather agreed with her. They had nothing on this guy. And while they could follow up with the toy store, he didn't see much point. It was time to go.

"No, Mr. Fishbourne, I don't believe that'll be necessary." Leo stood, trying to take some care not to loom over the stage manager, who remained sitting before them. If he did file a report of some kind, there was no need to add intimidation to his complaints. "You have my card if you think of anything else?"

Fishbourne snorted and picked up his red pen, already looking back at his papers. "Certainly. I'll call if I see an adult even thinking about entering a toy store or park without a child to supervise."

Count to three, Leo. Count to three and get the hell out. And then you can figure out how to break the news to Emma.

Turning, Leo gestured for Denae to head out the door first, but his eye caught on a shadow in the hall.

Even before they got outside, he knew who he'd find.

Emma, lurking near Fishbourne's office and waiting for the rundown. Fantastic.

21

Emma stepped in front of Denae just as she exited Fishbourne's office. "What'd you learn? Where was he last night after I lost him?"

"Shhh!" Denae glanced back at the open office Leo was still exiting, and Emma rolled her eyes.

Who cares if the man heard me?

"Follow me." Denae pulled her along toward the stairwell, only stopping when they were all the way down the hall from Fishbourne's office. And then she whirled on Emma, all but pinning her against the wall.

"You're hurting. I get it. I sympathize. But let me make it clear. You step on my toes again when I'm doing my job, and I'll go straight to the SSA with a complaint. Then you can see what mandatory counseling feels like. I'm guessing Jacinda only suggested it after the briefing. Am I right?"

Emma was so stunned by Denae's outburst, all she could do was nod.

"Okay, then. So let's call it even. You gave us a lead nobody else could have gotten. We followed up, and now we can probably dismiss Ted Fishbourne as a person of interest.

That'll save us time, and we can get back to looking for Tommy Grant."

Emma's voice returned with a flare of anger. "What do you mean we can dismiss him? The guy's absolutely suspicious, and you can't blame me for being curious. What did you find out?"

"We found out we've got nothing on him. He's clean." Denae stepped back, giving Emma a little room to move, but she stayed with her back to the wall, facing off against her colleagues.

She stared at Leo, waiting for the punch line. "But—"

"But nothing. The man builds train sets in his basement, and that's why he was at the toy store last night. He showed us pictures that'd rival any diorama in a toy museum." At least Leo's soft tone contradicted the harshness of his message. "Denae's right. We can probably forget about him, but that'll be Jacinda's call. If she wants us to, we'll keep an eye on him. And by 'we,' I mean me and Denae or whoever Jacinda assigns. *You* need to leave him alone."

Emma held Leo's gaze another moment. She felt Denae's eyes boring holes into her head.

Suddenly, the soft tone Leo had taken made more sense. The man pitied her. One by one, she was losing her team's respect and support.

Emma's stomach turned, and she felt her throat tighten up. Leo opened his mouth to say something else, but she turned on her heel and fled into the stairwell.

Maybe she couldn't question suspects directly, but that didn't mean she couldn't investigate.

She hit the ground floor at a jog even as she heard her colleagues stepping into the stairwell above her, and she didn't pause. Right now, she wanted to be as far away from them as possible.

Ignoring a smattering of stage crew and performers,

Emma hurried across the stage and toward the door leading down to the tunnels. Unlike their first night at the opera house, the tunnels were now lit at every turn by spotlights and lanterns to ease the way of the investigation.

Her steps thundered on the metal stairs, and Emma wasn't surprised to see new cameras dotting the various landings as she moved upward.

Between the noise she made and the new electronics, she all but expected the portly Frankie Wilson to appear soon after she exited into the storage area...

That didn't quite happen—the storage building was large, after all—but as Emma headed to Frankie's station, she saw him turning down the aisle to meet her.

"Nice to see you again, Agent Last," the man stuck out his hand, shaking hers, "especially now. I was just about to call. Working a double today or I'd already be home."

"What do you have for me?" Her voice came out breathy, betraying her near-run to the tunnels. She made a point of taking a deep gulp of air.

"Two kinds of good news and nothing bad. Which kind do you want first?"

"Just hit me with it. Anything good is welcome right now."

He stepped back with a proud smile. "First off, everybody working security here was cleared. We all had alibis for when those kids were taken, but I guess you already knew that, yeah?"

Emma paused for a moment before nodding and offering Frankie her best poker face. She could feel her cheeks burning with the shame of realizing a civilian was more informed about the case than she was.

That's not good. Not good at all. Get it together.

"What else do you have? You said 'two kinds of good news.' What's the other one?"

He referred to a note card he'd had tucked into his pocket. "I figured out exactly when the feeds were changed over to play a recording. It was a few minutes before two a.m. on February twenty-fifth, and whoever did it was in the main opera house, not out here."

For the first time in days, the grin on Emma's lips was genuine. Nobody on her team had managed to nail that down, being preoccupied with interviews and other aspects of the investigation.

There's something you could have been doing instead of chasing after Ted Fishbourne.

"Good job, Frankie. Please tell me you know who was in the opera house at that time."

Frankie turned and headed back toward his security station, waving at her to follow him. "I was here alone in the storage building as usual, and there was one security guard over in the opera house. Beyond that, I can show you whose security badges were still logged in, meaning they were inside the building, because it was so late."

Frankie came to his desk and pulled up the security badge-tracking system, which appeared in the form of an Excel sheet. On February twenty-fourth, only a few badges had been used to enter the building after nine p.m.

"That was a Thursday, so there were no performances, which means a pretty quiet building, just like today." Frankie pointed to the short list of names in the building overnight between February twenty-fourth and twenty-fifth. "You've got me and the other security guard, and the system caught him on video at exactly two in the morning."

He then hit some keys beneath another monitor and pulled up footage of an older man casually patrolling through the space Emma recognized as the opera house's second floor lobby, near where the drink carts were stored. The time stamp on the footage read 1:59 a.m.

"That's old Rodney. Spry, sure, but not fast. Even if he mainlined caffeine. It would've taken him more than ten minutes to get from here to the security station in the opera house."

Emma considered the other security setup she'd seen, which mirrored Frankie's exactly. "And he'd have access to the CCTV network over here from that building?"

"Yeah, but like I said, it couldn't have been him. And I was here at this station just minutes before the changeover, so it had to be someone over in the main house setting the monitors to replay recent footage rather than record anything new."

Emma glanced back to the badge log-ons. "So besides you and Rodney, that leaves Ted Fishbourne, Jason Engelson, and a Wallace Chapman. Jason's the costar, right?"

Frankie nodded.

"And who's Chapman?"

Frankie pulled up an opera house badge belonging to a Wallace Chapman. Narrow-faced and frowning, acne scars marring his pale skin, the guy looked like a gazillion other white men living in D.C.

"He's one of the night custodians. Tends to come in for overtime Monday or Tuesday nights to clean up from the last week's performances and make sure things are set for another full week. Seems to be a little antisocial and prefers to work nights, but that's like most nighttime custodial workers, far as I can tell. Always takes the overtime shifts when he's the only one on duty."

Emma jotted the name down, then gestured to the other names recorded. "And why would Jason and Ted be here so late? This says Jason badged in at 9:28 p.m., and Ted's just shown as badging out at 4:02 a.m., so I guess that means he was there all night?"

Frankie tightened up his ponytail, sitting down in his

chair with a satisfied grunt. "Not really weird for them, to be honest. Ted works strange hours. He's here at night all the time, 'specially when he's going over potential scripts and audition film. Sometimes wanders over here to look at what props and costumes we've got on hand at odd hours. As for Jason, I swear it seems like he lives here since we started rehearsals for *Tristan und Isolde*."

Thinking back to the grumpy actor she'd witnessed during interviews, she tried to recall any red flags, but he'd only seemed short-tempered and tired. "Any particular reason he'd be more concerned about this show, that you know of? Sounds like it's a little out of habit from previous shows."

Frankie's eyes darted over to a little photo pinned to the corkboard next to his security station. It showed Frankie and a woman and child, who Emma guessed to be his family. "I've only chatted with him once or twice...but I get the feeling his marriage might be on the rocks. Maybe worse. It's a shitty world we live in, ain't it? Some people murdering and killing little kids, families struggling to stay close. Makes you wonder."

As Frankie peered at his family's picture, his frown seemed to settle in place, but Emma decided to press. "To focus on Jason Engelson for a second...think it's just hard to be out every night and survive on an actor's salary? Or you think there's more to it?"

"I wouldn't know." Frankie's eyes narrowed. "Actors are known to be difficult to live with, but I don't get to know 'em too well, being over here. You see a married man sleeping on a couch in a greenroom a few times, though..."

"I get it." Emma gave one more glance to the Excel sheet offering up their now much-tightened list of suspects. She fought the urge to smirk. They were down to three people, and Ted Fishbourne's name was still among them. "Thanks for your help, Frankie. You think of anything else, you call me. Oh, and is Wallace Chapman still around here this morning? Where would he be?"

Frankie hit buttons to scan between security camera feeds and stopped the flood of changing images when he landed on one showing a man mopping a restroom. "That's the main restroom off stage right. He follows his normal routine, he'll be working on that hallway by the time you get back over to the theater. Doubt you'll find Jason here on a Tuesday morning, but I'll leave a note for Antoine, the guy who relieves me. He'll message you if he sees him walk in."

Emma patted the helpful guard on the back and then hurried back toward the tunnels. Ted Fishbourne might be off-limits to her, but there was no reason she couldn't question a custodian.

22

True to Frankie's prediction, Emma found Wallace Chapman mopping the hallway that ran outside the backstage area. The man was tall and gangly, with his head bent to the task at hand as he ran his mop methodically along the tiles. He seemed even more ordinary than he had in his picture. Taller and more awkward maybe, but just another man who'd blend into any crowd.

And as if to emphasize his ability to merge with the scenery, he barely looked up at her as she exited stage right. "You need something, ma'am? If you're looking for the restroom, just be careful. The floor's wet."

"Wallace Chapman?" Emma flashed her badge as he stood straight, his eyes going a little wide at the sound of his name. "I'm Special Agent Emma Last. I'd actually like a few minutes of your time if it's not too much trouble."

A cautious smile came to his face. He chuckled and leaned on his mop, and she noticed a fine sheen of sweat on his forehead. "Don't know why you'd pay any attention to me, but sure, I got time."

She came to within a few feet of him, noting the way his

eyes followed her. He didn't seem nervous…just curious. "Three weeks ago, around two a.m. on February twenty-fifth, somebody messed with the security system's CCTV cameras and programmed them to replay footage rather than record what was happening like they normally would. You have any idea who'd do that? See anything that night, maybe?"

Wallace's eyes squinted together in thought. "I'm usually here Tuesdays. Let's see…last week, I didn't see anybody but Jason, sleeping off a few drinks in the greenroom." He put a hand to his mouth, looking a little too theatrical, if Emma was being honest with herself. "Sorry, I didn't mean to let his secret slip…"

Emma waved off the apology. "I take it the man likes to drink?"

"Never before a performance night, but he has his moments."

"What about the stage manager, Ted Fishbourne? Ever see him acting odd around here?"

"Other than all the time, you mean?" Wallace Chapman darted a glance over his shoulder, as if to check that nobody was coming, then looked back at Emma. "Seriously, though, Ted's been kinda stranger than normal lately. Maybe two weeks ago, three weeks ago…the weekends blur together, you understand…I caught Ted in his office, uh…"

Emma's heart sped up. "Caught him what?"

He frowned and lowered his voice, leaning toward her. "I don't judge most things, ya know, but…" He shook his head, hand going white-knuckled where he clenched the mop. "He was looking at photos of a kid on his computer. Not normal to be looking at a kid like he was. Ted nearly jumped out of his skin when I popped in to clean, too, and that ain't normal. It wasn't his kid, either, since this one was Black."

Emma refrained from pointing out that a white man

could certainly have a Black child. "Can you tell me what the child looked like in more detail?"

The custodian pursed his lips, his gaze going far away again as if remembering back. "Kinda short maybe? I don't know. I only got a glimpse of the screen. Hard to see."

"Did he wear glasses?" She remembered Daniel Jackson's ghost staring white-eyed through *Star Wars* glasses.

"Maybe. Yeah, I think so."

You've got him, Emma girl. Fishbourne won't be hurting anyone else now.

"Thanks, Mr. Chapman. That's just what I needed." She pulled out her card and handed it to him. "You think of anything else, you call me, okay?"

He nodded, and she was just about to head down the hall toward the theater exit when her phone pinged with a text message. It was an unknown number, but the message identified the sender.

This is Frankie. Jason Engelson just came out of the greenroom, headed onto stage opposite you.

Emma turned on her heel and headed back into the theater, where she spotted the man wandering across the stage toward the staircase leading into the orchestra pit. He looked like hell, creases on his face showing that he'd just woken up, his shirt only half tucked in. He rubbed a hand through his hair as if trying to tame it.

"Mr. Engelson, can I have a word?"

He came to a lumbering halt near center stage and watched her approach, brow lined with confusion. "Why?"

"To help with the case." Emma stopped in front of him, noting the scowl on his lips. "Tell me about last night."

"Last night?" Jason Engelson practically snarled, his hands going to his hips. "What's it to you?"

Emma stood straighter, making sure her badge showed at

her belt as she continued. "I'm guessing you slept here. Your wife doesn't care?"

His nose wrinkled, and he burped out a stale cloud of booze breath. *Lovely.* "Ted doesn't care if I sleep here every once in a while."

"Ted's not your wife." Emma waited for a response, but Engelson stared past her as if a circus were stealing his attention in the background. "Why stay here instead of home?"

He shrugged. "Why not stay here? It's my life. My choices and my private affairs."

Emma didn't see any reason to press him, at least at the moment. Fishbourne was more important than a drunk actor with a mess of a personal life, and by the smell of this guy, he probably didn't have the self-discipline to be kidnapping kids while holding up his end of the deal as an opera star. "Okay, fair enough. What can you tell me about Ted Fishbourne? Is he a train hobbyist like I've been told? Does he have children in his life, maybe a niece or nephew? A grandchild?"

He scoffed, his eyes coming back to hers for the first time since she'd approached him. "Ted? I've known him awhile, and…I can't imagine a train set holding his interest. He doesn't have the patience. I mean, maybe, but I've never heard him mention it."

Emma filed that away to mention to Leo. "And what about kids?"

Jason frowned, shrugging. "I have no idea. I feel like I'd have heard him mention it, but if it isn't related to a show, it doesn't usually get past Ted's lips. Stage managers get to have private affairs too."

Emma meant to ask about his own personal life, if only to eliminate him from her mental list of suspects, but her question was derailed. Fishbourne emerged from a prop closet and headed toward the stage exit. The one that led to the parking lot.

She glanced at her watch. Midway through a Tuesday morning, and he was leaving after being questioned by agents? Whatever he wanted all of them to believe about his life outside the theater, she'd never been surer that he was full of it.

"Excuse me, Mr. Engelson."

The actor didn't answer or call to her as she left him behind. That was just as well. Emma kept herself from breaking into a jog as Fishbourne hit the stage door and left the building.

She had no doubt as to where the man was headed. Wherever Tommy was, Ted Fishbourne would lead her there. Screw questioning him. That wasn't necessary. She only needed to follow him and find Tommy Grant before this creep sent him off to join his previous victims in the Other.

Getting the boy back safe would prove to her team she'd been right all along, and then maybe they'd lay off asking if she was okay and doubting her ability to perform.

23

Emma could practically hear Leo and Jacinda in her head as she tailed Ted Fishbourne out the door.

"Emma, what are you doing? Think about what you're doing! Please!"

"What did I tell you? Do you remember me telling you to leave Fishbourne to Leo and Denae? Stop!"

She told both of them to shut it and made for her car. One of their dead victims had led to her suspicions of the man, and she refused to ignore that.

Emma paused in between two patrol cars, remembering her first case with Leo and Jacinda. The ghost of Penelope Dowe had silently aimed a finger at Reggie O'Rourke, the ringmaster at the Ruby Red Circus.

Reggie was dirty. He had crimes in his past, and behavior that was relevant to the case, even if he wasn't the one killing all the circus performers.

Maybe the same thing's true about Fishbourne, *or maybe he's our unsub.*

Either way, Emma couldn't exactly call up Leo and

Jacinda to say a ghost suggested she pay closer attention to Ted Fishbourne.

She was on her own, at least for now.

Fishbourne was backing out of his parking spot. Emma hurried to her Prius and waited until he had rolled out of the lot before following him.

The stage manager kept a leisurely pace on the roads, making his way through the midmorning traffic without much trouble. Emma followed at a good distance, and Fishbourne showed no sign of having spotted her behind him.

When he turned into a neighborhood, where traffic thinned out, Emma kept farther back. Within minutes, Fishbourne had driven up his driveway, exited the car, and gone inside. Emma pulled to the curb a few houses down.

This is it, Emma girl. You're slapping Jacinda's orders right down the tube now.

But she didn't have much choice. Not when Tommy Grant could be tied up in this man's house with leeches sucking every ounce of his blood.

Jacinda and Leo would understand. They'd have to.

Emma got out and made a beeline for Fishbourne's property. Walking up the border of the front lawn, she edged herself between well-manicured bushes and the front windows. She was about to take a glimpse inside when the front door was yanked open.

"Agent Last." Ted Fishbourne sighed, sounding for all the world like a frustrated schoolteacher. "Can I help you?"

Well, shit.

Straightening, Emma walked out from between the house and bushes with as much dignity as she could muster. Fishbourne stood at his front door, red-eyed and glaring, but without any apparent intention to threaten her. She didn't see a weapon, or even a phone.

Emma stared back at him from the front walk, fighting the urge to hover a hand over her gun.

No need to escalate this. Not yet.

"I want you to tell me what you know."

"What I know?" He huffed, scrubbing both hands down his cheeks. "I'm tired of being harassed. You should be on someone else's doorstep, hunting down the psycho who killed kids under my opera house."

His *opera house. That's interesting.*

A smidge of doubt wormed its way into Emma's blood. A killer wouldn't take pride or ownership of anything other than killing. Nothing else would matter to him.

"Mr. Fishbourne," Emma evened her voice, more curious than ever what the man would admit to, "believe it or not, I'm just trying to return missing children to their parents. And I know the train set excuse is crap. That means you're hiding something. Whatever it is—"

He stepped back and pulled the door wide open, waving her in as if he were an usher and had only ten seconds before the lights went down. "The train set is crap? Allow me to prove you wrong, since you clearly don't know what the hell you're talking about."

Emma didn't hesitate. She had her gun and phone, and she could take this guy in a second. Just let him try to come after her, and he'd see the difference between attacking her and attacking a malnourished child like Daniel Jackson.

She stepped inside to a tile floor surrounded by a luxurious living area. He closed the door behind her—not locking it, she noticed—and swept by her to a door set into the wall just before the kitchen space began.

"Come on, Agent Last. Before you eat up my whole damn day with your nonsense."

Another worm of doubt crept into her. Fishbourne's irritation could stem from her having interrupted his killing ritual. She'd have to be on her toes and ready to react if he tried anything. With one hand hovering near her weapon, Emma followed him through the kitchen.

The room turned cold and the air thick with the presence of the Other.

A young girl, maybe five years old, rolled a wooden train back and forth along the edge of the kitchen table, making soft "choo-choo" sounds as she did. Emma had the sudden urge to sit down, attempt to play with her, and get some answers, but Fishbourne was still moving, none the wiser that she'd ever paused.

The door he led her through took them down a narrow, carpeted staircase into a well-lit basement that must have run the length of the house. At the bottom step, Emma caught her breath.

An elaborate train track wound through miniature terrain and buildings, across bridges and trestles, and spanned several long tables.

Emma didn't know what to say.

Or how the ghost she'd seen in the kitchen fit into it all.

Fishbourne stood in the center of the setup, ringed with tracks that all merged to a single bridge crossing on a hinged section of track. Fishbourne lowered the bridge and stepped back, arms crossed over his chest. But he wasn't smiling. He simply watched her, observing. "Welcome to my basement full of crap, Agent Last."

Emma was about to apologize when she noticed a photograph over his right shoulder. The framed picture showed Fishbourne with his arms around a woman and a young girl—the same ghost child she'd just seen. The man wore a proud smile that reminded Emma of the smile her own mother wore in the picture on her nightstand, and her throat tightened.

From the corner of her eye, she saw Fishbourne follow

her gaze. He wilted where he stood. "You all seem curious about my interactions with children. Well, there's your answer. They died…oh, God, it was near a decade ago."

Emma had to ask. "How?"

He paused long enough that she thought he might not answer. "We were on a ski trip. I got worn out early and went back to the lodge. Marie and Angelica got caught in an avalanche. They never had a chance."

"Mr. Fishbourne, I am so sorry. So, so sorry."

He kept staring at his family photo, and Emma sensed the void in the room. The man in front of her was empty of life, still mourning, and she herself might as well have been another of his little statues set up and waiting for a train that would never really stop for her. Her heart was an abyss that should have been full of emotion, but instead she felt only regret.

"I am sorry, really. Please know that. Life…takes people from us, and…"

"You've lost someone?"

"Yes. Last month, on a case."

"I won't ask who it was, because honestly, Agent Last, I really don't care. I know you've just been following your suspicions, which I have to assume you have reasonable grounds to have formed. But I think you've been unnecessarily cruel. You're just adding insult to injury."

Abandoning professionalism, Emma lifted up the bridge that allowed her to enter the middle of the diorama where he stood with his back to her. She approached the man, not stopping until she was at his shoulder, invading his space. Close enough to see the tiny, shuddering movements in his shoulders that signaled he'd begun to cry.

The little girl shimmered into view on the floor beside him. She played with her wooden train set at his feet. This little girl was so devoted to her father, but Emma's parents had never once visited her.

"Please believe me. I hate how cruel life can be, and I'm sorry I've been thoughtless. I've lost people, more than once. I know you said you don't care, but...he was the man I expected to marry. He was killed by the suspect I'd been tracking, because I made a mistake in estimating where he would strike next."

"You can't know that."

"What?"

Ted Fishbourne turned to face her, his wet cheeks glistening in the lamplight. "I said you can't know that your mistake is what led to the killer choosing who to kill. Or that you could've stopped him, even if you had known he would target the man you loved."

Emotion burned Emma's eyes. "I wish I could believe that."

"I can't know that staying on the slopes instead of going back to the ski lodge could've saved my wife and daughter. It's done, and nothing we did or could have done would change any of it. Because in that moment, when we made the decision that we think was the *wrong* one, we still made that decision. There's no going back to it, no matter how seductive it feels to try."

He was right, just like Leo had been right, and Mia, Jacinda, and Denae too. They were all right.

Oren's death wasn't Emma's fault and couldn't have been prevented, no matter what she did. Because she did make a decision based on the information she had, using the training she'd received and skills she'd developed.

But knowing she'd lacked the necessary skill, training, and information to save Oren's life didn't make it any easier to live with.

"I don't know how to stop grieving, and…" Emma's voice caught, Oren's image suddenly joining her mother's in her mind and stealing her breath.

"I may've been wrong about you, Agent Last. You do get it. It does feel like this is forever, doesn't it? Life's little joke. You get to be happy, and then, one day, everything ends and there's no going back. No going forward to something else, either, because how could you possibly replace what you've lost?"

Tears threatened, but she held them in. "I never would've thought you capable of…if I'd suspected anything like," she gestured to the photograph of his family, "I'm so sorry. I should go. You've had enough of me for one week."

Emma was about to say more when she glimpsed movement in the corner of the room, just as the space went a touch colder, the air a tad heavier. She knew before she looked who'd be there.

Daniel Jackson shimmered into view, crouching in front of the train and tracing the track with his empty eyes. As Emma gave him her full attention, the ghost's chin tilted toward her. He nodded before examining the train again.

Without bringing his eyes back to her, Daniel spoke. "This underground isn't sad. I like trains."

Emma froze, only half-hearing Ted Fishbourne asking if she was all right. She thought back to when she'd first seen Daniel and assumed he'd been pointing out Fishbourne as a suspect. The boy hadn't actually said anything or pointed at him the way Penelope had done with the circus ringmaster.

Daniel had stood by the stairwell leading up to Fishbourne's office and had only stared in his direction.

"Agent Last? Agent Last!" Fishbourne's hands hovered in front of her face. He waved them again as she met his eyes. "Are you all right? You seemed to black out there."

Emma gave herself a mental shake. "I'm fine. Fine. I should go now. Thank…I mean, I'm sorry, again. Please forgive me. I don't know what I was thinking."

"I'd say you weren't. You were too busy feeling, like me. I've gone after actors and stagehands at times, and it's always the same. They get pissed off, and I feel stupid for taking out my grief on other people."

"Maybe we should both get help."

"I'd rather forget any of this happened, if it's all the same to you."

Emma apologized again and excused herself, giving one last look at Daniel's ghost playing with Fishbourne's daughter. Both ghostly children sat on the floor smiling and pushing a train back and forth between them.

Upstairs, Emma made a hasty exit, holding in her tears until she hit the sidewalk and got back to her vehicle. She no longer cared who saw her cry or what anyone might think.

Getting behind the wheel, Emma buckled up and made a fast U-turn, aiming herself on a path back to the opera house.

Daniel Jackson's ghost had first appeared to her backstage, by the stairwell that led to the stage manager's office. He'd been staring at Fishbourne while Vance and Mia questioned the man, and Emma had assumed that to mean the man was somehow involved in or had knowledge of Daniel's murder.

But he had merely been facing in Fishbourne's direction, not pointing fingers. Daniel stood by the stairwell, beside an industrial mop bucket on wheels. The mop handle was leaning against the wall over Daniel's head.

Whether she'd lost some professionalism or not, her failure this morning had just turned the tide in determining their real unsub.

"Little Black kid, kinda short maybe."

Emma had been so focused on Fishbourne that she'd prematurely dismissed the other names on the spreadsheet Frankie Wilson had showed her.

She only hoped Wallace Chapman was still where she'd left him.

24

I'd never understood the phrase "living on borrowed time" until now. Proceeding without thinking further ahead than the next task, I'd been a fool, and it was now only a matter of time before that FBI agent pieced things together.

She'd looked unhinged, red-eyed and angry, but also determined. By comparison, I was a fool doing somersaults in a two-bit carnival. She'd catch on to me sooner than later. I'd never been a great liar—always a touch too casual, a touch too thoughtless—and once that woman got her head on straight, she was bound to see through me.

Despair had hung on her too. She might be the type to let the job work its way into her heart deep enough to stop it from beating, but I had no way of knowing how long that might take.

My hands shook as I changed out of my uniform, missing button after button. I wasn't *supposed* to be afraid. I wasn't *supposed* to care so much about life that the idea of being caught bothered me.

Amazing how things had changed.

I sat down in a chair to tie my shoes, fighting the urge to

throw up. Until recently, I'd have laughed at what was happening. I'd have welcomed a fate that ended with me on death row. Wasn't death what I wanted?

Existence still felt like a curse, true, but I wanted to take things just a little further before embracing the sweet relief of death. I wasn't done yet.

Surely, there was time for me to do more work before the inevitable end.

The Teachings are still where I left them, with my proof. I should take them before I leave.

And I would be leaving. My work at the opera house was meaningless in the larger scheme of things, and I saw no reason not to abandon my shift.

Shoes tied, I sat back against my little locker and thought about my next steps. The boy in my family's basement was near his final bleeding, but to ensure I had time to complete that mission and secure myself from discovery, I would need a distraction.

Jason Engelson, that bigheaded cheater.

I'd watched him come and go from the opera house, mostly keeping to himself except during rehearsals and performances. And I'd watched him slink off into the greenroom, where he kept a bag of toiletries and a change of clothes, along with his spare bottle of gin. He and his wife weren't officially divorced, but they soon would be. I didn't doubt it for a second.

The way Jason made eyes at Layla during rehearsals, and when they would kiss during performances…sometimes I'd swear it didn't even look like acting.

A lot of good it would do him. My dreaming about him showed me a man devoted to life's miseries, seeking solace in other people's celebration of his efforts because he couldn't find such solace within himself.

And wasn't that the truth of it all? That none of us could ever hope to find such solace?

Least of all a less-than-talented actor like Jason Engelson. He probably didn't have the self-awareness to realize we all knew about his failing marriage and drinking problem. His life was a textbook case of misery. Even so, he'd do just fine for my purposes.

Knowing he'd slept in the lounge decked out for opera subscribers, I left the custodial closet and headed upstairs. Jason wasn't anywhere around—probably down in the greenroom making coffee—but his coat was slung across a sofa near the closed-down bar area. His phone poked out of one pocket.

I took one of his overpriced gloves from his other pocket and put it on to grab his phone. Stuffing it, then the glove, into my pockets, I grabbed his coat and hurried back downstairs. If I could set the Feds on Jason's trail, I'd buy myself more than enough time to deliver little Tommy and maybe even collect another life in need of saving from this world's inevitable decay.

First, I went back to the custodial closet and put Jason's glove on again so I could stick his phone into a colleague's coverall pocket. With only three of us working at the opera house, that wouldn't grant me too much extra time, but it might slow the Feds down a bit.

They'd have to first find and then question poor Carl. The man was routinely late for his shifts, anyway, and I knew he liked to search around the seats for trinkets and money dropped by patrons.

It wouldn't be that great a stretch to propose he'd stolen an actor's smartphone in hopes of hocking it for extra cash.

That task complete, I headed for the stairwell leading to the tunnels. As I made it there and casually dropped Jason's gloves over the stairwell barrier, the door to the parking lot opened. I let Jason's coat hang over the stairwell, out of sight behind the short wall that prevented people from tumbling downward. A stagehand entered from the parking lot, holding a tray with four cups of coffee.

I waved to her. "Fuel for those in the trenches?"

"Don't you know it. We'll be lucky if we don't bomb on opening night next week. The whole dead kids thing kinda fucked up rehearsal schedules."

"I can only imagine."

She headed off to the auditorium where the rest of the crew were probably gathered for a prerehearsal meeting.

I leaned over the stairwell and checked to see if Jason's gloves landed near the door into the tunnels, and they had. It would look like he'd dropped them on his way in or out.

But I still had to collect the Teachings. Except I'd been seen standing here, and if anyone came by while I was down below, they'd see Jason's gloves. I could take them with me and leave them again on my way out.

No, the crew will be done with their meeting by then, and they'll see me come up. Going out the other way isn't safe either.

The Teachings would have to wait, or maybe I'd just leave them there forever. I'd learned what I needed to learn and had successfully put it into practice three times already.

They'll stay behind, then.

I would now go after Jason himself.

The greenroom was generally silent this time of day, but for when a rare matinee was planned. The exception to the rule was Jason. He used the kitchenette when he was on the outs with his wife. Which was most days of late.

I found him standing by the coffee maker, barely managing to stay upright. The stink of gin wafted from him as he leaned on the counter, jerking with…sobs?

Oh, how delightful. He's already done half my work for me.

Heaving a breath, I leaned on the doorframe of the room

Last Mercy   167

as if I were winded before I got his attention. "Jason, the security desk just got a call. Your wife is at the hospital."

The actor spun around, nearly toppling sideways. Tears streamed down his face as he looked at me. Red-eyed and reeking of drink, he couldn't have looked more pitiful. "What happened? Is it her diabetes again?"

Oh, thank you, Jason. You've given me everything I need.

"I think so. They said it was urgent."

"Oh, God. I just talked to her this morning. I promised her I'd—"

"Come on!" I waved at him, rushing into the greenroom and handing him his coat. In his flustered state, he complied perfectly and slipped it on. I grabbed him by the shoulders and hurried him toward the door before he had a chance to think. "You're in no shape to drive. I'll get you to her. C'mon!"

Jason stumbled along beside me, his face a mess of snot and tears, which he wiped on his sleeve. "I was gonna make it up to her. I love her. I can't lose her..."

"Come on!" I yanked him forward alongside me, and we moved at a jog to the nearest exit to the parking lot. Outside, I pointed at my car and guided him to the passenger side door.

Some cop cars were scattered around the lot, and I gave their front seats extra attention as we headed to my car, but everybody must've been inside exploring the tunnels or questioning whoever they could find. Good luck to them. I was leaving, and I was taking their soon-to-be new suspect with me.

He buckled himself into my passenger seat even as I reached into the back, searching around for the heavy wrench I'd stashed there weeks ago, just in case my go-to chloroform didn't work so well one night. Jason was in full-on panic mode now, searching his pockets for a phone that was now tucked into Carl's coverall pocket. "I gotta call the hospital. Which one is she at? Did you hear—"

The wrench caught him in the back of his head, sending a hollow *thud* echoing through the car. Jason collapsed forward mid-syllable. I waited for him to sit up and stare at me, but he remained slumped against the chest strap, and I glimpsed blood trickling through his brown hair from where I'd struck him.

Shrugging out of my coat, I put it over the seat behind him so he wouldn't bloody my car—didn't want to scare the next child I snatched up, after all—then reached across him to lean the seat back. That done, I pulled him back to a more natural angle and let him recline into the seat. Sleeping, to all appearances, even if I could hear his breath shuddering in and out.

How a head wound would make his breathing so jagged, I didn't know, but I also didn't care. The important thing was that he was unconscious.

I started the car and pulled out, considering my next step. Taking Jason along with the children wasn't a total departure from my mission. By stealing him away from the world, I was stealing yet more false happiness. And, realistically, only doing what Jason would eventually have done to himself. He had been so bent on self-destructing recently.

My family's old home was in a distant neighborhood, across the Sixteenth Street divide and deeper into the poorer side of the city. But I diligently followed the speed limit. It wouldn't do to get a cop's attention.

After navigating the streets, even forcing myself not to dream about any of the pathetic citizens I passed by, I finally pulled into the drive outside my family's home. I kept my eyes open for any neighbors, but the area had gone to crap, and anyone still living nearby was too busy staring zombielike at a screen, devoted to more fantasy and make-believe happiness they would never experience themselves.

With the side door to the house hanging open, I put Jason back in his initial slumped-over position and tugged my coat out of the car. The damn thing was covered in blood—Jason had ruined it—but at least I wouldn't need it for much longer. Laying the thing on the ground, I maneuvered Jason's dead weight out of the car and onto the makeshift stretcher. I hadn't checked his breathing again since knocking him out, but I suspected the actor was dead.

That was fine, though. My goal had been to use him as a distraction for the Feds and hide him, not treat him to the same, slow unwinding I gave the kids. No amount of instruction or encouragement would get Jason to accept death as a form of salvation. He'd have fought me to the end, so devoted was he to life's unending litany of torment.

Alas, poor Jason, your final curtain call has come.

I tugged him into the house, dragging him along the walk via my old coat. I bent down and checked for a pulse. Nothing. I almost clapped with delight.

No need to bother tying him up.

I stuffed his body beneath the card table set beside the old washer and dryer, getting a kick out of the way I was able to fold him into an unnatural position. A crack sounded as his neck broke when I slammed my foot into his head, shoving him farther into the shadows. He was gone now if he hadn't been before.

There'd been no sound yet from below, but I put an ear to the basement door just in case. The boy I'd picked up last night ought to be really suffering now, losing more blood than his admittedly overweight body could stand to give up, so I doubted he had the energy to keep his eyes open, let alone call for help.

But I couldn't just trust my ears. I had to see him, so I

crept down the stairs. True to my expectations, he lay on the basement floor, still as a sleeping lamb, as my friends performed their ministrations to this suffering.

He's almost ready for the final bleeding.

Satisfied with his condition, I headed back outside.

My trusty little car sat waiting for me, ready for the next bit of business.

The Feds would eventually discover that Jason and Ted were innocent—I knew that—but in the meantime, I was free to do as I wished.

I'd make the old Chapman home a proverbial mausoleum before I was done with it.

25

Emma pushed past the masking curtains and entered the backstage area, looking for Jacinda among the people clustered around the space. She'd called her on the drive over from Ted Fishbourne's house, giving Jacinda an update on what she'd learned from talking to the man.

The SSA hadn't said much in response to the information. Still, she'd agreed to search for the custodian—reluctantly, though, from what Emma had read in her voice.

But from the amount of activity backstage, she'd followed through.

Finally spotting the SSA in conversation with two uniformed officers, Emma beelined for the corner of the space where they stood near a mop and bucket left leaning haphazardly beside the entrance to the greenroom. She saw no sign of Daniel's ghost, however. Maybe now that she'd arrived, he no longer felt a need to direct her.

Sliding to a stop in front of Jacinda, Emma searched the area for her team members and the janitor. "Is he here? Did you find him?"

"Calm down." Jacinda frowned and pulled her aside, away

from the officers, until they were out of sight and earshot of anyone. "He's supposed to be here, but nobody's been able to find him. Leo and Vance are checking his duplex as we speak, and we've already looked in the custodian's closet here. The only thing we found was a phone that appears to belong to Jason Engelson. It was tucked into a pair of coveralls hanging near the lockers."

"Were they Wallace Chapman's coveralls? They were, right?"

Jacinda met her gaze. "No, Emma. They weren't. The coveralls belonged to another custodian here by the name of Carl Long. He's been contacted and has an alibi for every one of the nights in question because of his second job as a school custodian."

"So we're going after Chapman or Engelson? Or both?"

"We're pretty sure the phone was either planted or represents somebody's poor attempt at hiding evidence. Regardless of who put the phone there, we're pursuing leads in the best way we know how. Like I said, Vance and Leo are visiting Wallace Chapman's duplex. Denae and Mia will be following up with a visit to Mr. Engelson's, as it appears the actor has left the building…without his phone."

"I'll go—"

"Stop." Jacinda glowered at her, speaking low. "Let me finish. You should know that we've discovered a pretty compelling piece of evidence that implicates Jason Engelson. His gloves were found near the entrance to the tunnels, and a call came in claiming he was messing around with the cameras near the storage building—"

"Who made the call?"

"It was anonymous—"

"That doesn't make sense." Emma went backward in her mind, piecing together everything she'd heard and seen. Jason Engelson was just a sad drunk. Wallace Chapman was their killer…he had to be. "Nobody with a lick of sense would be messing around the tunnels or the security cameras right now. We have people everywhere, and they've been here since Sunday night. Our unsub has to know that. Jason Engelson *definitely* knows that."

Jacinda frowned, pursing her lips and taking a beat before she spoke. Too calmly for Emma's taste. "Be that as it may, we found his gloves by the tunnel entrance. And not all killers are smart, Emma. Especially when they begin escalating and making mistakes. You've seen it happen time and time again, and I'm surprised to see you so quick to forget. Should I be revising my recommendation to make bereavement leave mandatory?"

Emma's fists clenched at her sides—she couldn't help it—and she fought to keep her voice even, despite the skepticism in Jacinda's face. "If our unsub was Engelson, there's no way he'd be that stupid, even if he was escalating. I just talked to him this morning!"

Jacinda's eyes narrowed. "You talked to him too? You were busy."

Swallowing, Emma tried to ignore the implications of that comment. "That's beside the point—"

"Where was Jason Engelson when you saw him? Do you know where he was headed?"

"He was here." Emma gestured toward center stage, glancing around despite herself. Although, if they found him sooner rather than later, they could clear him and get on with chasing the real unsub. "And I don't know where he was going. Maybe to shower, considering he smelled like two-day-old bathtub gin."

Jacinda sighed, rubbing at her temple.

"Look, Jacinda, the glove thing has to be a trick. The custodian Wallace Chapman is our killer. He has to be—"

"And a few hours ago," Jacinda spoke quietly, leaning in so

that only Emma could possibly hear her, "you were absolutely sure it was Ted Fishbourne, the stage manager."

Shit.

Emma licked her lips, fighting through a quick stab of self-doubt. Jacinda was right, but so was she. "That's not the point. Suspects change. I spoke to the security guard at the storage building too. He gave me a list of everyone who could've had access to the tunnels and CCTV feed. On the day the feed was tampered with, only five people's badges were recorded. Two security personnel, Jason Engelson, Ted Fishbourne, and Wallace Chapman."

"That narrows things for us but isn't a smoking gun. And, as I've said, Emma," bitterness and frustration were clear in Jacinda's tone, "we're looking into both Engelson and Chapman already."

"You're wasting time with the actor. He's not our guy. Wallace Chapman described Daniel Jackson to me to a T. He was trying to shift attention away from himself and back on Fishbourne. We have to find him wherever he is, or we're going to have more dead kids—"

"That's enough." Jacinda stared hard at her, sighed, and then took a card out of her pocket and handed it to her.

Emma could only stare down at it.

"That's Mark Skaja's card. He's a grief counselor. Thank you for bringing all this to light. You've helped immeasurably, but you've also acted in direct opposition to my orders, and on more than one occasion. I want you to get your priorities straight and call Skaja. That's your assignment now. You're suspended, with pay, but off this case. I'll take possession of your badge and weapon, Agent Last."

The card glared up from the palm of Emma's hand, all but accusing her. She found herself speechless. Utterly speechless.

"You disobeyed a direct order," Jacinda reached out and closed Emma's hand around the card, "and harassed an innocent man in his own house. As far as I can see, your behavior today is a direct call for help. You need to stop pushing your problems away and get that help. Your badge and weapon, please."

A bubble of emotion caught in Emma's throat, but she wasn't even sure whether it was rage or horror or sorrow. Not when Jacinda was taking her off the case, they had a missing kid, and Emma finally knew who they needed to be chasing.

The sound of a wolf howl jarred Emma where she stood. If she hadn't known better, she'd have said the howl made Jacinda's hair tremble in the very air, but whether the sound came from the Other or Emma's own imagination, she knew it wasn't any part of Jacinda's world.

She choked on a breath, looked around for some other agent or one of the uniformed officers, as if anyone in the room might back her up. Turning to face Jacinda, she found herself shaking her head. "You can't—"

"Emma, don't force me to make this more punitive than it already is. Last time I'm asking. Badge and weapon."

With a shaking hand, Emma withdrew her badge and handed it over, then unholstered her gun. She passed it to Jacinda, whose face wilted with sadness as she held Emma's gaze.

"There's nothing you can say or do to change my mind, Emma. I'm sorry, and please, call Dr. Skaja. Today."

Emma's mind went blank. She found herself trudging toward the exit she'd come through just minutes before. Shattered.

Stagehands glanced her way as she passed, as did a few cops coming up from the tunnels, but Emma didn't stop until she got to her car. What was she supposed to do now?

She couldn't go home. She couldn't face her empty apartment knowing that she should be out on this case. And yet…if she went searching for Engelson or Chapman, she was certain to run into other members of her team who'd no doubt know she was off the case.

Talk about humiliating.

Emma could just imagine the uncomfortable pity she'd see in Leo's or Mia's eyes if they had to send her home. The awkward *what do I do now* expression she'd see on Vance's face, or the insistence she'd see on Denae's.

Swallowing down emotion, Emma started her car and pulled out of the parking space. She turned toward home when she got to the street but knew that wasn't where she'd end up.

Not today. And while going anywhere but home might make everything worse, everything harder…she didn't see that she had much choice.

26

Leo circled the side of Wallace Chapman's duplex with Vance, searching for any sign of either foul play or the man himself. Denae had just texted that she and Mia were en route to Jason Engelson's apartment. Leo wanted to be with them, not just to be closer to Denae. This errand to a custodian's pad was a waste of his and Vance's time.

Through the windows, he glimpsed packed bookshelves, a worn couch, and a stack of recycling that included takeout containers and Easter-themed cardboard from a bargain-sized package of soda. Easter was close, the purchase would've been made recently, and trash wasn't lying about to suggest the duplex's occupant was either unraveling or unable to take pride in his space.

Examining the corners of the unit, Leo searched for any sign of medical equipment, jars, or dirty water like Carla Alvarez had described to them. Or a fish tank, maybe.

Where does your garden-variety serial killer store his murder leeches? Where would I keep them if I were such a person?

Leo cupped his hands around his eyes, blocking out light

that cast a glare across the windows. But try as he might, he saw nothing suspicious in Chapman's place.

"See anything?" Vance gestured over his shoulder. "Nothing in back but dead trees. Bed's unmade, but I'd be shocked if a bachelor ever made his bed."

Leo forced a laugh, gazing around the property. True, the place was dilapidated, but it did seem occupied, so Leo guessed the address on file with the opera house employee records was accurate. They certainly had no reason to doubt that Chapman lived here.

Outside, trash cans sat at the corner waiting for pickup, and a snow shovel leaned against the tired siding of the duplex. The yard was a sad mishmash of broken asphalt and muddy, brown grass, depending on which direction you looked, but Leo guessed that couldn't be blamed on the tenants so much as the landlord.

He thought back to what Jacinda had said, about the leeches being a medicinal variety and possibly even captured from the wild.

"Do you know if leeches like it hot or cold?"

Vance shrugged. "Got me. I think Mia has most of the information about them. Want me to text her?"

"No. I'm just shooting in the dark here, thinking maybe we could spot some kind of special storage tank or refrigerator, if that's where you'd store them. I wish we could see into a bathroom, get a look at the tub, just to confirm, you know?"

"I already got a look at the bathroom through a window around the back." Vance held his hands out when Leo's head jerked toward him. "There's nothing here, man. I'll show you if you want. The door's wide open to the bathroom, which is off the master bedroom. Toothbrush and soap by the sink, shower, and the edge of a toilet. No fish tanks or barrels full of muddy water and leeches."

Well, that's something. Maybe Emma is just wrong.

Vance pointed to the empty driveway. "We've seen all we're gonna see, and it doesn't look like his neighbors are here."

"What do you want to do?"

"Give Emma a bill for wasting our time based on her instincts. Even if we point at Chapman being in the opera house when the security footage got tangled up, no judge is going to jump to a warrant from that. We'd need more for probable cause."

Leo sighed, watching the curtains in the windows for any sign of movement. Then he turned and headed back to their SUV. "Better see if Mia and Denae had any luck at Jason's place, yeah?"

Vance grunted his agreement. "I'll drive. Just in case we need to get there fast."

"I'm never living that down, am I?"

"Nah, but that's okay. We all have our quirks."

Leo returned the comment with a raised eyebrow and a smirk, but he let his colleague have his fun. He didn't need to know the reason for Leo's caution behind the wheel, and it wouldn't do any good to make him feel guilty anyway.

After buckling into the driver's seat, Vance dialed Mia, putting the phone on speaker.

"No sign of him at his place either," Mia spoke quickly, "but his soon-to-be-ex-wife says he's been unraveling over the last few months. Drinking more than ever. She also told us that Jason always wanted children and she didn't, and that's a big reason for their split-up."

Leo couldn't imagine a man who wanted children would devolve by taking out his angst on kids—more likely, the target for such anger would be women in this situation—but he'd seen weirder things. Especially since he'd joined the

VCU. "Mia, did she say whether she could see him being capable of anything like this?"

Mia grunted. "They might not agree on much, but you should've heard her defend him. Said he'd never do anything so horrible. I mean, of course she wouldn't see that. Who wants to admit they were married to a monster?"

Vance thanked her and ended the call, promising to check in again if something came up. He rotated his neck. "You want to keep looking for the custodian or start helping with the search for Engelson?"

Grimacing, Leo couldn't resist gazing back around the duplex property. He was torn. The urge to keep looking for the man came mostly from his loyalty to Emma, and he knew it. But they had absolutely nothing to work with. Nothing but her "instinct."

As much as Leo hated to admit it, Emma's instincts weren't firing on all cylinders right now. Not that instincts were trustworthy at any point, no matter whose. Their best chance at closing the case without any more dead kids turning up seemed to be finding Jason Engelson as quickly as possible.

From somewhere outside the vehicle, a wolf howled. Impossible in the middle of D.C., but Leo heard it. He shifted his gaze to Vance, searching for any reaction, but the agent was only waiting for an answer.

Another howl rang out, chilling Leo's blood until he felt like the nerves might make him scream.

"Let's join Denae and Mia."

While Vance got the SUV started, Leo texted the lead detective at the opera house, asking him to keep an eye out for Chapman and to alert Jacinda or another of their team as soon as the custodian showed up. If he did come back, Leo could split off and question him at the opera house. He owed Emma that much, at least.

Vance nodded at Leo's phone as he pulled away from the curb. "All good?"

"Yeah." Leo gazed at the detective's speedy reply in the affirmative, which should've satisfied him, but it didn't.

He punched Emma's name in his contacts list and waited for her to pick up. Five rings later, the call went to voicemail. He hung up and tried again, but she still didn't answer.

Fighting the urge to throw his phone out the window, Leo stuffed it back in his pocket and stared forward. The run-down neighborhood around them blurred into the background as Vance hit a major street and headed directly for Denae and Mia's location.

I have to stop worrying about her. Put all the concern into a corner for now. Whether I'm imagining wolf howls or not, this isn't the time. We have a criminal to catch.

Despite Vance's raised eyebrow, Leo pulled his phone out again and texted Emma. If she wouldn't pick up the phone, he'd damn well make sure she at least knew that people cared about her.

Nothing and nobody at Chapman's place. Will let you know if we find him. Please take care of yourself. Call if you need me.

Vance sighed. "Texting Emma? Mia says she never picks up anymore. Or replies to texts, so good luck with that, I guess."

This time, Leo held onto the phone and simply nodded in reply. He didn't have the energy to talk about it and didn't want to invite Vance to air any further grievances about their colleague, no matter how off-kilter she was lately.

More and more, he felt like Emma was reaching a breaking point. A ledge he'd have to talk her down from. But before that happened—and hopefully it wouldn't—they had a child-killing unsub to catch.

That was his job. Emma's job was grieving.

Right now, there was nothing else for it.

27

Emma parked across from Oren's studio, near where she'd become distracted and lost track of Ted Fishbourne the day before. She got out of her car and forced herself to stare at the Yoga Map's front door.

It looked no different, except for the real estate agent's *For Rent* sign in the window. The other glaring difference was the absence of Oren's little red hatchback, which had always occupied a spot in front of the studio or no more than three car lengths from it.

Emma turned her attention to the studio once more. With the windows shuttered and depressing, the *For Rent* sign made it abundantly clear the studio was closed for good. The place exuded none of the peace or solace Emma had so often felt when standing in this exact spot.

When Oren was alive.

Driving up to the studio—or, more often, walking since her apartment was so close—had always put a smile on her face. She would sense Oren's warmth even before stepping inside for his classes. Clearing her mind hadn't always been possible, but just being at the Yoga Map left her feeling rejuvenated.

Ready for whatever came next.

But so much of that feeling had come from Oren, from his deep, caring voice.

A chill shot through her, and she momentarily worried that Oren's ghost would arrive to accuse her of failing to protect him.

She only let herself relax when the afternoon's weak sunlight warmed her cheeks yet again.

She'd always loved D.C. in late March, the way winter was giving in to spring and buckling under the pressure of blooming flowers and prettier days. Today, though?

Today, the spring breeze and the crisp air were more of an insult to the despair she felt rippling through her heart. The day should be dark. Gray and angry and depressing.

Her phone buzzed, and she glanced down to see a text from Keaton. He'd been trying to get in touch, like everyone else she called a friend. And she'd been ignoring his attempts for the last few days too.

But she owed him at least a reply, acknowledging he was trying to help like the good friend that he was.

I can't talk now, Keat. I'm sorry. I just can't.

She stuffed her phone away and crossed the street to the studio. Being there was probably a bad idea, but Jacinda had made it clear that Emma needed to deal with her feelings. So that was what she would do. Let the grief counselor pick up the pieces later, assuming Emma could bring herself to call Dr. Skaja at all.

Peering into the Yoga Map through the glass, she caught a glimpse of the bloodstained floor and whirled away from the sight. A pained and mournful howl vibrated the air. Emma's back hit the cool glass of the window, and she slid down to the sidewalk. Tears fled down her cheeks even before her ass hit concrete.

It took her a moment to realize *she'd* made the frightening howling sound.

She had her face in her hands, given over to sorrow without any concern for what passersby might think. The air went cold around her, the atmosphere thickening.

"Oh no, not now." She shook, keeping her eyes shut. Seeing Oren wasn't something she could handle right now. Not now.

"Underground is evil, isn't it?"

That's not Oren's voice. It's too high-pitched. Too...young?

Emma tried to get her breathing under control. She took another minute with her eyes closed, telling herself she deserved the break. If the ghost disappeared before she looked up, so be it. She could imagine easily enough who the prepubescent boy's voice belonged to, but Daniel hadn't really helped her before. She didn't see why he would now.

Still, once she got her breathing and her tears under control, she raised her gaze to find the white-eyed ghost standing beside her. His *Star Wars*-themed glasses glinted, making his creamy gaze all the creepier. Instead of focusing on his face, she let her attention rest on his hands, which were clenching and unclenching by his sides. The nails were bitten to the quick, his fingers and wrists too skinny by half.

"Why didn't you just point to Wallace Chapman earlier? The case could be over now." Emma glared at him but knew there was no point. Chapman hadn't even been around during that first night of questioning, so Daniel couldn't have singled him out even if he'd wanted to.

Well, not without speaking...

"Or you could have told us," she pushed herself to her feet, leaning on the glass, "that your kidnapper was the custodian."

"The underground is evil." He shifted on his feet, clenching his hands faster and faster. "It's where sadness leads. Everything is sad there."

Emma sighed, trying to take her mind back to the case and fully off her memories of Oren.

"I'm sorry everything is sad there." She crouched to face him directly, not caring who might stop and stare. "But what underground are you talking about? The tunnels? Somewhere else? Where is it?"

"It's where the sadness leads." Daniel brought a ghostly hand to his mouth and began biting a nail that was already bloody. "Underground. Tunnels. Basement. Everything's evil there. And sad."

"Basement? Like a house basement?"

Daniel didn't answer.

Even as a spirit, he's still terrified.

Emma had to fight the impulse to reach out and comfort the child-sized ghost, knowing it wouldn't work. But this wasn't getting them anywhere either. She was just about to ask him what the killer looked like, to confirm they were at least on the right track now, when Daniel disappeared.

The Other's signature cold front vanished as suddenly as the ghost had, leaving her alone in the pretty midday sun that had so annoyed her earlier. And it still did, along with the new mystery of whatever basement Daniel had spoken of.

Leo and Vance hadn't mentioned a basement in Chapman's duplex. Maybe Chapman lived somewhere other than the duplex Leo and Vance had visited. Maybe Daniel was just talking about the tunnels. Maybe there was a bunker somewhere.

Maybe. Maybe. Maybe.

Or maybe she was wrong about who they were looking for. Again.

I'm losing my mind. I must be.

She couldn't forget Jacinda's expression when she reminded her of the certainty with which Emma pursued Ted Fishbourne, only to be proven fully and embarrassingly wrong. She'd *known* Fishbourne was their unsub…just like she now *knew* Chapman was.

New tears broke through, and she nearly slapped herself in her haste to wipe them away. When her phone rang, she picked it up and answered without even thinking about it.

"Emma, finally. Are you okay?"

"Leo." Emma nearly choked, trying to steady her breath. "I'm fine. I mean, I'm not. Don't believe a word of it. I'm not fine."

Shuffling came through on his side, then the slam of a door. "Where are you? I'm coming to get you."

Emma glanced across the street to her little white Prius waiting for her. With her luck, she'd crash it between the Yoga Map and her apartment, despite the distance being so short. Plus, she just didn't have the energy to argue. Not anymore.

"I'm at the Yoga Map."

"Dang it." The words had been spoken under his breath, not meant for her to hear.

Unlike her usual response, the old-fashioned curse didn't make Emma smile today. She didn't have the energy for it.

"I'll be there in fifteen minutes. Stay put."

Emma nodded, choking out, "Okay," before she hung up. And then she slumped back down to the sidewalk, just as broken as poor Daniel Jackson's ghost.

28

Tommy knew he shouldn't look at the things on his arm. He really, really shouldn't.

They were right out of the horror movies his mom always told him not to watch, like some prop or special effect.

But they weren't props. They were alive and stuck to his skin, sucking his blood away, and the worst part was he couldn't even feel them unless he looked.

He didn't know when they would stop feeding on him. Would they fall off and crawl away somewhere? Would they just stop drinking his blood but hang on until they got hungry again? What if one fell off and slimed its way to some other part of his body he couldn't see or reach?

Tommy was aware of them, so he couldn't stop himself from looking. He watched the leeches drinking his blood, sometimes squirming where they hung from his skin.

And there was nothing he could do about it.

He tried wriggling his ankles and wrists against the zip ties, but it was no use. He grew weaker and weaker with every hour, and the ties hadn't lost any of their strength. All he managed was to pinch the remaining nerves in his wrists with each little attempt at loosening them. Hurting himself instead of the Soda Can Creeper's plans.

That's what he was calling the man who'd kidnapped him. At least in his head. The ridiculous humor of it helped him feel a little less scared, even if he already suspected he'd die down here before he ever got a chance to make his friends laugh at the nickname.

At first, Tommy thought he'd get material for the best meme ever. He'd get away and post it to Discord or maybe the Snapchat account he'd started with a secret email address. Then he'd finally get some good attention at school instead of the usual bullying he had to deal with because he was the chubbiest kid in almost every class.

A sliver of brighter light shot down the stairs, and Tommy shifted sideways to look up. But he didn't call for help. The Soda Can Creeper had swatted him earlier that morning for trying that. If anybody was in a position to help, they'd be down here already.

The Creeper's lumbering steps began thumping down the stairs, blocking much of the light. Tommy squinted around the movement, only realizing what the man was carrying as he got closer to the bottom of the stairs. He'd known it was big and heavy, but…

"Is that a person?" He choked on the words, and the Creeper squinted at him. As if he'd expected Tommy would already be dead, maybe.

"What does it look like?"

Tommy inched backward as far as he could. The Soda Can Creeper dropped the body in a heap by an old water heater.

"Is that person dead?"

"Looks like it." The man kicked the limp body, and his head thumped into the heater with the same sound his mom's shoe made when she kicked their aging oven in frustration. "I wish I could've kept him alive a little longer, but not everything goes to plan. You're old enough to know that, aren't you?"

Tommy stared, unblinking, at the body. His eyes dried with the weight of the sight, but he couldn't look away. "Are you going to kill me too?"

The Creeper gave him the same smile he'd offered on the abandoned playground. "Yes, Tommy, of course. Don't worry…your time will come soon. The misery will end, just like this poor soul's struggle with life ended earlier."

Tommy shook his head. He thought of his one good friend at school, Carey, and how impressed he would be if he'd managed to survive. When he told him about the dead body and the leeches, Carey would want them to write a story about it. Something else Tommy might not get to do. "I don't want to die, mister. I want to go home."

The Soda Can Creeper moved up closer and crouched down in front of him, where he patted Tommy on his knee as if he were a puppy. Cringing back from him did no good…he just reached out and held on. "That's exactly why I can't kill you yet. Because you still want to go home."

Freezing up under the grip, Tommy tried not to even breathe. Maybe if he didn't react, the guy would let go.

Frowning, the man glanced back at the body, then scratched at one of his acne scars.

"Tommy, my friend, you must understand that death is a release from misery. I am the only true friend you have because I'm willing to release you from this struggle, from this farce called life. My friends are helping, you understand."

He brushed his fingers down Tommy's arm, sending a shiver of fright through him. He flinched away, but the Creeper held on, gripping his wrist and turning his arm side to side, wiggling the leeches.

"Yes, I believe they are helping you quite well. But these

may be done feeding for a while. I'll have to swap them out with some other friends. Let's do that, shall we? It's really important to me that you understand what a favor I'm doing for you."

Tommy wanted to argue but couldn't find the words.

Besides, the Soda Can Creeper clearly wasn't waiting for an answer. He leaned forward and admired the leeches up close, stroking one with a finger.

"There'll come a time when you will no longer want to live. Then your final bleeding will occur, when you understand that nonexistence is preferable to existence. We'll celebrate that revelation together. I'll erase you from this Earth, and the pain will end."

Tears began leaking from Tommy's eyes. This was the part of the story he wouldn't tell Carey about, even if he got the chance. It was too real.

"Your time is coming soon, Tommy. Try to appreciate the end, won't you?"

29

Emma remained curled into herself in the passenger seat of the Bureau SUV, leaving Leo to keep on talking at will. He sounded like every television big brother character she'd ever seen, offering advice she hadn't asked for. He'd started out by asking if she was hungry, if she needed anything, and then gone back to the same refrain from his text messages.

She didn't mean to be ungrateful. She simply didn't know what to say to him at this point.

"Want to talk, I'm here for you. Hell, we all are." He glanced sideways at her, turning onto her street at a snail's pace. "Instead of obsessing over the case or trying to deflect, though, you've got to sit and feel your feelings. You just have to. I know it hurts, but it's the only way forward."

Leo kept talking, but she sat and pictured Oren. Reminding herself that they'd had something special and had been working to make even more of it, but he was gone.

The thought brought a short sob raking from her throat, and she ducked her gaze away as Leo turned her way. "Emma, it's not your fault he's gone."

Again, she nodded.

"Please, say it." Leo pulled against the curb outside her building, unbuckling his seat belt in a clear sign that he meant to stay right there with her until he was satisfied she was okay. "I know survivor's guilt when I see it, Emma. Please, say it's not your fault."

"Mia made me do that last night."

"Okay. Maybe that helped you get through until this morning, but here you are. So let's try it again."

"It's not my fault." Her words came out in a whisper, but maybe it was a step.

Leo seemed to think so, as his voice sounded a little more solid when he spoke again. "You have a couple old friends coming by later."

Keaton and his sister, I bet. Should have known the team would call Keaton.

"People who care about you, like we do," Leo reached over and gripped her hand, squeezing, "and I hope you'll let them in. Talk to them some, okay?"

The pity in Leo's voice was too much to refuse. "Okay."

Before he could belabor things any further, she snapped open her belt buckle and climbed from the SUV, taking care to appear steadier than she felt. The last thing she needed was for Leo to walk her to her door.

She didn't turn back as she opened the front door to her building, but when she reached the staircase, she glimpsed the tail end of Leo's SUV pulling away. That was something. He trusted her enough to get inside on her own without being monitored the whole way to her apartment door.

Upstairs, she managed to make a cup of coffee and pull a box of crackers from the pantry.

When she'd emptied her mug and the urge to nap offered some numbness, she didn't fight it, just fell on the couch.

A firm knock at her door startled her awake. The second

knock pulled her to her feet with the memory of Leo's comment about old friends coming by.

That had to be Keaton.

"Coming!"

She opened the door and was wrapped up in a hug instantly.

"Took you long enough, Last." Neil Forrester had his arms around her before she could process his presence. His beefy arms weren't as solid as in the past, but the man knew how to hug. Emma glimpsed Keaton smiling over Neil's shoulder, a squint in his eye that gave him *the cat who ate the canary* look.

She pulled back and stared at her former SSA. "Shouldn't you be in Connecticut?"

He laughed and pushed past her into her apartment. "Flew in this morning. Keaton picked me up. You got anything to eat?"

"Uh, no." Emma glanced back to Keaton, accepting his hug next. "I can't believe you guys are here."

Keaton held her tighter, none of the awkwardness from their last meeting in the embrace. Maybe she'd gotten more accustomed to Leo as her partner, but this man was still her same old best friend. "Of course we're here. I was already thinking about showing up out of the blue, and then Leo called last night."

Emma paused as she took that in. Leo had called them.

Leo.

She broke the embrace with Keaton and waved him to come in. As he and Neil investigated her fridge and cupboards, Emma thought about the way Leo had simply driven away.

When Emma daydreamed about having a sibling, the way Autumn Trent had her half-sister, Sarah, she always imagined someone who knew what she needed and made sure it happened.

The way Leo made sure Neil and Keaton got the message that the one thing Emma desperately needed right now was the company of trusted friends.

In that moment, thinking about everything that had happened since the morning, Emma realized the case wasn't her primary concern. She knew it should be, and at any other time, it would have been.

But right now, Emma's primary concern had to be herself.

Neil shut the fridge and frowned at her. "You never did learn to cook, did you?"

She found it in herself to grin. "And you never did learn not to be hungry, huh?"

He patted his slight paunch. "The few days I went hungry are the reason I have no hair left. And besides, my favorite Chinese place is still just down the street. I called in the order on the way over. Should be here in a few minutes. My treat." He then whipped out his phone. "I'm also going to order you some groceries."

Keaton gestured for Emma to join him as he headed for the couch.

Stunned by their visit, Neil's surprise lunch, and Leo making all of it possible, Emma simply sat down in the armchair kitty-corner from Keaton, regarding him. His baby face hadn't changed in over a month since she'd last seen him, of course, but his brown hair was cut shorter now.

No, actually, lines of light-pink, healing skin striated his face.

Something must have happened on one of his cases. That would make a good, safe conversation topic. A case. She'd lead into that.

"Thanks for coming." Emma sighed. "You didn't—"

Keaton put a hand out, gripping hers. "You're my best

friend, Emma, and you lost someone who meant the world to you—"

"But I'd only known him for a couple months!" She bit her lip, fighting the urge to cry again even as she tucked her feet under her, shrinking into the couch and looking away. This wasn't supposed to happen. This was supposed to be friends coming over to chat, to talk about life, and what they'd been up to. Not to dwell with her in her grief. "We were still really new. I should be able to get past this."

"*Should* is like *almost* when it comes to horseshoes, Emma. It means less than nothing."

Neil came over to crouch in front of her, forcing her to meet his eyes. "It's not about how long you knew someone. It's how much they meant to you, whether you realize it or not. I didn't meet this man, Oren, but just from the way you talked about him…from what you didn't say as much as what you did…I know losing him had to feel like hell on Earth for you."

Emma felt tears building, again, and couldn't hold them back.

Keaton lifted a box of tissues from the end table and handed it over. "You have to accept that it's okay not to be okay. Take time to grieve and to think about the future without him."

Just the very idea started Emma's mind on a spiral. The future. Without Oren. Every morning from this moment on, she would have to face a new day that didn't have Oren there with her.

But then Neil gripped her hand, pulling her back. "And you've got to talk to people, Emma. Let your friends be here for you. Especially this Ambrose guy. I like him. He's good for you. You just have to let him be."

All the unread texts and unreturned calls in Emma's phone burned in her hip pocket as she searched Neil's blue eyes. She'd always known the man as rock-steady, controlled, and dependable. Maybe if anyone knew what they were talking about, her old SSA did. She sniffled and accepted the tissue box from Keaton so she could blow her nose, buying herself time before replying.

Then the doorbell rang, and Neil made a show of groaning as he got to his feet. "Late lunch, here to save the day. Let's eat, Last. You'll feel better."

Leo was smart, calling them. I've got to thank him for knowing who could help and for not being afraid to make it happen without asking me first.

When Neil brought the Styrofoam boxes to her coffee table, Emma tucked into the meal with a hunger she hadn't felt in weeks. By the time they'd finished and eaten their fortune cookies, she'd almost forgotten how sad she'd been just moments before. Keaton and Neil were both yawning and patting full stomachs.

She waved at the empty dishes laid out between them. "I can clean up. You guys should go to your hotel and get some rest. That much food would put a moose in a coma."

Neil sighed. "I propose Lucy's Diner tomorrow morning at seven…no objections, Last." He put up a hand, and she settled into her chair.

"Lucy's sounds great. You guys have done more than you know. Seriously, thank you. I'm good, and I'll see you tomorrow."

Keaton stared hard into her eyes for a second too long but finally nodded. "Okay, then. See you tomorrow. I'll come get you in the morning, okay? Maybe early enough for a run?"

Emma wanted to say yes and felt like she should. But the longer they stayed, the harder it became for her to ignore the day's earlier sadness.

"Maybe not that early. But I reserve the right to change my mind and call you. Deal?"

Keaton grinned and nodded.

Two long hugs later, Emma locked her door and stepped back. Her friends had been yawning, but she actually felt rejuvenated. The sadness was still there, but it wasn't pressing down on everything. On top of the coffee and brief nap she'd had earlier, the meal had done wonders for her focus.

Which was exactly why the case was back on her mind.

A child was still missing, and she knew where to start looking.

She pulled out her phone and texted Leo.

Thanks for calling the guys. This really helped. Meanwhile... status report? Pretty please with a cherry on top?

A minute passed, and then another, until she worried he wouldn't answer. Finally, her phone buzzed in her hand.

Warrant out for Engelson's arrest. Haven't found him yet. Let you know when we do. Take care of yourself.

Emma stared at the text, waiting for some mention of Wallace Chapman to materialize.

Her team was chasing after a man who had nothing to do with the abductions or murders at the heart of their case, let alone the latest kidnapping.

She gave an eye to the stacked dishes in her kitchen, but the determination building up in her blood couldn't be denied.

"I'm sorry, Oren. Someone else needs me right now. *I* need me. But I'm not forgetting you. I promise I'm not forgetting…"

Without allowing herself to doubt her next steps for another moment, Emma grabbed her coat and headed out the door. Her feet hit the sidewalk, purposeful and directed.

She'd left her car outside Oren's studio, which wasn't that far. She'd walked to his classes plenty of times.

It was unfortunate she didn't know more about Wallace Chapman, because he really could be anywhere. So she'd just have to start with the one place she knew he'd recently been.

The opera house.

30

Leo had skipped lunch with the team to take care of Emma, which left him to enjoy a brown-bag sandwich and chips in his vehicle. He sat outside the VCU offices, scanning his messages as he finished eating. Keaton and Neil reported that they'd made it to Emma's place and reassured him she was good to go, at least for now. That was the news he'd been waiting for.

It meant he could finally give his full attention to the case.

Jacinda had put out an APB for Wallace Chapman, much as she and the rest of the team, except for Emma, seemed to think it was a futile effort. Still, they couldn't write off the custodian just yet. It was even possible both he and Jason Engelson were involved somehow, either as partners or with one blackmailing or in some other way manipulating the other.

With those possibilities in mind, Jacinda had also prepared the affidavit requesting a warrant to enter and search Jason Engelson's apartment. The judge had signed off because Mr. Engelson had been less than forthcoming that he hadn't been living at home with his wife for quite some time. That, coupled with the gloves found and reports of Engelson being in the opera house overnight, compelled a pretty quick judicial review of Jacinda's affidavit.

The team was ready to execute that warrant, with Vance on his way to collect it. Denae and Mia were still inside, finishing up with Tommy Grant's mother. They'd be joining Vance at Engelson's place, and Leo intended to join the search.

Technically, he was supposed to be ensuring Emma followed through with Jacinda's directive to stay off the case. But he'd done that, right? It sure felt as though he had, and reading Keaton's message again boosted Leo's confidence even further.

She's good. Just had a huge dinner. Neil's treat, obv. Waffles at Lucy's 7 a.m.

Leo sent back that he hoped to join them. As he finished, he spotted Mia and Denae climbing into a Bureau SUV. He started his vehicle and followed them out of the lot.

Jason Engelson's ground-level apartment was in a nice neighborhood not far from Emma's, and they arrived in minutes. Rather than parking out front, Leo drove through the nearby lots at his yaya's pace, searching for the man's car. By the time he parked, Vance had texted that he was en route with the warrant.

While Mia continued to knock on Engelson's door and Denae called Jacinda with an update, Leo scanned the parking lot, eyes peeled for any cars trying to slink away. All he spotted was Vance arriving in a Bureau sedan.

He pulled up beside Leo's vehicle, waving at the team with the folded warrant in his hand. "No answer yet?"

Mia stepped away from the door, shaking her head.

"I'll get with the building manager to serve this. Hang tight."

While Vance stepped away to find the apartment office,

Leo and the others kept a close perimeter around Engelson's unit. When the quiet started getting to him, he stepped up to bang on the door again, announcing, "FBI, Mr. Engelson. Please open the door."

Denae laughed. "You know we did try that. Was it twice, Mia, or three times?"

"I'm going with four. My guess is Engelson's skipped town."

Leo did his best to laugh with them. His anxiety around the case kept him on edge, looking for anything that might lead them to confirm their unsub's identity and location. "You're probably right about him skipping town. I checked for his car on the way in but didn't spot it."

Denae winced. "Sorry, we forgot to tell you. His car is still at the theater."

"So he possibly ditched his identifiable vehicle?" Leo fought back a groan. Smart unsubs were the worst.

"Right." Mia glanced at Denae, frowning. "He could have left in a rideshare, a taxi. Or the subway."

Leo gazed at the darkened windows of the apartment. "And he's not at the theater himself, we're sure?"

Denae shrugged. "Uniforms are searching the tunnels… again…but so far there's no sign of him. We even tried his almost-ex, and she hasn't seen him in close to two weeks. They talked early this morning, by phone, but she didn't make it sound like they had plans to meet up. The words 'attorney' and 'divorce' were used at least twice as many times as his name."

"Divorce can easily be a triggering stressor for a killer." Divorce, job loss, and death of a loved one were stresses that could all drive a person over the edge, leading them to do things they wouldn't do under other circumstances. Those pressures were part of the reason Leo was concerned with Emma's mental well-being at the moment.

"I agree." Mia stepped aside as Vance and the apartment manager bypassed them on the way to the door. "Jason's probably drinking heavily, and he's grumpy. Stressed. But not *kidnapping kids and torturing them with leeches* level of grumpy and stressed."

"You don't always know." Denae gripped her elbow and led the way after Vance and the manager. "But we'll get him, Mia. And save Tommy. Engelson can explain himself then"

Leo could sympathize with Mia. The problem was, they'd picked up exactly zero red flags. Evidence like the gloves and Jason's name appearing on a login list might have aimed them his way sooner, but what possible motive could he have for killing children?

I guess that's why we're about to search his apartment, to find out.

Vance made a beeline for the bedroom while Mia and Denae split up between the bathroom and kitchen. Leo wandered the small living room.

A single armchair sat on one side of the space across from a television with a layer of dust over the screen. A small bookcase and desk occupied the side wall. The bookcase held scripts in binders, a few biographies, and tomes on pronunciation.

A closed laptop sat on the desk. Judging from the dust print around it, the device hadn't been moved in a while. On the wall above the laptop, a corkboard held a collage of photographs showing Jason Engelson and a woman roughly his age.

Both of them were smiling, posing in different locales around the city and beyond.

Happy.

Leo opened the central drawer and found a bill book and a legal pad. The top sheet of the legal pad had a listing of names with phone numbers placed beside them. A few quick searches on his phone identified them all as divorce attorneys.

Not much to puzzle through there.

Denae knocked through drawers in the kitchen and sighed with disgust. "All of this guy's pots are gathering dust. He must live on takeout."

"And liquor," Vance waved a hand behind him as he came from the bedroom, "because there's a veritable bar in there."

Leo aimed his voice toward the bathroom. "Any luck, Mia?"

She ducked her head out with a frown. "This guy has every over-the-counter painkiller known to man."

Vance nodded, seeming unsurprised. "For the hangovers."

"And," Mia raised an eyebrow at him with a quirked lip, "a shelf of hair products and moisturizers that rivals even yours, dear Vance."

Denae chuckled, but Leo slowly turned in place, taking in the small apartment as a whole. The place was clean, but musty. Like the heat had been left on and their guy hadn't come home in a while. Add that to the scattered pictures and the dusty desk, and he wondered if Engelson was avoiding it. Practically living at the opera house, like his pile of clothes in the greenroom suggested.

"Guy doesn't have much of a life here," Denae slammed the fridge door shut, "unless you count liquor and a roof over your head as luxury."

Mia opened the other drawers in the desk, which held nothing more than files labeled with various billing companies. "His wife said that disagreement over kids was the main thing that set them apart."

Leo showed them the list of names he'd found. "All divorce attorneys, so he's at least taken the step to start looking."

Mia shrugged. "Could be he thought about it one night

after he'd had a few drinks. He comes up with a list, but that's as far as he gets because he isn't there in his head yet. He's not ready to take that leap."

Vance and Denae both nodded, with Denae throwing in her own take. "It could be he's just avoiding making that decision by camping out at the theater. It's one place he's always the star of the show, right? He feels at home there, getting all the applause and attention. Until the lights go down, at least."

She, Mia, and Vance began trading suggestions about where Jason Engelson might have fled.

As much as Leo wanted to think the actor could be their unsub, the more his colleagues discussed the possibilities, the more he doubted they had any reason to be standing amid the ruins of the man's life. It felt like more of an intrusion than anything that might give them a lead on catching and stopping a child killer.

Leo shook his head. "Does this place really feel like the home of someone whose pastime is murdering kids in a cellar?"

Mia grimaced, but didn't disagree, and neither did the others.

Leo pointed at the shelves of scripts, then at the pictures. "Jason seems organized. Even if he's going through a divorce, or just speculating about going through a divorce…and this place is simple, bare bones…I don't see evidence of a guy willing to do something so god-awful as killing children. I see the home of a guy who still cares about the future. He's studying these scripts for upcoming shows." He then flipped open one set of pages to show them notes. "This script is for a performance scheduled for next month. The date's on the first page. We're seeing exactly what you'd expect of a guy like this."

Mia ruffled her gloved fingers through some of the bill

files in the drawer Leo had left open. "Killers can compartmentalize—"

"Right," Leo shifted on his feet, antsier than ever, "but look at the killer's process so far. Taking kids…and not from anywhere around here…to torture them and then strangle them? That speaks to an unsub with some real delusions or a very specific methodology built around his perceived mission. But this apartment?" He gestured around them, praying the others would see what he was seeing.

"This apartment," Denae sighed, "if it belonged to a killer, would be more what you'd expect of a passion killer who'd go after people he knew personally, or someone who's doing what he's doing for a very specific reason that would have everything to do with outcome and nothing to do with process."

"Someone who'd care that people wound up dead, but not so much how." Mia rifled through another script, then held the title page up for them. "Probably not someone making notes on a script they're going to be working on next summer, either, since you'd expect our unsub to be pretty preoccupied with other matters."

"Even if it's a psychological mismatch, I'm not sure where that leaves us. And we have his gloves and his name on the list from Frankie Wilson. Like it or not, Jason Engelson had the opportunity and at least some of the means to commit these crimes. Motive is still a question, but we can't cross him off yet."

With that summary from Vance, Leo wanted to smack his forehead into the wall, because he couldn't argue with that logic.

Vance eyed the room, then pulled out his phone. "I can see you're all of one mind here, but I'll text Jacinda and update her. See what she thinks, and then we can figure out next steps."

Denae nudged Leo with her elbow. "You okay? You look like your lunch just decided to disagree with you."

"It's nothing."

The truth was, Leo didn't want to agree with Vance, but he knew the man's conclusions were sound. They couldn't just ignore Jason Engelson because it felt right. Evidence could point them places they weren't ready to look.

Whether I like it or not.

31

I pulled my dead father's sweater from the front closet and flapped it against the wall, ridding it of mothballs and dust. The thing had been a Christmas present from my mom one year, and I doubted it had ever been worn. It would help give me a respectable air today.

I headed out the back door to pass by my friends' home—the old family pool, long neglected and filled with a filthy murk that might, technically, have been water. To me, it represented both opportunity and a pure reflection of the inevitability of failure all life-forms faced.

Rot, putrescence, decay.

Pulling up a sleeve, I dragged my fingers through the slimy water before submerging my arm up to the elbow. I sensed them collecting around me, swimming for the warmth they sensed emanating from my flesh.

No matter how cold and tortured I might feel inside, the spark of life remained, and my friends knew how to find it.

I yanked my arm up, smiling when I found three of them attached below my wrist. I caressed them, whispered promises of the meals they would enjoy, and one by one, gently pulled them free and set them back into the filthy pool.

Shaking my arm dry, I wiped away trails of algae before tugging the sweater sleeve back down. With a last look at the pool, I waved to my friends and set out to hunt.

I wandered toward a yard-turned-junkyard lined with rusted husks of cars. It sat at the neighborhood's edge, near the overpass that separated these suburban ruins from the freeway.

And there, in that yard, a small blue coat held a huddled figure.

Closer up, I recognized the form of a miserable little girl I'd seen scavenging around the neighborhood before. She was crying and holding her wrist. Blood trickled out from between her tiny fingers.

Kneeling before her, I gave only a cursory glance at the surrounding homes. Nobody around here cared about wounded or needy children. I knew that better than anyone, having been raised in this neighborhood by two adults more concerned with their own grief and anger than the needs of their child.

My mother and father were my first and best teachers about the futility of taking breath. And now I would pass along their lessons to this girl.

"What's your name, little one?"

She held her arm, now more scared of me than her injury.

I prompted her a second time. "Are you hurt? What's happened?"

"I cut myself on the metal, and there's nobody here."

"To help you, you mean?"

She nodded, scrunching her nose.

"Where are your parents?"

"I don't know."

"You don't know? That sounds awful. Can I help you?"

The little girl held her arm out, displaying a small cut in her flesh. I made a show of shaking my head over the little wound. It would heal in mere days if cleaned and left alone.

Well, assuming she's had a tetanus shot. Otherwise, I could be saving her from far worse suffering in the days to come.

"Oh, that looks like it hurt!"

She gave me a serious nod.

"We have to make sure a bad cut like that doesn't get infected."

"No, it's okay. My mom can help. I see her now. She's over there."

I spun to see a woman in a matching coat shuffling around beside a tent set up in an overgrown area near the underpass. She hadn't looked our way yet, but I didn't know how I'd missed seeing her before. This would make the task infinitely more difficult.

Standing straight, I looked down at the girl. "Well, your mom seems busy. I could always take you to a doctor and then bring you back. What if I go ask your mom if that would be okay? Can you wait here while I do that?"

Her eyes grew wider. "Yeah, but…me and Mom don't have any money for a doctor."

I gestured for her to crouch down again and stay put. When she did as directed, I breathed out my relief with a smile. "It's your lucky day. I'm here to help. I'm Linden. Now, can you tell me your name?"

She dithered, and I worried the mother would notice us, so I prompted her with a nudge of my toe against her little sneaker. "It's polite to introduce yourself. My name's Linden, and you are…?"

"Alice."

"Well, Alice, I know a doctor, and he can help you out free of charge if you come with me. Now just wait here while I go talk to your mom. And keep your arm covered.

We don't want to get any blood on your nice blue coat, do we?"

The girl popped up from her crouch and glanced toward the overpass. Her mother remained where I'd seen her, pushing around boxes and mounds of what she probably thought of as possessions, but which were clearly items pulled from a dumpster.

Probably the closest to actual possessions Alice has ever known. Good thing I arrived to help them leave it all behind.

I waited until Alice had settled back down before I wandered toward the mother and their "home." The rusted-out car would obstruct Alice's view unless, like most children, she was a curious sort. Even if she did see what I was about to do, I had no reason to worry.

The neighborhood was otherwise empty, which was probably why she and her mother had chosen to camp there. Fewer predators to worry over.

They hadn't counted on me showing up, of course.

If Alice saw me killing her mother, she'd probably come running over on instinct. Even if she did run away, I could easily catch her. The chloroform rag in my pocket would take care of the rest.

The mother startled as I approached, backing up against the concrete of the overpass and frantically reaching into her coat. "You want something?" Her hand flashed from a pocket.

Shiny metal caught my eye, but I ignored the little penknife, focusing instead on her eyes. "I'm here about Alice, Mrs...?"

"What about my Alice? What hap—"

She tried to cry out, but I'd acted with all the speed I could muster. One hand grabbed the wrist with the tiny knife while the other slapped the rag over her nose and mouth. I pressed hard, pushing her backward and going down with her as she fell against the mounded trash and effluvia behind her.

I heard the girl crying, "Mommy! Mommy!" and her little feet pounding our way. How delightful that she was doing just as I'd expected.

The mother ceased her thrashing as the chloroform did its work.

Little Alice was there now, beating on my back. "Stop hurting my mommy! Stop it!"

If it hadn't been so sad, I might have smiled at the girl's determination to protect the one who'd so badly failed to protect her.

It didn't take much to bat her flailing little fists away and slap the rag across her face just as I'd done with her mother. I hugged her to me and retreated into the tent, just in case anyone driving on the overpass happened to look down at the disused ruin of a neighborhood these people called home.

When Alice went still, I made certain her heart was still beating. Her mother was already stirring outside. I quickly reclaimed her, pressing the rag over her mouth before dragging her inside the tent. I thought it'd be perfect to have mother and daughter both meeting their end side by side, but that would mean leaving them here and coming back with my car to move them.

I'd taken enough risks already, acting as I had in such haste, in public view.

Wadding up the old sleeping bag that Alice and her mother used for a bed, I pressed it over the woman's face, sealing off her airways completely. I held it there with one hand and all my body weight while I occasionally reapplied the rag to Alice to keep her under.

The mother bucked and spasmed beneath me as I held her down.

When she finally went still, I collected Little Alice in the sleeping bag and slung her over my shoulder, along with a dirty blanket that looked as though it'd been used as a pillow. That, I draped across my shoulders, covering Alice completely. I would look no different from any homeless person, haggard and hung with the trappings of destitution.

I moved along with a clumsy step, encouraging the world to see me as a broken soul. The sleeping bag stank of mold, and the blanket felt wet against my collar. Perhaps the child had soiled it. So much the better…it would give me one more thing to wave in her face as proof of her life being nothing but a miserable waste of time.

My parents' home loomed ahead, and I pointed to it, despite my companion having no conscious awareness of anything I said. "That's my house, Little Alice. I have friends there. Friends to take away your misery forever."

Inside, I made quick work of binding Alice, just as I'd done with young Tommy downstairs. Thinking of the boy made me excited. It had to be close to his time, finally. I yanked Alice up from the floor and hefted her under one arm. She stirred but remained unconscious. I knew that wouldn't last, so I hurried her downstairs.

The basement door creaked as I opened it, and I grinned at the effect. Would fear make Tommy's blood run faster? Not that my friends could pick up the pace. But the thought of Tommy's heart pushing his blood more rapidly…ah, it gave me thrills.

I was halfway down the stairs when the boy began speaking, his voice now a cracked, dead whisper of what it was, coming out in fits and starts. The words spilled out faster when he glimpsed the girl I held, and he sounded sick with desperation. "You can't keep killing people, mister. My mom'll miss me. You can't do this. Please, stop. Let us go, and we won't tell—"

My boot thumped into his leg, and he stared at the spot where I'd struck him. "Shut it, Tommy."

He cried, and I ignored him as I tended to the girl. I'd apply my friends to her soon, when she could watch me do it. For now, I only tied her up beneath the heavy worktable bolted to the floor. Let her wake up to watch Tommy bleed dry, and then see how she felt about living.

When I stood straight, the boy was sobbing like an infant but still too alive for his own good.

Maybe when I came back, Tommy's final bleeding would be complete, and I could deliver him.

Upstairs, I closed the door on them, blocking in the pathetic little cries from the boy. The sound was promising, but he still needed time.

The old home's windows were dusty with grime, but I cleared a little spot and stared out at the street.

What would my parents think if they were watching me? From Hell or whatever afterlife they'd gone to? Perhaps they'd be disgusted, lying to themselves about having raised me better. Or maybe they'd be indifferent, still so focused on themselves and each other that I barely existed to them.

But the thought of them watching suddenly made a chuckle break out of my throat. It was raw and unending, and I couldn't remember when I'd last emitted such a sound. Because the truth had finally hit me. What would really have horrified my parents was finding out they had an afterlife at all. There couldn't be one, though. Not really.

My chuckle died as quickly as it had risen. The prospect of life after this was unforgivable.

To escape this existence, only to have to suffer through another. That would be horror on top of horror. No, nothing awaited me, nothing but wonderful death.

There was no sense worrying now.

Not when I had children depending on me.

Because, I realized, I'd changed my mind. I didn't care if the girl was conscious to see me applying my friends to her arm or not. Tommy could watch me do it, and that would be enough.

I'd go outside now and collect them for her, and then we'd just see what came next.

32

Emma flagged down one of the few performers hanging out in the backstage area, keeping her voice low in case other agents happened to be around. "Any idea where the custodian's office is?"

The floppy-haired young man raised an eyebrow at her. "You mean Chapman's chambers? Yeah, I think they searched it earlier. You back for more?"

Emma nodded, playing along and hoping the actor didn't pick up on her not having shown him a badge. Or any ID, for that matter. "Just coming in to double-check we didn't miss anything."

"Good idea. It's out that door," he gestured to the same door she'd gone through to find the man mopping earlier, "and hang a left. Go through the double doors, and it's two or three doors down, on the right. Labeled *Custodian Closet*, so you can't miss it."

"Thanks." Emma hurried for the door and went through it without pausing but drew up short. A uniformed officer stood outside a door halfway down the hall where Emma had found Chapman earlier.

The officer glanced her way and lifted a hand to wave at Emma. "Coming in to search again?"

"No," Emma shook her head, "wrong turn. I was looking for the bathroom."

She backed out before the officer could say anything else and desperately hoped she hadn't just given the cop a suspicious vibe.

Because you're sure as heck acting suspicious, Emma girl.

Thankfully, the performer she'd spoken to was no longer in the backstage area. On the off chance the cop did come out to check on her, Emma made a beeline for the restrooms on the other side of the space, near the stairwell to the tunnels. Inside, she washed her hands, making a show of wiping them dry with a paper towel.

Upon using the foot pull to open the door to exit, she found the cop was nowhere around. The performer Emma had run into was now going over lines off to the side with two members of the chorus. Emma gratefully observed them all turning away from her, deep into their practice and clearly not wanting to be disturbed.

Wallace Chapman's locker might be out of reach, but the location where Jason Engelson's gloves had been found was right out in the open. Emma headed down the stairwell to the tunnels, thinking she could at least examine them for any sign of recent passage.

Or maybe Daniel will show up again and tell me which part of the underground he thinks is the saddest.

Of course, she hadn't spoken to the management, and even if she had, Emma wasn't technically allowed to be acting with Bureau authority. At least, not as it related to the investigation underway.

She'd come this far, though. Was it worth the risk of ruining any case they might have by poisoning the tree? Anything she found, even if it proved or simply indicated culpability, could be called into question without proper authority for her search.

She looked at the door leading to the tunnels. She could call Leo. Or Jacinda. She should call them.

As soon as the thought hit her mind, she dismissed it. Neither of them would approve of what she was doing, and Jacinda would undoubtedly give her more than mandatory bereavement leave. More like mandatory *buh-bye, see ya never* leave.

Deciding her future was effectively sealed, and that Jacinda would do what Jacinda would do, Emma recommitted to saving Tommy Grant. That meant confirming what she'd come to accept had to be true. Wallace Chapman was their unsub. She just needed evidence to support that conclusion.

First, she cast her gaze around the base of the stairwell, looking for anything that might indicate someone had recently passed through. Of course, technicians would have examined the gloves themselves, but had they dusted the stairwell thoroughly for prints or snapped photos of the area after the gloves were found?

Photos she could neither confirm nor deny, but she spied no trace of fingerprint dust. Taking out her phone, Emma tapped the flashlight app and held the device under her arm while she pulled on a pair of inspection gloves. That done, she pushed open the tunnel entrance door.

Taking a moment to let her eyes adjust, she headed down the hall to the room where Carla Alvarez was found. It looked the same, except for the remnants of crime scene tape still stuck to the brick around the entrance. Scuffs in the dust showed where numerous officers, agents, and technicians had wandered through over the past few days.

As Emma stood in the room, she tried to place herself in the mind of a man who would so purposefully harm a child, and in such a grisly fashion as their unsub had to Daniel Jackson, Jessica Howard, and Carla Alvarez.

What's got you so fixated on hurting kids? Why are you doing this to people who have nothing to do with all the pain in this world?

Those children hardly had a chance to learn what it meant to be happy, much less to have caused harm to someone else. And even if they had, they were kids. By their nature, children did impulsive things, and sure, sometimes that meant they did hurtful things. But never with purpose behind it.

Not like the man who applied leeches to Daniel's and Jessica's arms and then strangled them to death in these tunnels.

A deep blast of Other cold swelled around Emma, making the already claustrophobic space of the tunnels even tighter. Emma turned in a circle, shining her phone's flashlight into every corner, scanning the small mounds of dirt and grime where the floor and walls met.

The withered, red-haired form of Jessica Howard's ghost stood near the wall opposite the entrance. Daniel's ghost stood beside her.

"It's sad underground. I don't like it down here."

Jessica's ghost nodded. "He takes you where the sadness leads. Underground here or underground there. It's all sadness."

This was the first time Emma had heard her ghost speak, and she'd said something that caught in Emma's mind. "Where is there, Jessica? Is it another room in these tunnels?"

Both ghosts shook their heads, and Daniel leaned down. Emma wondered if he would tie his shoes, because the laces on both looked frayed and loose. His clenching fists unfurled, and he wiped ghostly fingers across the floor instead, like he was trying to pick something up.

When Emma moved closer, the ghosts vanished, taking the deep cold of the Other with them. In their place, illuminated by the beam of Emma's flashlight app, was a loose brick at the bottom of the wall.

She squatted down and reached for it, pausing with her fingertips just inches from the brick.

If this was a hiding place containing evidence of Wallace Chapman's guilt, she could be ruining the investigation just by touching it, gloved hands or no.

But if she found such evidence and left it undisturbed...

She reached for the brick again. It slid out easily, revealing a deep cavity in the wall. Stuffed into the space were several pamphlets collected in a file folder and three slim books held together with what looked like the strings of an old mop.

The books and pamphlets all featured eye-opening titles.

"*The Conspiracy Against the Human Race*, *Bringing People Over to Your Way of Thinking*, and *Teachings on Pessimism as True Intelligence*. Lovely." The pamphlets were titled *Better to Have Never Been* and *Embracing Your Depression for a Better You*.

Emma set them all out on the floor and snapped a quick picture before replacing the suspect's literature in the cavity, in the exact position she'd found it. She wasn't ready to alert Leo to what she was doing, but when she did, the picture would tell its own story.

She was about to leave but noticed one more brick farther down the wall poking out. Sidestepping in a squat, Emma reached for it and wiggled it free with her gloved fingers.

A single book occupied the hiding place this time. It was an old high school yearbook, which she laid on the floor and opened. A newspaper clipping and a small stack of other pages slid from between the flyleaf and front cover.

"Woman Drowns in Swimming Pool While Drunk Husband Watches."

Wow. Talk about a headline.

Emma scanned through the clipping quickly, self-explanatory as it was, but the information still chilled her. The woman at the heart of the headline had been a Maureen Chapman who'd lived in Briarwood, a suburb of D.C. She'd drowned in the family's pool after slipping and striking her head on the edge.

That was the public story anyway.

The pages that had fallen out with the clipping told a different story. Emma lifted them, noticing the heavily overwritten word *proof* in a jagged scrawl on the top page. She flipped through the stack and took in a deep breath. They were printouts of police logs going back twenty years or more. All of it was public information and searchable, with the right forms submitted to the right agencies.

From the look of things, Wallace Chapman had been requesting police logs for Briarwood. He'd circled and underlined certain reports, most of them for "domestic disturbances" at a residence on the eight hundred block of Linden Lane. A few other reports listed "noise complaints," and in one case, a charge of drunk and disorderly had been filed against a Zachary Chapman, aged forty-nine.

Emma held the police logs and continued scanning them. The last page was a scribbled mess of notes and writing, with a repeated refrain.

Nothing changes, nothing changes, there's no point. No one cares and nothing changes. This is all the proof I'll ever need.

Emma understood something new about Chapman now. And having had her own experience with the depths of despair and misery, she knew how seductive certain thoughts could be. Thoughts about ending that despair and putting a stop to the misery.

But Emma's suffering hadn't led her to bring others into that dark and destructive place, had it?

She thought of Leo's face when she'd told him not to screw up the investigation into Ted Fishbourne, after Jacinda had pulled her away from conducting direct interviews with their people of interest.

Of Mia gripping her hand and smiling from across the table. *"It's not your fault..."*

Of Denae, pinning Emma to the wall, insisting she needed to get straightened out so she didn't fuck up their investigation.

Even after all that, Leo still came to her outside Oren's studio. He collected her and took her home, taking time out of his day and leaving the investigation in everyone else's hands. And he'd called in Keaton and Neil because he knew they could help.

Looking around at where she squatted in the dusty, grimy tunnel chamber and thinking about her friends and colleagues, Emma knew what she had to do.

She took photos of the yearbook, the clipping, and police reports, then replaced it all as she'd found it and pushed the brick back to conceal the cache.

Emma then retreated to the tunnel entry door and went into the stairwell, where she tapped out a text to Leo. Her finger hovered over the send button. What if she were wrong? Backing out of the message, she started a new one to Frankie Wilson.

Is Wallace Chapman still around the theater?

Emma doubted he would be, but she had to check. She couldn't fuck this up. While she waited for the reply, she looked up the address of Chapman's old family home, knowing that would likely be the next step.

Sure enough, Frankie's reply came in seconds.

Supposed to be here but left early. Didn't give a reason or sign out.

Emma was already climbing the stairs as she closed the message app and pocketed her phone.

She had to get over to Briarwood ASAP. It was far too easy for her to imagine Wallace Chapman tormenting his newest victim in the dungeon of a house he'd grown up in.

The custodian had to know they were closing in on him, especially after that talk she'd had with him earlier. What better way to paint more suspicion on someone else than make it look like they'd fled? Especially if that person was already showing signs of being at his wit's end.

Wallace already tried to aim me at Ted Fishbourne. Now he's moved on to Jason Engelson.

At her car, Emma pressed send on the text for Leo. For a moment, she considered waiting to receive his reply, but the thought of Tommy Grant suffering whatever misery the deranged custodian intended pushed her into action.

Wallace Chapman had been moving faster and faster. By now, he'd be restless, wanting more. And Emma couldn't let another child disappear or die. Not on her watch.

33

I thumped back down the main staircase, the worn carpet barely offering a buffer to the wood. Hell, the carpet had been worn when I'd lived here decades ago.

Whole house is falling down around me. Maybe if I find another base...but where?

I'd done a circuit of the upstairs and the main floor, trying to distract myself. Trying to pretend I wasn't this dissatisfied.

Because the truth was, I no longer wanted to be caught or killed. I wanted to keep up my work indefinitely.

What were the lives of four children in the grand scheme of things? Hadn't the Teachings advised that every human life was ultimately a life lived in vain? They were nothing, that was what. Four was such a small number.

Those two I'd left dead in the opera house had been a good start, even if the third had been saved. And I had two more downstairs, whose deaths I hoped would satisfy some of the angst I felt now. But did four lives really make a difference? Would I really be living in accordance with the Teachings if I stopped now?

Back at the front windows, I ripped down the ratty curtains and stared out at the wasteland of Linden Lane. I didn't think anyone had seen me abduct the girl and bring her back here, but I had no way to be sure.

The house across the street had a car in the driveway that I didn't think had been there when I'd pulled in, but someone could have been home all along. Peering outside and just waiting to see something they'd alert the cops to if given the chance.

Part of me still hoped to end my suffering, but another part wanted to believe nobody was aware of who I was or what I'd done…that I could keep going and get away with this forever, stealing away child after child until my legacy was written on tiny grave markers across the East Coast.

I went back to the basement door and put my ear to the wood. Like everything else in the house, the timber was weak and thin, barely capable of masking sound. Through it, I heard the children whimpering behind the gags I'd added after my last visit to check on them.

The boy was nearly ready now, even though he still seemed to think the world might deliver him to safety after all.

That brought a small smile to my face. Each cry meant one more release of energy and hope. One more sound sent emptily into the dark, the echoes of which would remind these children of how alone they were.

How miserable they were.

I couldn't wait to end their suffering. To feel them go limp in my arms.

I moved to the window that looked out on the pool that now lay like a swamp, full of dark water and rotting leaves. My mother had died there, lulled into nonexistence by the cool water as my father sat nearby, drinking himself toward death. The oval body of dark water and muck had never looked more like a grave site than it did now.

Watching my mother slide into the pool after slipping on the wet concrete and hitting her head…it had all looked so calm and simple. So certain.

After she died, I sat with my legs dangling in the water, each day for weeks and weeks, swirling my feet in the exact spot she'd fallen, thinking about joining her. All it would have taken was to knock my head against the edge of the pool, just as she'd done, and then roll into the water, unconscious.

I could never bring myself to do it, of course. Instead, I used her tragedy to fashion my purpose moving forward.

The actual swamp outside my neighborhood had proven to be a treasure trove. At first, I'd thought it an answer to my prayers. I could lie down in the murky water, weighed down with my own resentment at being forced to draw breath at all when my mother no longer could. The surroundings, so gloomy and dismal, would do the rest, and I would slip beneath the water, just as my mother had done.

That wasn't how things had played out, though. I was not prepared for my body to reject the idea of drowning, and so I failed in that attempt. But in splashing to the edge of the swamp, finding salvation in the tangled roots along the shoreline, I had discovered something else.

My friends.

And now they were my fellow residents, living here in the old swimming pool where my mother died.

Perhaps I'd drop the children's lifeless bodies in there. The pool couldn't smell worse than it already did, thready with decay and the rot of vegetation. I'd seen a dead rodent floating in the sludgy water not long ago, so the children would have even more company.

Of course, they wouldn't be alive to enjoy it.

I retreated from the window and went into the kitchen.

A picture of my parents stared back at me from the wall, all their sadness hidden from the camera lens. Mom was in a bathing suit by that damn pool, Dad grinning with his arm around her. The house looked brand-new behind them, gleaming in the summer sunlight.

If only the truth of their relationship had been revealed in that picture. Mother's arms would be covered in the bruises she so often wore. My father's face would be twisted into the snarl he could never quite shake, no matter how drunk he became. Even in sleep, the man's lips would pull tight, as if his dreams, like his life, only angered him.

That picture was a lie. I slammed my hand against the frame. The glass shattered, and the frame split apart.

It felt good. Powerful.

I turned to an old kitchen chair, picked it up, and smashed it on the floor. One leg shot off and hit the wall. I turned to the cabinets and wrenched at the doors until they broke free from their hinges. Tearing apart this kitchen that my mother had taken such silly pride in—and the place where my father had mistreated her the most—felt incredible.

I threw a cabinet door across the room.

Cries built in my throat as I tore apart the kitchen with my bare hands and then moved on to the living room. I kicked over the old iron grate in front of the fireplace and nabbed the poker to stab at the brick mantel. Chips of brick and dust flew against my face as I thrust and slashed at it with all my might until the poker handle broke from the shaft, leaving me with a splintered shard of wood in my hand.

Staggering back, I breathed deeply, filling my throat with dust. I coughed, then screamed as I swung the fireplace poker at the couch.

It tore apart in moments, padding and fabric shredded to reveal rusty springs and a splintered wooden frame.

I didn't care if anyone outside heard me. The roller coaster of purpose, of questioning, had become too much. I just wanted everything to be over.

Everything. This house. Those children. My life. I just wanted it all to be over.

A deeper scream tore out of my throat, a roar more ragged than the others. I dropped the poker, my arm having gone weak, and got on the couch, stomping and jumping until all the energy and rage left my body.

In the remnants of the living room, I sat on the floor, staring at my destruction. My parents would have been disgusted. At that notion, a little bit of warmth ran through me. I suspected what I felt was *accomplishment*. Destruction *was* my purpose, whatever the objects being destroyed might be.

My attention fell on the old sweater I'd worn out to get the girl. Hanging beside it, the length of rope called to me. That was my tool for deliverance.

Their final bleeding was likely now complete. It was time.

34

Driving through Briarwood, Emma could understand why the place had barely been a blip on her radar. The place wasn't poverty-*stricken* so much as poverty-*dismantled*.

Everywhere Emma looked, signs peppered the landscape offering property for sale or rent. So many of the homes were in states of such total disrepair, she'd be surprised if anyone purchased them. She couldn't tell which homes were abandoned, which might still be livable, and which ones still had hopes—however bleak—of providing shelter for future families. Even the driveways boasting cars were so overgrown that Emma doubted those vehicles still ran.

And on some level, Emma understood why. One end of the neighborhood abutted the highway system, with no outlet and a homeless encampment underneath an overpass. The neighborhood was encircled with closed businesses, condemned apartment complexes, and park-to-ride lots. One street she'd passed on the way in had backed onto a railyard.

The place was just *dead*.

Emma couldn't even imagine the difficulty of trying to convince someone to move here.

Her phone pinged with another text from Leo. He'd sent three already, all of them frantic demands that she think about what she was doing before she put everything at risk of ruin… again.

It wasn't like her to do this, and she knew that. But since Oren's murder, Emma hadn't been feeling like herself.

She wasn't even sure what "feeling like herself" meant anymore. Sending that text to Leo, letting him know what she'd discovered, had felt like exactly the right thing to do at the time. Now, though, driving through Wallace Chapman's neighborhood, looking for his family home, Emma wondered if maybe she should have kept quiet.

Maybe she was supposed to be there alone, to face off against this monster, her misery versus his.

The Chapman family home was coming up on the right.

Emma parked two houses down by the curb behind a beat-up Chevy, then moved up toward the Chapman house. It stood at the top of a shallow slope and behind a stand of scraggly trees.

She didn't see a car in the drive, but if Chapman was there, he could have pulled into the attached garage. Moving from tree to tree once she got to the yard, she slipped closer and closer. A rickety but still effective privacy fence bordered the backyard.

Emma advanced across the weedy stretch of dirt between the house and the dividing fence. When she peeked over, she found a leaf-littered pool, stinking with decay, and crumbling lawn furniture, all speaking to a space long abandoned. An overturned grill had been left to rust beside the pool.

She pushed back from the fence, considering whether to look for a gate and investigate the back windows. The crash of broken glass inside diverted her attention, and she raced to the front yard. A guttural, masculine yell nearly made her fall backward in surprise. The yelling continued, rageful and manic in its intensity, followed by violent batting and banging, which trailed off into laughter that could've been weeping.

Emma waited for more sounds or an indication of where the man might emerge from if he came outside. When she heard nothing, she darted around to the side of the home again, checking every window she passed.

From where she stood, she saw a figure looming against the inside of the window, menacing a fireplace poker at…a couch.

Chapman is attacking his furniture. Okay.

He embarked on another unintelligible rage fest, and Emma inched away from the window, moving around the front of the house toward the garage on the opposite side. The handle on the main door held when she tried it, so she kept moving around the building.

A little way down past the edge of the driveway, she noticed a window near ground level, overgrown with hearty weeds bent on overtaking the house. When she crouched, she found nothing beyond excessive dirt and blinds.

But what she heard, though muffled, was the unmistakable sound of a child crying. No, two sets of whimpers.

Two children, at least.

She stared harder into the black, abysmal basement space, certain she detected movement.

Between what she saw and heard and the adult-sized temper tantrum happening upstairs, Emma lost any doubt she might've harbored until now. She pulled out her phone to type a message to Leo, seeing his multiple attempts at getting her to stand down.

Emma, do not engage. Do not pursue. You're risking everything.

"That's nice, Leo. Tell me something I don't know."

Denae and I are en route. Vance and Mia are with Jacinda, right behind.

That, at least, was a relief. Emma typed out her message and hit send.

Wallace Chapman is the unsub. 11981 Linden Lane in Briarwood subdivision. Verified sound of child crying in basement and perpetrator present on main floor. Unhinged.

Leo's reply was fast and unsurprising.

Wait for us. ETA 20 minutes.

Unfortunately, Emma couldn't wait for them. Not with a child crying inside, likely two, probably being bled out by leeches and facing strangulation if she didn't act soon. Jacinda would react however she chose if Emma played the rescue tune from *The Lone Ranger* again, but she didn't have much choice. Her first duty was to save those children.

Bureau chiefs can drag you over the coals all they want, Emma girl. Two kids are about to be killed in this house unless you do something.

She bent to examine the window again and froze at the sound of footsteps inside. Adult-sized footsteps, thudding down a staircase.

I'm out of time.

Emma stood, braced one hand against the brick of the house, and kicked her boot against the glass of the basement window as hard as she could. It shattered, and she kicked again and again to clear any shards or fragments that could slice into her. That done, she dropped to her butt and used both feet to remove the rest of the glass, kicking it inward, preparing to torpedo herself inside before Chapman could reach the children.

Her feet and lower legs went in, pushing the blinds aside

and giving her a brief view of the blacked-out basement with two huddled forms on the floor.

In the brief moment she spared to examine the children's forms, Chapman arrived.

With a roar, he raced forward, grabbing Emma's ankles. He gave a sharp yank, tugging her through the small window.

Bits of glass scraped her back and arms as she fought to hold herself outside the house. This was not how she intended to launch her attack. Her palms slipped with blood as she was pulled inside, falling awkwardly against a small shelving unit. Stabs of pain raced along her ribs and spine as he forced her onto the floor.

Nearby, the whimpering and crying grew louder, but the area was so dark, her eyes still hadn't adjusted.

She bucked and twisted, trying to free her legs from Chapman's grip, but he only yanked on her harder, knocking her head against a heavy table leg as he dragged her deeper into the darkness.

35

Close your eyes. Center yourself. Breathe, Emma girl, breathe.

Channeling Oren's deep voice, Emma did as he would've instructed. Her ass thumped along the ground, her squirming doing no good as she tried to protect her head.

Lurching up, Emma leveraged her way forward to grab his arm where he held her ankle. As she yanked him off-balance, he landed half on top of her.

She moved to roll him sideways and maneuver over him, but he was stronger and bigger, with the basement on his side. His back hit an old water heater, stopping her from rolling onto him, and his hand went to her throat.

His other hand fisted up and slammed into her head, knocking her skull back into the cement floor. Emma grabbed for his face. He was too heavy on her, and his hand remained around her neck.

But her eyes had adjusted now, and she could see him clearly enough.

His angry, pockmarked face sneered down at her with none of the easy ignorance he'd displayed that morning in the theater, his sweaty hair sticking up in all directions.

He spit in her face.

As Emma jerked her head sideways, she found herself face to face with Jason Engelson, his neck twisted in the wrong direction on his body, staring at her from beside the water heater. Eyes wide open. Dried blood streaked down his temple.

He was very, very dead.

"Oh, shit!" With adrenaline fueled by surprise, she kicked up, loosening Chapman's grip, and rolled away from him. As she caught her breath, choking in air, she caught sight of a little girl bound a few feet away.

But when Emma returned her focus to Chapman, ready to launch herself at him, her heart crumbled.

She was too late.

He held his other hostage in front of him like a shield.

It was a boy who matched the description of Tommy Grant. In the dim light, the boy's mouth opened and closed, gasping for air around a gag. Both of his arms were bare and completely covered in leeches. He wobbled in Chapman's arms, bound at the ankles with a heavier rope secured to the shelving unit she'd been dragged over.

But Chapman gripped Tommy tight, that angry sneer still on his face. He held a shard of glass to the boy's throat, menacing the skin with the jagged edge just enough to cause an indent, even though he hadn't broken through flesh. "You can't stop me. You wouldn't dare. One wrong move and he dies."

It wasn't too late to save these kids, but the lunatic was right. Emma couldn't risk doing anything that might compel Chapman to push the glass into Tommy's throat.

The girl cried softly beside her, struggling to breathe under her gag. Like Tommy, the girl had leeches covering both arms. Her eyes were wide and aware, which meant Emma had time and could focus on Chapman and Tommy.

She turned back to the killer, testing her estimation of his awareness. Would he follow her, step for step, to keep Tommy between them?

Emma moved to the left. Chapman took an equal step to his left, pivoting just enough to hold Tommy in front of his center mass. Emma had to smile, as grim as the situation was. She'd been right about him—that he'd protect himself. That meant she might end up being right about him in other ways.

"Let the boy go, Wallace. You don't have to kill him."

"I recognize you." Chapman wiggled the shard of glass, drawing an agonized whimper from Tommy. "You don't understand what I'm doing. The misery I'm saving them from."

"I'm going to save them. All you're doing is creating the misery. I know that's something you're familiar with. So am I."

"You?" His astonishment appeared genuine. "Know misery? What could someone like you know about what it means to suffer like I have? To know that every breath is a curse and every sunrise an omen of more pain and sorrow to come?"

"You'd be surprised. To hear you describe it like that…it's actually a pretty familiar feeling." Raw emotion crept into Emma's voice. She allowed it. Anything to convince him. "Why don't you do yourself a favor and give up? Let me save these kids from more misery and suffering. Just because you and I know what real pain is like, that doesn't mean we need to bring other people down with us. Let the kids go, and we'll talk. Deal?"

"You're not going to save anyone. I'm…I'm the one who's going to save them." In the dim light, the man swallowed heavily, as if considering her words. "Me…not you."

Emma's mind stilled for a moment, shell-shocked by the emotion in his voice. Desperation, yes, but also hesitancy.

Maybe what she'd said had sunk in, made some impact. Tommy wavered, and Chapman jerked him upright, holding him tight to his chest, that damn shard of glass still against his throat.

Tommy looked thinner than in the pictures Emma had seen. Paler and less substantial. And tear tracks ate through the dirt caking his sallow skin.

Chapman repeated himself. "I'm the one who's going to save them. Not you." But even though the killer's hands gripped Tommy as hard as ever, his voice gave him away.

The man was having doubts.

"You want what's best for them, don't you? You want to save them." Emma nearly choked on the words, as if her throat were filled with blood. "You're trying to do what's best for them. Like...like nobody did for you?"

Chapman took a step back, yanking Tommy along with him, and a dot of blood appeared where the shard of glass touched his throat. "I *am* saving them. And you know nothing about me!"

Emma tried her movement test again.

For each step she took, Chapman mirrored it, keeping the boy between them, pressing harder with the glass against his fragile throat. They were at a stalemate. Emma just had to bide time, holding him off from killing either child, and hope that Leo and the team would get there soon.

"You'll understand," the man whined, weaving in place as he held Tommy. "When I kill this boy and you watch, you'll see how much better off he is once he's dead."

Tommy jerked against Chapman, bouncing his bound hands off the man's arm where it crossed his chest and held him tight, but the struggle did no good. Wallace Chapman had the determination of the damned on his side, holding him steady.

The boy screamed behind his gag, and Emma waited for

the sound to die before she spoke again, eyeing the blade of glass digging into the child's neck.

"Did you know Tommy loves baseball?" Emma waited for Chapman to process the question, buying time.

He squinted at her, leaning back with Tommy held tight to his chest.

"His mom works late so she can afford to buy him tickets to the games and equipment. He's a catcher on his team at school. Did you know that?"

Tommy goggled with amazement at her, tears running down his face. Emma willed him not to contradict her, to understand what she was doing. Hell, she'd make a damn baseball fan out of him if this saved his life, so it wouldn't be a lie.

"You don't know anything about these kids, Wallace. They aren't like you. They aren't like me. They have hopes and dreams. Tommy wants to play catcher for the Red Sox when he grows up, and he's got the talent for it. He's good. You'd see trophies if you went to his home."

Chapman shook his head, his hand trembling. "No. He'll fail. He'll just fail and be more miserable—"

"And the little girl you left to die, who we rescued from the opera house? She's a dancer, Wallace. A good one. Jazz and ballet. Even with her scoliosis, she still practices every week with her class. She's got an amazing future ahead of her. Because *we* rescued her. Did you know that?"

"You're lying."

Emma held her hands out, as if she would take Tommy from him. "Just let Tommy go, Wallace. Please."

"So he can suffer? Like I did? Like everyone does?"

"No, Wallace. So he can learn how to live through the suffering. Some people do that, and it makes them stronger. You just never found a way."

The glass jittered against Tommy's throat, and Chapman's

arm dropped by a fraction of an inch. It wasn't much, but it might allow Emma to grab him before he could kill the boy.

"Let him go, Wallace. He doesn't need your help to be okay."

"You're a liar. The Teachings warned me about people like you. People," he spit on the floor, "are the worst. They're the reason everything goes wrong in the world, and the world would be better off without any of us in it."

Emma wanted to keep trying. She wanted to believe she had something more to offer that might convince Chapman to let the kids go and let her take him into custody. But the sneer on his lips, the way he'd chosen to hide behind a child…

She spit to the side as if in reply to his comment. "You're pathetic."

The little girl, all spit and vinegar herself, apparently, jerked her head up and down in agreement. She bared her teeth around the gag and screamed, "He killed my mom!"

Her words were muffled but clear enough. She might be weak, but Emma's taunts had brought some life back into her.

Good.

Emma shifted her leg, planning to move fast to the right, then correct to the left and grab Chapman's arm before he could sink the glass into Tommy's neck. As she did, Chapman laughed and scraped the glass up Tommy's cheek, drawing a line of blood that welled sluggishly and began seeping down his face onto his shirt.

Emma froze. She put out one hand. "Stop, Wallace. Stop, please. Don't hurt him."

"I'm not hurting him. I'm saving him. And look at you, so confident just a moment ago, but now? Now that you see him suffering, you can't bear to look at it, can you? That's what life is. It's suffering and pain. And if you can't bear to look at it, then maybe you should accept that you're not prepared to live either. That's what my parents did. They suffered, and they gave up on the idea of ever changing their lives. They were pathetic, not me."

"Wallace, please. Let the child go."

"There it is again, your desire to stop the pain. You're the pathetic one!" Wallace tightened his grip on the shard of glass, blood beginning to leak between his fingers. He let loose a mad cackle that echoed around the room.

While the girl squirmed to get farther away from him, Tommy shuddered and wailed in his grip.

The howl of a wolf ripped through the air in the distance, taunting Emma along with this killer's unhinged philosophy. With it, a spike of anxiety nearly stilled her blood, and she wanted to throw up.

But she didn't. Because she'd heard something else too. A vehicle pulling up outside.

And Chapman had been too distracted to notice.

36

Leo double-checked his phone as they turned the corner onto Linden Lane. He hadn't received any further updates from Emma, which meant she'd probably gone inside, against his advice and Jacinda's orders to stay away from the case entirely.

Denae parked right in front of Emma's glaringly white Prius, the little car sitting against the curb as if to mock Leo.

What the hell is she doing to her career and her life? If she's in there dying...

He led the way toward the Chapman property, Denae on his heels. Vance, Mia, and Jacinda pulled in across the street, and he left it to them to follow. Rather than waiting, he drew his weapon and sped up as he crossed the dead lawn.

A broken window beckoned halfway down the side of the house.

Indicating the entry point to Denae, Leo jogged forward in a crouch. Behind him, he heard Denae whisper-shouting a command for Vance and Mia to fan out and cover them.

"You don't know what they need!"

A man's voice rumbled up from the window, as angry as

it was threatening. Chapman was downstairs.

Leo bent closer and heard Emma answering him, "Neither do you, Wallace. So let's talk about it, okay? I'm not even armed right now. I'm just here talking to you. What if you put down the glass and we just talk?"

She spoke in a calm voice with a tenor of concern and fear. She was either less than confident in the moment, worried for a child's safety, or possibly injured. Man, but he hoped it wasn't the latter.

The window was too small to offer any sort of vantage, let alone with broken blinds hanging over the opening and the basement being dark. Leo stepped away, softly as he could, and met Denae's gaze. She nodded toward the front door, and he gestured her forward. Another wave brought Mia and Vance up.

"Cops are covering the back," Mia pointed at two uniforms jogging up through the side yard, "and more are covering the garage and driveway. Time to go in?"

"Emma's in there buying time. It's now or never." Leo tried the front door, jiggling the handle, but it was locked. He stepped back, and with the others covering him, kicked out the lock. True to his suspicion, the old door gave way with little more than a crack of defeat, and they were in.

The house was wall-to-wall destruction on the inside, with overturned furniture, bits of broken glass, and couch stuffing covering the filthy carpet. He opened the door beside the front entrance just to check and found a wall of cobwebs and coats. Waving the others inside a second later, he stalked toward the kitchen.

An angry yell—the perp's—echoed out of a partially ajar door in the kitchen. Leo nudged it the rest of the way open with his foot. Below, Emma rambled on about awards for math that Tommy had earned, but Chapman was wailing over her that he needed more time.

Denae nodded at him to go, and he moved onto the staircase landing.

What lay below was dark, barely lit by the kitchen behind him and the small broken window Emma must have gone through. Leo flicked the light switch beside him, not hoping for much, but some bare bulbs came to life below. Wallace screamed out a curse, Emma told him to calm down. Leo rushed down the stairs with Denae right behind him.

As the basement came into view, Leo heard a wolf howl, but this wasn't the time to stop. The first figure he saw was a tiny girl bound and tied beneath a worktable. She was small and unfamiliar, but her eyes were wide with life and desperation.

Emma stood against the far wall, below the broken window with her hands held out as if encouraging calm, palms forward.

Her gaze barely darted to Leo as he descended, but he saw some relief flow into her eyes.

Denae's hand was on Leo's shoulder as she followed him down the final few steps. When they got to the bottom of the stairs, though, his spine went rigid, and he felt Denae back up a step. Emma was facing off with Chapman, who held a shard of glass to Tommy Grant's neck.

The madman was in the corner of the room, using the boy as a shield. Emma wasn't armed, and Leo didn't have a clean shot. Denae circled out from behind him, leveling her gun on Chapman.

"You need to put the glass down, Wallace." Leo sighted on his head, praying the man would listen. Neither he nor Denae could take the shot like this. Not with Tommy in the line of fire. "It's over."

The killer's face scrunched, as hopeless as any expression Leo had ever seen.

Shit. He might just stab the glass into Tommy's throat.

37

I knew it was over. I did. Tommy was shivering in my arms, and I had two FBI agents aiming guns at me.

I didn't want to die by cop. I didn't want to bleed out on the basement floor where my dad used to try to fix radios, used to teach me how when he wasn't busy beating my head against the dryer for not remembering to clean the lint screen. He was dead now, and I was glad he no longer faced the screaming miserable void of his life.

But I didn't want to die at all anymore. Recognizing that was as liberating a thought as I'd ever experienced. More so than when I first decided to show others the path to release and true freedom. Leaving suffering behind was still the truest way forward, but…I choked back a laugh before succumbing to a fit of giggles.

How funny to realize I didn't want to be erased, despite everything. Even after all I'd gone through, all I'd suffered, I would rather not leave the world. Because I did have purpose now, much as that conflicted with my worldview. A worldview that'd led me down this path of killing as if the future held nothing for me.

Just as the Teachings had instructed me to believe.

And if reality had remained so bleak, if life, *my* life, had remained purposeless and meaningless, then of course I would have welcomed death. But I had a reason to remain now.

A reason to exist.

My hand slipped with the blood running off my palm from gripping the glass shard at Tommy's neck, but I gripped it tighter. The shard was the only thing keeping me alive. And I still needed to finish my mission somehow.

"You go back upstairs." I glared at the two agents, willing them out of sight. "You do it now, or he dies."

The woman at his side shook her head, her long, tight curls bouncing around her ears. "That's not happening, Wallace."

Confounding me, the man stepped sideways, putting himself between me and the squirming form of Little Alice, still tied to my table. He clicked his tongue at me, as if scolding me for tracking mud into the house, another thing my worthless father used to beat me for.

"Drop the glass and let the boy go, Wallace. If I have to shoot you, I will. I won't miss either."

I forced hardness back into my voice. "You want the kids to see me die?"

The girl screeched from behind her gag, and I understood her without trying.

"*Kill him!*"

If only it were that easy.

The man shrugged, maddeningly. "The girl's behind me. Tommy's not looking at you. Agents Monroe and Last and I won't lose sleep watching you die. Is that what you want?"

The woman's lips hardened into a line.

I looked at the first agent who'd broken in. She was closer

now. They'd tricked me, distracting me so she could move in and try to snatch Tommy when I wasn't looking.

I pulled myself tighter into the corner, shrinking down as much as I could behind my shield.

The boy went loose, drooping against me, either from fear or blood loss. I yanked him upright, hard. "Don't move, you hear me?"

The guns on me didn't waver, but Tommy nodded and went a little stiffer.

I knew I only had two choices for how this day ended. I'd be dying or going to prison. At this point, those were my options.

And I absolutely did not want to go to prison…but if I dropped this little baseball lover, that was exactly what would happen. If I went ahead and killed him, my fate would be the same. They might shoot me, but they might not shoot to kill.

Between the choices, I preferred death. That was the original goal, after all. If I couldn't take Tommy with me, so be it. That meant I had only one choice left.

38

"Will you kill me if I let this boy go?"

Emma's throat nearly closed. There was that desperate doubt she'd heard a hint of earlier. Chapman was lost and looking for a way out. But he wanted an escape from life, not just this basement.

She breathed deep. Telling the truth was sometimes harder than lying. "I know suffering. I know misery. Just a few hours ago, I swear to you, I wanted to shrink into myself and die."

Leo flinched visibly, and Emma knew he'd heard the catch in her voice that revealed she was speaking the plain truth. But it was too late to stop now. Chapman's wild eyes became dark pools of doubt and pain, and she imagined they mirrored her own…and that he'd see it in her too.

"Wallace, listen to me. Hear it in my voice. I know what it is to want a release from pain."

As purposefully as she could, Emma let her back slump just a bit. Her chin tilted up as she relaxed her neck. She hoped Chapman recognized in her stance some of the weakness and helplessness that had been working to grind her to dust over the last few weeks.

Over her lifetime, if she was being honest.

She needed Chapman to see the pain in her that echoed his. To believe it.

Emma bit her lip and softened her voice, ignoring her fellow agents to focus on Chapman. "Just let him go, Wallace. Let him go, and this will all be over, just like you want. I understand you. Existence is a curse, right? You're miserable, and thought they were—"

"They *are* miserable!" His shout racked him, and he backed against the wall, pulling Tommy with him.

Leo flinched. "Right. Right. And I understand what you want. That you're tired of being miserable. We're on the same page, Wallace, I promise." He lifted his weapon an inch. "We'll save you from your misery."

Emma willed her voice to remain steady, even as she doubted the conviction of what she was saying. "You don't really think we care whether you live or die after the way you left those children in the opera house, do you?"

The lie sounded good even to her, and Chapman nodded.

His breath seemed to slow, evening out. Some of the desperation left his expression.

He's beginning to believe you, Emma girl. Just tell him what to do.

"Wallace, I want you to let Tommy go, and then my partners will release you from this misery."

She silently willed Leo and Denae to roll with her story. Out of the corner of her eye, she saw Leo give a small nod. Once again, they were on the same page. She had to gamble that Denae would follow suit.

"I'd prefer to take us both." He glanced down at Tommy. "I must complete my mission."

Emma gritted her teeth. "That won't happen. If you kill

that child, we'll take you to jail. And you know what happens to people who go to jail because they've hurt children." She nodded at the boy. "Your choice."

She watched an array of emotions flash over Chapman's face. Just like any bully, he didn't like when the tables turned.

Only Emma's heartbeat filled the silence as he considered his options.

After what felt like a million years, Chapman lessened the pressure on the glass shard, but kept Tommy held to him. The boy's lips shook around the gag, and he clenched his eyes shut. "I'll lower this kid enough that you can shoot me. I promise to drop the glass."

Shit. It wasn't the answer she'd been hoping for, but it was better than nothing.

Emma swallowed. "Let's do that, Wallace. Whenever you're ready."

Chapman rose above Tommy's head, coming up from the crouch he'd been in. He stood a bit straighter still, so that Tommy's head was at his chest.

But Leo didn't shoot him, and he didn't drop the glass.

"Shoot me!" His eyes went wider, staring at Leo and Denae. "*Shoot me!*"

"Drop the glass!" Denae yelled.

He reached his arm around Tommy to hug him tighter, and he repositioned the glass in his bloody hand to tear through the boy's neck.

But the boy wiggled free, darting toward Emma.

Chapman stumbled forward, slashing at the air right behind the child.

"I said, drop the—" Denae's command was cut off by gunfire.

Leo's bullet hit Chapman in the upper arm, sending him spinning and toppling forward.

Emma caught hold of Tommy and shoved him behind her.

Chapman staggered in Emma's direction, still gripping the glass shard.

She stepped forward to meet him, catching his arm below his elbow, stepping to her left and hauling him around in an arc. Blood flowed down his wrist, dripping onto Emma's hands as he fell back against the heavy worktable.

Denae shifted, and Emma saw her trying to get a better firing angle.

But Chapman wasn't giving her an opportunity. His face twisted with fury, and despite the blood flowing from his wound, the madman fought with a strength Emma could barely match.

Leo came up beside her, bending Chapman's arm to the side, until Chapman kicked Leo right in his kneecap. The agent buckled, his gun clattering to the ground.

Chapman back-kicked Emma next. Combined with the blood pouring from Chapman's hand, the force of the blow made her lose her grip. She stumbled backward, landing hard on her tailbone. Shard of glass still in hand, he leaped on top of Leo.

All Emma could see were Leo's hands shooting up to catch Chapman's arm as the shard of glass came slicing down at the agent's face.

But even as the sharp edge fell, Emma rolled for Leo's gun. Snagging the weapon from the floor, she sighted on their perpetrator. "Chapman!"

He looked up, saw the gun aimed at him, and focused past the barrel on her eyes.

"Wish granted." She fired twice, sending him onto his back.

But the shots sounded strange to her ringing ears. Emma looked over and saw Denae, weapon drawn, and realized she hadn't been the only one to fire. As soon as Chapman had cleared Leo, Denae had taken her shot too.

Denae offered a small nod, but her face was grim.

Across the basement, Chapman lay still. Blood pooled beneath him, fanning out along the basement floor.

Emma held the gun on his form as Mia and Vance rushed down the stairs, Jacinda right behind them. Leo was groaning and holding his knee.

"Son of a bitch kicked my knee out. Dammit!"

Denae pulled Tommy over to the stairs, then went to help Leo, leaving the boy in Mia's care. Vance freed the girl under the table with Jacinda's help. She started babbling the instant they had the gag out of her mouth.

Emma stepped over and confirmed Wallace Chapman was dead, checking his pulse and giving a shake of her head. "He's gone for good."

As Jacinda approached, a displeased set to her lips, she offered no congratulations.

"We'll discuss this in the office, when you're all approved to return to work, Agent Last. That will occur after your suspension and mandatory bereavement leave are up. We'll consider that time to run concurrently with two weeks of administrative leave while we investigate this use-of-force incident."

Everyone shuffled their feet a little, but Jacinda wasn't done.

"Agent Ambrose, Agent Monroe, I'll be collecting your badges and weapons as well until the investigation is complete."

Emma stood frozen, her ears still fuzzy from the gunfire in the enclosed room. She met Jacinda's eyes and saw nothing there but quiet certainty.

"Do you have any questions, Agent Last?"

Emma shook her head and handed over Leo's weapon.

39

As she neared Oren's old studio, Emma slowed her steps. Her back still ached from the struggle in the basement and being dragged over chips of glass two days before. It would have been so easy to just stay in bed, but the walk had felt necessary. The Yoga Map's same old sign hung ahead of her like a sad beacon, calling her toward a life she couldn't have anymore.

She'd tried to practice a series of stretches Oren had taught her to loosen her hips and lower back, but she'd only made it through the first two poses before giving up. Though she'd thrown her mat back into her coat closet in frustration, she had every intention of trying again when she got home.

Just a little bit at a time, Emma girl. Keep going.

On autopilot, Emma kept going.

Wrapping up the investigation had taken an eternity. Leo was transported to the nearest hospital for X-rays on his knee, as Wallace's kick had been well-placed, dislocating the kneecap—a patellar dislocation. But it had popped back into place on its own. He'd be able to walk on it and return to full duty in a few days wearing a knee support, but full recovery would take about six weeks.

After all the chaos, Emma had gone home with Mia and slept on her couch. Early the next morning, they'd met Keaton and Neil for an early breakfast—at which point she'd gotten a well-deserved lecture from Neil—and spent the day with them before they headed back to the airport.

Now, restless after a full day of sitting her apartment, she was here.

She walked past the Yoga Map's front entrance and around the corner, avoiding the stretch of sidewalk where Oren used to park his car. He'd often sat on a bench there to get fresh air between classes—though she always told him it smelled more like car exhaust and fried chicken from the nearby fast-food place.

Emma stopped walking. She waited for the chill of the Other to arrive, closing around her. It didn't. No ghostly Oren sat on the bench, either, staring at her with empty white eyes.

She took three steps, and she was there, standing right in front of where he would've been seated. Still no icy sensation. Still no Oren.

The metal was cold when she sat down, but no colder than it would normally be after sunset in early spring.

Emma took several deep breaths. Her shoulders sagged under the weight of knowing this was probably going to be her routine for the next two weeks. Jacinda had been clear about a number of things after the M.E. had come to remove Jason Engelson's and Wallace Chapman's bodies. Most of all, Jacinda had expressed her understanding that Emma was not the type of person who could avoid rushing to someone's aid.

"I've admired that about you from the beginning, Emma. What needs to happen now is for you to understand that no amount of devotion to helping others will ever outweigh the need to follow

rules. We can't be a team if one of us is making up a different set of rules."

Jacinda was right. She'd been right on every occasion before, too, such as when Emma tore off after Kenneth Grossman or raced away on foot in pursuit of Adam Cleaver—murderers who'd committed heinous acts of violence and who justified their actions with their own sets of rules.

Just like Wallace Chapman had done, and just like Emma had been prepared to do herself. But it wasn't until he turned his attention on Emma, and actually threatened Leo, that she used deadly force. Just as she'd been trained.

Even with the knowledge that they'd stopped Wallace Chapman, she struggled to accept it had been the right move to kill him. It was what he'd said he wanted, and what she'd felt compelled to do, in the moment…

But it was an act of taking a life, and no amount of training or counseling would ever change that.

She had to believe it was worth it. Once she'd seen Tommy reunited with his mother, Emma began to relax. A little at least. And the girl, Alice Bundy, had been taken to a shelter in town. A man claiming to be her father had been located there, and after his identity was verified, she was released to his custody. Emma hoped their lives would improve but knew that homelessness was often a lifelong challenge for children born into such situations.

Even if Alice did make it out of homelessness, her mother wouldn't be there to see it.

Police confirmed a sleeping bag and blanket had been found in Chapman's home, and Alice identified them as belonging to her and her mother, Whitney Bundy. Emma asked the girl what her mother looked like. Uniformed officers confirmed the description matched that of a woman's body found in a tent near the overpass.

Emma wasn't sure what to say to the child. Denae had stepped in and shepherded the girl away.

Thank goodness the father was still alive and seemingly able to care for Alice. For now, the girl was safe, just like Tommy, whose mother had apparently found some choice words for her nosy neighbors. Her son would be letting himself in and out of the apartment as he pleased from now on. Both kids would need counseling, without a doubt, but even a tough life with memories of trauma was still a life worth living.

Deep down, Emma had never doubted that, and she knew she never would.

She put a hand out, resting her palm over the bench seat where Oren would have sat. He would sit right in the middle of the bench, taking up more space than necessary. It was his one uncharacteristic quirk that always made her laugh.

"Oren, you manspreader. I miss you."

Her mom would have liked Oren, Emma felt sure. Her dad wouldn't have understood him, but he would've liked him too. It might've taken a few meetings, maybe several, over coffee—in public—but Oren would've grown on him.

If only they all could've met. Emma pictured that for a few moments—her and her parents as adults, sitting around a table with Oren—and she chuckled at the idea of him trying to convince her dad, over dinner, to try yoga. The serious lawyer probably would've asked him when he planned on growing up, or else humored him so laboriously that Emma would've laughed all of them away from the table.

What would her mother have said, though? How would she have responded to Oren demonstrating triangle pose right in the middle of dinner?

It occurred to Emma that she hadn't thought about her mom for a while. With every day that passed without her mother's ghost appearing to her, Emma felt further and further away from the glimmer of memories she had of the woman. Even though Gina Last had died when Emma was just two years old, somewhere in her psyche, there must've been a flickering of history, a hint of what her mother had been like in life.

And all I have is a photograph that keeps falling over.

Maybe it was time to stop wondering who her mother had been, or what she'd been like.

But did that mean her mother's ghost had no reason to reach out? And what about Oren's?

Sitting on his bench, taking up his space, Emma couldn't think of a good reason to avoid the Other or to avoid thinking about Oren's ghost.

Maybe he would end up like her mother, distant and gone. But if he did appear, the least he could do was explain why he sat on this bench like a self-absorbed dude on the subway instead of a yogi.

And maybe he would accuse her of not being able to save him. But she had an answer to that question now.

She'd had no way of knowing what Adam Cleaver had in his mind, because the man's mind had been fractured in ways that couldn't be anticipated. He hardly knew what he was thinking himself.

Emma took a deep breath, closed her eyes, and forced herself to stop pushing the Other away.

How much time passed, she wasn't sure, but when the air thickened and chilled around her, she already knew who she'd open her eyes to see. The presence was undeniable.

After all, he was the reason she was there. And his ghostly knee was invading her personal space, just as if he'd actually been sitting beside her.

Seeing Oren sent a sharp pang through her chest, but his

dazzling smile was the same as she remembered it. That smile, and the hand that reached up to brush hair from his white eyes, made it a little easier.

"I'm so sorry, Oren." Tears began leaking from Emma's eyes, and she had to clutch her knees to keep from reaching out and trying to touch him. "I should've been able to save you. I should've been there. And if I'd only spent more time with you while I could, maybe things would have been different. Maybe we'd have been on vacation that week, and you…"

She broke off, shaking her head.

Beside her, Oren leaned forward with palms together, fingertips pressed to his lips. He'd been sitting like that and waiting for her to finish, letting her vent, his smile dimming as he listened.

"Emma, it's okay. It wasn't your fault." He reached over, hovering a hand above her knee. "Your heart has always been in the right place, and it's one of the reasons I fell in love with you."

Giving up any pretense of holding back tears, Emma trembled where she sat. Her vision blurred. "I love you too. And I miss you. I miss you so much."

Oren's smile returned, sure as ever. Patient as ever. "It's okay, Emma. Let the hurt come out. We're going to miss each other. But I love you. You're an incredible woman. What you can do is incredible, too, if you'll only stop pushing your talents away. I can't think of a more deserving person."

Emma could barely see him through her tears now, but she forced herself to take in his words, his long, complete, clear sentiments. Was he breaking the rules talking to her like that? So plainly? Were they both just a couple of rebels? She hadn't known that about him in life.

But if Oren believed all this of her, that had to mean something. She had to accept what he was saying as true.

"I can't stay, Emma…"

Emma's heart thundered, a silent plea against the inevitable. This had been too fast. She needed more time. "No, not yet, Oren. After so long—"

"I'm sorry." He smiled again, then stood, his white-eyed gaze holding hers in the way of the Other. "I shouldn't even be talking to you, but I need you to remember that you can use your abilities for good. And don't ever doubt that I'll be watching over you and supporting you in every way I can."

"But I miss you. And I have so many questions about the Other!" Emma's hand hovered in the air between them, yearning for a touch that would defy their cruel divide. "If you can only stay and tell me—"

He staggered to one side as if he'd been pushed. He glanced off into the distance, at something she couldn't see.

"The Other is seductive, it's dangerous." The words were rushed, fear in each syllable. "And it's reaching for you."

A wolf howled. The sound chilled Emma deeper than the Other's presence had when Oren had appeared.

"I have to go, Emma." He backed up a step. "I'm sorry. I have to."

Time was a traitor, and Oren's form wavered before blinking out completely.

As night swallowed the last vestiges of his presence, Emma was alone again. The chill of the Other bled away into the night air after him, as if it had never been. The echo of his words was the only proof he'd even been there at all.

Emma put a hand on the bench where his ghost had sat. She slid her palm over the metal as if collecting his memory and clutched that hand to her chest as she forced herself to stand.

The End

To be continued...

Thank you for reading.
All of Emma Last series books can be found on Amazon.

ACKNOWLEDGMENTS

The past few years have been a whirlwind of change, both personally and professionally, and I find myself at a loss for the right words to express my profound gratitude to those who have supported me on this remarkable journey. Yet, I am compelled to try.

To my sons, whose unwavering support has been my bedrock, granting me the time and energy to transform my darkest thoughts into words on paper. Your steadfast belief in me has never faltered, and watching each of you grow, welcoming the wonderful daughters you've brought into our family, has been a source of immense pride and joy.

Embarking on the dual role of both author and publisher has been an exhilarating, albeit challenging, adventure. Transitioning from the solitude of writing to the dynamic world of publishing has opened new horizons for me, and I'm deeply grateful for the opportunity to share my work directly with you, the readers.

I extend my heartfelt thanks to the entire team at Mary Stone Publishing, the same dedicated group who first recognized my potential as an indie author years ago. Your collective efforts, from the editors whose skillful hands have polished my words to the designers, marketers, and support staff who breathe life into these books, have been instrumental in resonating deeply with our readers. Each of you plays a crucial role in this journey, not only nurturing my growth but also ensuring that every story reaches its full potential. Your dedication, creativity, and finesse have been nothing short of invaluable.

However, my deepest gratitude is reserved for you, my beloved readers. You ventured off the beaten path of traditional publishing to embrace my work, investing your most precious asset—your time. It is my sincerest hope that this book has enriched that time, leaving you with memories that linger long after the last page is turned.

With all my love and heartfelt appreciation,
Mary

ABOUT THE AUTHOR

Mary Stone

Nestled in the serene Blue Ridge Mountains of East Tennessee, Mary Stone crafts her stories surrounded by the natural beauty that inspires her. What was once a home filled with the lively energy of her sons has now become a peaceful writer's retreat, shared with cherished pets and the vivid characters of her imagination.

As her sons grew and welcomed wonderful daughters-in-law into the family, Mary's life entered a quieter phase, rich with opportunities for deep creative focus. In this tranquil environment, she weaves tales of courage, resilience, and intrigue, each story a testament to her evolving journey as a writer.

From childhood fears of shadowy figures under the bed to a profound understanding of humanity's real-life villains, Mary's style has been shaped by the realization that the most complex antagonists often hide in plain sight. Her writing is characterized by strong, multifaceted heroines who defy traditional roles, standing as equals among their peers in a world of suspense and danger.

Mary's career has blossomed from being a solitary author to establishing her own publishing house—a significant milestone that marks her growth in the literary world. This expansion is not just a personal achievement but a reflection of her commitment to bring thrilling and thought-provoking stories to a wider audience. As an author and publisher, Mary continues to challenge the conventions of the thriller genre, inviting readers into gripping tales filled with serial killers, astute FBI agents, and intrepid heroines who confront peril with unflinching bravery.

Each new story from Mary's pen—or her publishing house—is a pledge to captivate, thrill, and inspire, continuing the legacy of the imaginative little girl who once found wonder and mystery in the shadows.

Connect with Mary online

- facebook.com/authormarystone
- x.com/MaryStoneAuthor
- goodreads.com/AuthorMaryStone
- bookbub.com/profile/3378576590
- pinterest.com/MaryStoneAuthor
- instagram.com/marystoneauthor
- tiktok.com/@authormarystone

Printed in Great Britain
by Amazon